Readers love *Rebel*
by RHYS FORD

By RHYS FORD

Published by DREAMSPINNER PRESS
www.dreamspinnerpress.com

Savior

RHYS FORD

Published by
DREAMSPINNER PRESS

5032 Capital Circle SW, Suite 2, PMB# 279, Tallahassee, FL 32305-7886 USA
www.dreamspinnerpress.com

Savior
© 2018 Rhys Ford.

Cover Art
© 2018 Reece Notley.
reece@vitaenoir.com
Cover content is for illustrative purposes only and any person depicted on the cover is a model.

Trade Paperback ISBN: 978-1-64080-862-1
Mass Market Paperback ISBN: 978-1-64108-122-1
Digital ISBN: 978-1-64080-861-4
Library of Congress Control Number: 2018944477
Trade Paperback published September 2018
v. 1.0

Printed in the United States of America
∞
This paper meets the requirements of
ANSI/NISO Z39.48-1992 (Permanence of Paper).

To Michelle and Maite, who kept me company while I pulled through this book and cheered Mace on.

And to Jules, who told me, "No, you didn't go over the edge there." Let's hope she's right, because she wasn't right about us being able to eat all that cake.

Most of all, this book is dedicated to Yoshiko, my beloved Writer's Cat, who stoically battled through a lifetime of sunbeams, belly rubs, and beating up the dog because she felt like he needed a smacking. I will miss you so much, baby girl. My laptop is lonely without your company, and my heart will always hold your purrs.

ACKNOWLEDGMENTS

To my beloved Five—Penn, Tamm, Lea, and Jenn. Through thick and thin and through dangers untold, you are my true, constant stars. Kind of like a constellation… but with more bickering about tea and someone losing their knickers. I felt this was so true to form I'm using it again.

Much affection and love to my other siblings—Ren, Ree, Mary, and Lisa. And of course the San Diego Crewe—Andy, Steve, Maite, and Felix.

Thanks will always go to Dreamspinner—Elizabeth, Lynn, Naomi (who suffers my insanity), Liz and her team, and everyone else who works so hard to polish what I send them. So much admiration for all of you.

A special shout-out to Micah Caudle for putting up with me. Dude, I owe you every bit of coffee you can drink in your lifetime.

ONE

MASON COULDN'T remember the last time he'd eaten, but that was normal. Money was tight, so food was scarce—something his ten-year-old mind accepted without question. That was a lesson he'd learned a long time ago. He'd also learned to be thankful for the shelter he'd been given. Complaining only strained his father's already-frazzled nerves, and Mason still clearly remembered how deeply the cold had gotten into him when he'd been taken up to the rooftop and left there overnight, something he'd driven his father to do because he hadn't been grateful for what he had.

His ribs and hips ached with the memory of the frost and the bitter wind he'd been unable to hide from that night. When the sun got too high in the sky, Mason had wondered if he'd been forgotten and would have to suffer another night in the frigid winter weather, but the heavy steel door had cracked open and his father's gruff voice ordered him to hurry up and get inside.

It'd been too hard to walk. His limbs were unresponsive, but Mason knew that if he didn't move, the door would close and that imagined night would become real. He crawled past his father's legs, and his knees caught on his heavy work boots, but he made it inside before the door closed.

His life was made up of closed doors, hunger, and now an impenetrable silent darkness.

This time the hunger was different. This time it came with a thirst Mason couldn't shake and a fear that pressed in on him with a fierce, monstrous will. He couldn't hear anything or see anything in the close confines of the closet his father had shoved him into.

"Stay there," his father ordered. "Don't make any fucking noise until I let you out. Do you understand?"

Mason barely had time to nod before the door closed and he heard it lock—a small, inconsequential click that shut his world down and left him in a three-by-three space with nothing but his own breathing to keep him company. He did everything he normally did to pass the time when left to himself, and then he slept… anything to avoid the dead silence.

His hunger grew, but the silence never broke.

It was impossible to tell what day it was or even how long he'd been behind the closet door. Even when he accidentally kicked one of the walls when his cramped leg spasmed uncontrollably, his father didn't respond.

No matter what, his father *always* came and pounded on the door if he made a noise. Sometimes he even opened the door to teach Mason to be quiet.

But this time his father *didn't* come.

They hadn't been in the apartment for more than a few months the first time his father shoved him into the hall closet and told him to stay put. There were angry voices out in the corridor, and then his father's fingers were in his shirt, in his hair, and he was tossed into the closet before he could catch his breath. His father had no time to give Mason a water bottle or anything to soften the roughness of the industrial-grade carpet the landlord put in every room.

Mason was so very tired of the silence and darkness, but the door wouldn't budge, and he was too small and weak to do anything but pound on the walls… if he dared.

And he would *never* dare.

Sleep came more and more often, or at least that's what it seemed like, and every waking moment felt like the scrape of a knife against his spine. He was too tall for the space, and he couldn't get comfortable. His knees and elbows ached from being bent and scraped raw by the acrylic carpet. His fingertips were sore, and one blistered and rubbed to a swell when he tried to scratch through the wall. He felt the bump grow, and when it burst, he was so thirsty he put the injured tip on the flat of his tongue, as grateful for the salty water as he was for the closet he was given to hide in.

And still the silence never broke, until one time he woke up coughing.

There were colors now in the darkness—fantastical sprites and murmuring voices speaking about things Mason was probably too stupid to understand anyway. His father always told him that. It was one of the things he was told to be grateful for, because the only thing being smart got him was beaten.

He wasn't cold anymore, but it was getting harder to breathe. His eyes burned, and his throat felt as torn up as his elbows. No matter how hard he tried to swallow, he couldn't get any moisture in his mouth, and his tongue felt swollen and heavy and pressed against his teeth. It'd been so long since he'd heard something other than his own movements, Mason was startled to hear the quiet crackle.

The silence had broken, but he was now too weak to move.

There were definitely voices, and Mason tried to scream for his father, but nothing came out but a croak. He ached everywhere, and as the crinkling noises slowly turned to a full roar, Mason clenched his fist and flung it at the door. He needed to get out because the air was too thick and he couldn't catch enough of it when he breathed.

Just when Mason thought he couldn't hold on any longer, the darkness cracked.

There was a slice of light, and then Mason saw the monster who'd opened the door. Or it could have been an alien robot from one of his stories, the kind he saw in the old black-and-white movies he watched late at night when he didn't have to be kept away. The monster reached for him, and Mason tried to get loose, but the closet was too small and he was too little and too tired. The thing's hands closed over his arms. He should've been too old to be scared—he'd just turned ten—and despite what his father told him, Mason was pretty sure monsters weren't real.

This one was very real. It was man-shaped and yellow-striped with squiggles on it—words smart people would know but someone like Mason could never understand—and the monster breathed funny. It hissed and spit behind its single frosted eye. The air it brought with it was filmy, hard to see through, and smelled of burned toast. Then Mason saw the man's face caught inside the eye.

It was a mask of some kind, and he wanted to laugh at his foolishness, embarrassed by how stupid he was, but he didn't have enough air to breathe, much less chortle. The man's hands were still on him, and he lifted him up while another pseudo alien worked to get a plastic triangle over Mason's face.

The man terrified him. Mason struggled to make sense of his fear and loathing of what the man was and give in to the palatable relief at being found. For him the monster became a man who would expose him to the world and go against everything his father had pounded into his head.

He didn't know who he was more afraid of… his father or the man rescuing him.

"I've got you, kid," the man said through his mask. He looked angry, and Mason struggled to apologize, fearful of the power in the man's arms. "Just lie back and relax. I'm going to get you out of here… just… hold on. Everything's going to be all right."

Twenty Years Later

"MONTENEGRO!" MACE knew he didn't have to yell, but the adrenaline pouring through his blood made it impossible to do anything but shout. "Let me do a final check, and then we're clear. I've got 4B and 4A to check over."

"Copy." Mace could hear Rey's amusement loud and clear through their connection. "I'll hold the hall. You go do it, but make it quick."

He always made it quick, but Rey liked to remind him, especially when time was tight. This fire was slow moving and losing its power. The call that had begun as an inferno started by a balcony barbecue grill was now a weakening, sputtering bank of flames trapped between two fire crews. Still, nobody would turn their back on the building until it was called in as an *all clear*.

For Mason, that meant doing one final sweep of every room.

It was stupid… and he got shit for it sometimes… but like a lot of things Mason couldn't put into a box and lock away, he wouldn't be able to rest until he checked every door and every closet in the area they'd been assigned. Often there was no need, but the few times he didn't, he itched beneath his skin for days, and a nagging sense of something left undone haunted him until they went on the next call.

The search was less of an obligation and more of an onus, a burden much heavier than the breathing apparatus and gear he carried into the fire—a legacy of sorts, a sword and shield he had picked up the moment he earned the right to call himself a firefighter.

"Just remember, Crawford, we've got a pot of Dungeness crabs over at the house waiting for us." Rey's voice echoed through Mace's helmet. "And I haven't seen Gus in three days, so… hurry it up."

"Hold your horses, Montenegro," Mace scolded back as he opened a hallway closet door. "I need, like, five minutes."

They were in a part of the building that hadn't been touched by the fire itself, but the walls showed signs of smoke damage. Dark gray curls of soot brushed over yards of ivory-white paint. The owners had been evacuated before Mace and the others moved into that end of the floor, but there were signs that a child occupied the small, boxy apartment— either that or they had a very spoiled puppy that slept in a bed shaped like a racecar in a room right off the kitchen.

With the power turned off, it was a little dark, and the afternoon sun was hidden by other buildings that crowded in over the apartments, but there was enough light for Mace to see the closet was empty.

He swept through the rest of the apartment, and his boots left deep tracks over the area rug in the center of the living room. There was no avoiding the filth of a fire or spreading it when they walked around. No matter how careful they were, fire brought destruction and everything that came with it. It was part of the job to wade through the mess and pull out what lives they could find.

The carpet was crispy under his feet, but the crunch came from a bag of chips spilled on the floor rather than the scorched remains of a rug. Whoever decorated obviously felt there was no such thing as overkill, because no matter where Mace turned, there was another piece of furniture blocking his way.

"Hey, Montenegro, when I'm done here, can we see if anyone from 4B is downstairs?" Mace's voice echoed in his helmet, turning him into a Sith Lord when he spoke. "You can tell them their place is intact but just a little dirty. Maybe the chief will let them come up and get some things, but no one's going to be sleeping here tonight."

"Can do that. You about finished? Crabs. Family dinner. Gus," Rey drawled. "You know… just reminding you."

"Yeah, asshole. I know. You want to get laid," Mace grumbled back. "I'm coming out after one more door check in here and a quick scan of the other apartment. Then we can call it clear."

"What the hell is he doing? The floor's empty." Another voice broke over the communication, the querulous whine of one of the newbies assigned to the station to earn their chops. "We should have been out of here by now."

"It's a thing he's got to do. Also, we operate under a 'better safe than sorry' motto in this house." Rey's calm voice dropped a register, and an undercurrent of menace echoed through the line. "So we're going to wait as fucking long as it takes, because it's what he needs to call the job done."

"Ten minutes, tops," Mace promised. "And quit yelling at the kids. Don't want to scare them off the job, Montenegro. The sooner they graduate, the sooner we don't have to work double shifts to cover."

Fire was a fickle thing. No matter how many times Mace had been told not to anthropomorphize the flames, it always seemed like fire had a mind of its own. Ravenous and unyielding, it ran and leapt along the inside of walls, sometimes playing hide-and-seek with the men and women who'd been sent to kill it. But if there was anything Mace knew, fire—despite not being sentient—had a fucked-up sense of humor.

So it came as no surprise when he opened what should have been the last closet door he'd have to check before calling the building clear… and found the back wall being eaten up by flames.

"Crawford, what do you see up there?" Their battalion chief's voice broke over the line. "We're reading a hotspot—"

"Found it. It's gone into the apartment next door." Mace ran through the building schematics in his head. There'd been little space between the walls on the other floors. The thick wooden framing was solid and gave the fire a lot of fuel but little space for someone to slip through. Mace didn't think the closet would be any different. "It's in 4A. Don't think I can go through the wall."

"Did you call that space clear?" the chief asked. "If not, get through the door and check."

"Got it. Place is riddled with studs, and the fire is moving fast. Going 'round to the door. Montenegro, send the crew 'round, and we can get it contained before it spreads."

"See you in a second, Crawford," Rey responded. "Floor crew, move east."

As soon as Mace heard his best friend give him the clearance, he unlatched his suppression equipment and began to move, hoping to beat the flames before they consumed the other apartment. It was hard going. Moving quickly in fire gear was difficult, and he was hampered by furniture and tight spaces, especially in San Francisco's narrow housing. Mace's pack caught on the wall as he went through the apartment's hallway, knocking a picture frame off the wall. As he negotiated the living room, with its obstacle course of sofas and a coffee table, he caught a glimpse of something shifting.

The floor rumbled with the sound of firefighters entering the area as Mace checked the apartment's doorknob. They poured out of the hallway to Mace's right, and he gestured toward the apartment he'd just come out of and guided them with curt instructions to the closet space. Rey jogged over with a hook in his hand, and Mace took up position next to 4A's door, ready to enter once Rey broke in.

"Check the knob?" his best friend teased.

"Yeah, locked." Mace angled his shoulders to give Rey as much space as he could. There were times when someone couldn't make it out. Mace had pulled out more than one person from a deadly situation and had nightmares about the moments he hadn't been able to get there in time. This was *not* going to be one of those times. "Break it down, Rey, and let's hope no one's inside."

415 INK was a dream.

And Rob Claussen knew it.

415 Ink was a legend of sorts, a Camelot of inkers with skills Rob could only dream of. Situated across of Fisherman's Wharf on Jackson, the tattoo shop was constantly busy with walk-ins. That ensured a steady paycheck, but working shoulder to shoulder with some of the best artists in the business made the busy shop the dream of a lifetime. In the few months since he'd been given a shared stall at the pierside shop, he'd sucked up many tricks of the trade from master inkers like Ichiro Tokugawa and Georgie Baker. Barrett, himself a master of American Traditional and Neo-Traditional, spent time patiently tattooing a piece and explaining his choices to Rob whenever he was able to.

It was a dream job. It was a dream shop. And even though he probably would never have a permanent station like Barrett Jackson, Gus Scott, or Ivo Rogers, three of the five brothers who owned and worked there, he could see how the experience was priceless. Hell, he could see it in his own work just in the few months he'd been there.

At twenty-five he should have been further along his tattoo career, but his stint at Berkeley threw him off the rails for a couple of years. By the time he'd gotten his head on straight, he had to play a lot of catch-up with other artists his age. So when the spot at 415 Ink came up, Rob didn't think he had a chance in hell of getting it. Yet Barrett saw something in Rob's work, and the brass ring Rob thought he would never be able to grab was suddenly in his hand.

He was scared shitless he would do something stupid and let it go.

That something stupid was Mace Crawford... and his something stupid walked right into the shop through the back door just as Rob locked down the front of the place for the night.

He'd been about to shut off the lights in the shop's lounge area when he heard a noise coming from the back door. Panicking, Rob grabbed the broom they used to sweep up the shop and turned the corner, intent on doing bodily harm. Instead he bounced off of a very delectable stretch of legs and shoulders named Mace Crawford.

From the look on Mace's face, the devil had been chasing his tail. There was a wildness to his eyes, a haunted expression on his too-fucking-gorgeous face. He'd been on a run or was midjog, because he wore a pair of black drawstring pants slung low enough on his narrow hips that Rob could see the red band of his underwear peeking up on one side. His short-sleeved red T-shirt clung to Mace's hard chest and flat belly, tightly enough to show every muscled ridge on his torso and leave enough to the imagination that Rob's mouth watered at the thought of peeling the slightly rain-dampened fabric off of the man's body.

The art on his upper arm was exquisite. Its lines flowed around the curve of his shoulder and down toward his elbow. Neo-Traditional in style, it was a simple piece at first glance, a shout-out to the old-school flash plastered to the walls of most shops—a knight's helm in profile tucked against a few licks of flames and a sweet red rose at the bottom—the tattoo was definitely Mace. The colors were blended seamlessly with a dab of the old style's standard palette and a nod to the old seadog inkings from the past. Like Mace, it was a stealth piece, seemingly easy to do but complicated as all hell if someone really knew what they were looking at.

The ink was as heartbreakingly gorgeous as the man himself, and Rob wanted to lick that too.

It wasn't fair for a man to be as handsome as Mace Crawford was. Sure, life was never *really* fair, but Mace was a kind of bad karma that made Rob wonder if he'd spent his former life suppressing civil rights or talking on the phone loudly during a movie in a theater. He didn't want to lust after Mace. He hated nearly everything about the man, but at the same time, he had long, involved daydreams about taking Mace into the shop's back room and doing wicked things with him on the art table they couldn't even leave a drink on.

And dammit, Rob was half convinced Mace knew it.

Mace's bright blue eyes saw everything and judged it all. There was a hard arrogance in his gaze, a streetwise weariness folded into a steel-firm assuredness that Rob hated, but it was Mace's aristocratic beauty he disliked at first sight.

Rob spent most of his time staring at Mace and reminding himself he didn't like perfection. He wanted—longed—to catch the attention of a man who was real, not a construct of masculine tropes. He hated himself for wanting to run his fingers through Mace's sun-streaked dirty-blond hair or bite at the plump of his lower lip. Rob disliked the tickle he got in his belly when Mace's too-white smile made dimples in his cheeks, and he particularly loathed the ache in his chest when the tall, muscular firefighter laughed with his golden rumble of a voice.

But most of all, Rob hated how Mace's gaze landed on his face and flicked away as though Rob meant nothing.

"I just… needed some water," Mace said softly as he pushed his way into the cramped space by the back door. He filled the area, stealing all the air, and Rob tried to shift to let him past, but all he seemed to do was make matters worse. They tangled, and Mace sighed. "Hold on. Let go of the broom. Or just… put it down."

Up close, Mace Crawford smelled like a light hint of sweat, fresh linen, and lemon zest, another checked-off box of impossible manly things. It wasn't fair. The guy was out running and literally smelled as fresh as a spring morning, whereas Rob… was probably more fragrant. Rob stealthily sniffed at his own T-shirt and tried to remember if he had pulled it out of one of his dresser drawers or from the pile of could-be-worn-again clothes he'd stacked on a chair in his room.

Of course the sniff didn't escape Mace's notice. "What are you doing?"

"Nothing," he muttered back. "What the hell are you doing? Here, I mean. Aren't you guys supposed to be having a dinner thing tonight? And how did you get in?"

Mace towered over him. As much as Rob loved his Filipino French mother, he wouldn't have said no to being as tall as his much older half brothers, especially when trying to hold his own against a gorgeous demigod. Rob fell into childish mind games when Mace came around, and no matter how often he reminded himself he didn't need to prove anything to anyone, old habits and insecurities were hard to break.

"That was over hours ago. I stopped by, grabbed a beer, then left. Look, I went on a run and just stopped in to grab some water." Mace dangled a set of keys in front of Rob's face. "I own the place, remember? You going to let me in?"

"Sure, I can do that." He didn't get a chance to step aside before Mace edged past him and their chests brushed, setting Rob's skin on fire. He closed his eyes, took a breath, and shook off his body's response to Mace's touch. "Seriously, you just came here for some water?"

"Yeah, just for some water," Mace repeated as he stalked over to the lounge. "Wasn't looking for anything else, so you don't have to worry about entertaining me."

"There wasn't anywhere else you could have stopped? Convenience store? A bar?" Rob dogged Mace's heels, determined not to salivate at the sight of his hard, full ass flexing as he walked. "I've got to close up."

"Owner, remember?" Mace jangled the keys again and then tossed them onto the table in the middle of the lounge. They skidded for a few inches and came to a stop at Rob's discarded jacket. "You don't have to stay. Go home. Not like I can't lock up behind me. If you've got a problem with it, call Bear. I'm sure he's up."

Rob had every intention of leaving. His hands were on his jacket, and he'd done one final check on the safe and bolted the front door closed. There was absolutely no reason in hell for him to stay, especially since Mace was right—the guy was one of the owners. He could dance naked in the middle of the shop, and the only person who could give him shit about it was Barrett.

But there was something wrong. In the few months he'd been at the shop, he'd never seen Mace look… off. It was as though something that usually kept the man up had crumbled inside of him and he was holding himself up by sheer will. Rob knew what it looked like when someone was about to break down. He'd seen it in the mirror about a million times, and Mace Crawford was falling apart.

"What's wrong?" Rob took a step toward him, torn between touching Mace and running as far away as he could. It was one thing to lust after Mace in secret, but asking him to open up and begging Mace to shut him down wasn't something Rob wanted to experience. But when Mace turned around, Rob saw the glitter of pain in his clear blue gaze, and he forgot all about leaving. "Dude, what the fuck is going on with you?"

"There was a kid... in a room she shouldn't have been in, in an apartment *someone else* said was clear. By the time we got to her, she was pretty fucked-up, and I don't know if she's going to make it." Mace paced a bit in front of the water cooler. Then he stopped, tilted his head up, and closed his eyes. "That's what the fuck's wrong with me. Now, let me grab some water and get out of here... because no matter how pretty that mouth of yours is, you're not going to be able to kiss it and make it all better, no matter how fucking much I want you to."

TWO

"AND HE just… *left*?" Lilith, Rob's best partner in crime and Goddess of Housing, paused halfway up the stairs to their third-floor apartment. "Just dropped that on you and booked? God, what an asshole."

If Rob had the breath to agree, he would have, but standing at the back end of a sofa angled up a flight of narrow stairs wasn't exactly the time to pick up a conversation he'd started on the first floor, and glaring at Lilith wasn't going to do him any good. Once his childhood best friend got on a rant, there was no stopping her.

"Can we talk about it after we get this thing inside?" Rob jostled his end of the couch, hoping to jog Lilith's awareness that they were trying to move him into her newly inherited place. "It's kind of heavy."

Lilith looked down at him as though he were insane and not holding up the other side. "I know you. You can't stand secrets. You hate leaving junk mail unopened because it *just* might be something good."

Lilith hadn't taken another step. If anything, the couch was getting heavier, and not for the first time since he'd pulled it out of a free-to-take trash pile outside of a Russian Hill apartment, he was reminded that the knobby fabric was scratchy and uncomfortable on bare skin. It was also a pink plaid that would have had a better home as a jacket and skirt set for a Beverly Hills teenager than a sofa, but beggars couldn't be choosers.

Since he was impoverished, that was nothing a king-size sheet from the dollar store couldn't fix. If only he could say the same thing about Lilith, who was taking another breath and still hadn't moved one inch from the top of the stairwell.

It wasn't that Rob wasn't happy about moving in, but the building, like most of Chinatown, was built before air-conditioning—and freight elevators—was a thing. Still, there was an indescribable and magical vibrancy to the neighborhood.

Oddly enough, Rob felt like he was coming home.

Even though he'd spent time in the district before, it took on a different light now that he was going to live there. It gave him a new awareness as he unloaded his life into the old building's cramped front lobby. Lilith had given him a brief rundown, knowledge gleaned from years of visiting her grandmother, who'd owned the apartment before she passed away. Her place had been two one-bedroom units at one time, but Lilith's grandparents had the foresight to purchase two street-facing apartments that mirrored one another and knock down walls to combine the living rooms into one long space and enlarge the kitchen. There was a powder room off of the living room—the space probably carved out of a closet or pantry—but on the other side of the main space there were two good-sized bedrooms with separate sitting areas and bathrooms.

It was a dream in a district where space was at a premium and usually cramped. Parking was problematic, and there was a too-much-of-a-temptation home-style Chinese deli on the corner with roast pork loins and Peking ducks hanging in the window to lure customers in. Lilith was dismissive of the bakery in their building and told him to grab food at the deli instead, but it was the meat market in the storefront next door that caught his interest.

He'd never lived someplace where he could find foods like his mother cooked, and the market showed great promise.

The district felt old but welcoming in a way he hadn't experienced before. The sights and sounds of people on the street were like the staccato flow of his mom and aunts chatting. Even though the language was different, gestures and facial expressions were so similar that Rob had to do a double take. Still, he felt a little bit outside of everything, like a lost child looking through a window into a world he should've known but that he had been denied.

His father always insisted his mother leave her culture and language locked away in a box where Rob couldn't get to it. He'd grown up not understanding when she spoke to her relatives on the phone, and only discovered things like *adobo* and *sisig* from a Filipino food truck parked near his college.

It enraged and saddened him, but when he begged his mother to share that part of herself with him, she refused and told him he was his father's son before he was his mother's.

Walking away from his family had been hard enough to do, but turning his back on his mother broke Rob's heart.

Still, over the past year, it'd gotten better… so much better… to the point where she would periodically drop by the shop to visit. He hoped he could coax his mom to come into Chinatown to see his new place, provided he could get the couch up into Lilith's apartment before he let go and it killed him.

"Lil, I love you, but this thing weighs five hundred pounds, and I still have to unpack." His arms were aching, nothing like the soft throb along his forearms after a long day of tattooing, and Rob felt the beginning of tremors in his thighs. "Just. Move. Back."

The fear in his voice must have spurred something in her lizard brain, because Lilith took a dramatic breath and began to cautiously back up through the open door of their apartment. It was slow going, probably because the front room was littered with the bits and pieces of his life that he could put into a box or ten. There'd been a time when he'd had a bedroom the size of Lilith's Chinatown apartment, but those days were so far behind him, they could've happened to another person.

Rob took a tentative step up to the next stair tread. In fairness he *had been* a different person then, one with less ink and driven by someone else's ambition. He'd been Robert back then, a stocky off-brand knockoff hoping to fit into a family line he had no business being in, putting his shoulder to a grindstone he'd tried to convince himself he didn't hate, and working toward someone else's dream.

"Not anymore. They can all go to hell," he muttered to himself as he reached the landing and nearly dropped the couch when he tried to take another step up. His foot landed with a thump, and Lilith shot him a dirty look while she tried to hold her end up. "Sorry. I thought there were more stairs."

No one would ever call him graceful. As much as Rob loved to dance, his body was made for other things, none of which included ballet or any kind of sport that required coordination or teamwork. He always seemed to zig when he should have zagged, and his family's oddly innate ability to read the minds of their fellow sportsmen escaped him. His father despaired at his attempts to play tennis and racquetball, and once commented that perhaps his youngest son was better suited for something more in keeping with his brutish blood and should take up football.

It hadn't been the first disparaging volley against his mother's ethnicity, and certainly not the last. Over time Rob would learn to ignore the slings and arrows lobbed at him, noting his half siblings never spoke that way about her in front of their father, but Rob was fair game.

And he'd gone along with it, hoping to earn everyone's respect, to get them to overlook that he was a golden-skinned changeling born into an aristocratic clan and see that he was good enough to stand shoulder to shoulder with them.

It'd been easier to walk away than to change their minds.

"Let's just drop it here," Lilith said as she let go of her end just as Rob got through the front door. He had to scramble to avoid his feet being smashed under the weight of the heavy couch, and as he danced back, the front door swung and its knob dug into his spine.

"I swear to God, it's like you took out an insurance policy on me and are trying to kill me," he grumbled as he rubbed at a sore spot near his kidney. "I'm going to shove it toward you so we can open the front door all the way."

"Sure, if you need to." Lilith's imperious response came as she flung herself onto the far end of the couch. "I am *done*."

Lilith was God's response to a much younger Robert's prayer for a best friend. She'd come through the door of his high school English class wearing a sequined tank top, black skinny jeans, and high heels that added three inches to her already six-foot-tall, stick-thin body. At the time, he'd been suffering under the delusion that he was straight, and somehow the statuesque, confident young woman with her severe black bob and bright red lipstick was the girl of his dreams... kicking Annette Gresham, a commonplace cheerleader and honors student, out of the top spot.

Sadly for Rob's unrequited heterosexual delusions, Annette Gresham soon became Lilith Walters's dream girl, something he learned when he screwed up the courage to ask Lilith out on a date, only to be asked if he had the buxom Annette's phone number and could they make it a threesome.

Lilith liked to say that her offer brought him to his senses about being gay, and Rob had to admit there was more than a little bit of truth in that statement, especially since his first reaction to her suggestion was a total lack of interest in something he'd heard his older brothers chortle about. It was the first step down his own personal yellow-brick road, and Lilith was certainly his Glinda... if Glinda the Good Witch ever looked like she moonlighted as a dominatrix.

Unabashedly bisexual and unapologetically hedonistic, Lilith was still possibly the most grounded person Rob had ever met. When his former landlord evicted Rob from his studio apartment so the man's son could move in, Lilith offered him the second master bedroom in her place. He'd said no before, so Rob didn't think the offer was even on the table, but Lilith, the sister of his heart, insisted.

"The place is huge and paid for," she reminded him. "Remember? Crazy grandma? The only thing that would piss my family off more than me inheriting this place is if I set up a den of drunken debauchery in it, and you, Robbie boy, can be my first victim."

She was lying, of course. Not about her family being pissed off—because apparently the enormous Chinatown apartment should have gone to one of the old woman's sons instead of her German Chinese granddaughter—but rather that Lilith would set up anything sketchy in her grandmother's place. She loved the old woman who'd watched her in the afternoons when she was little and insisted on attending every single one of Lilith's art shows, including the performance pieces where everyone was nude except for their papier-mâché chess-piece helmets. He'd sat next to Ma-Ma during that one and spent the night trying not to laugh at her running commentary about how one of the dancer's dicks bounced about as he sproinged across the stage.

The old woman died a month and a half ago, leaving everything to the granddaughter who made her laugh.

Rob put his shoulder to the couch, grunted dramatically at Lilith's extra weight, and kicked the door closed behind him. Collapsing facedown on the sofa, he landed on her thighs with a sweaty plop and made certain he rubbed his wet T-shirt all over her bare legs.

"Oh God, it's like you're smearing sashimi all over me," Lilith gasped. "Get off of me. Get off so I can show you the best part about this apartment."

"I thought the low rent was the best part." He grunted again and rolled over to let her out from under him. "That and the endless hot water. Oh, and it's closer to the shop, so I don't have to get up two hours before my shift to make it in on time. Okay, why the fuck didn't I move in here before?"

"Because you're a fucking idiot, Robbie." Lilith kicked at his shoulder playfully and got off the couch. She stepped around his boxes and motioned toward the bank of windows that faced the main street. "But you haven't cornered the market on being stupid. All of this time Ma-Ma lived here, and I never once noticed the view. And most of the time, there's nothing to see because everything's all closed up, but dude, when they roll up those doors, it's showtime. Just like right now."

"What view? You've seen one Chinatown street and you've seen them all," Rob grumbled after her as he reluctantly got off the couch. "What is so special about—"

Lilith was right... *again*. She was a fucking idiot. Her grandmother lived in the place for decades. She came over from Hong Kong to marry and then raised three boys and one girl while her husband worked himself to death. By the time Lilith came along, the apartment had seen the family expand well beyond its walls, but Chinatown probably hadn't changed much. So it would've been impossible to not notice the fire station across the street.

A fire station that apparently pulled its trucks out in front and made its fire crew wash them down.

Traffic was definitely slowing, more because the streets were cramped and cars had to move around the fire truck's front end that jutted into the road. But Rob also imagined it had something to do with the four muscular men dressed in tight T-shirts and hip-hugging pants having a water fight with a couple of garden hoses.

"I used to wonder why she had these chairs here," Lilith said as she dropped into one of the two soft-bodied wing chairs set in front of the window. A small round wooden table with water rings on it sat between them, while a small jade rat kept a plastic cream-and-sugar set company on the windowsill. "I'm kinda mad at her for not sharing this with me. I like to think of it as her last gift to me—an apartment with air-conditioning and a view that can make you sweat."

There was something familiar about one of the men soaping up the side of the truck, and Rob blindly searched for the chair's seat with his hand as he sat down. He knew those shoulders, those thighs, and even from three stories up, he could almost make out the cocky sneer on the man's gorgeous mouth when the bubbly sponge he threw found its target and struck a familiar Latino firefighter in the face.

"Fucking hell, that's the asshole." Rob leaned forward as though somehow those extra few inches would change his mind. "The one I've been telling you about."

"I thought you said the asshole was the owner of the shop?" Lilith gave him a side-eye from her sprawl over the chair. "He tattoos, and he's a fireman on the side?"

"No tattooing, but he does own the place. Or at least... some of it. There's five of them. They're brothers," he groaned and rubbed his sweat-and-grime-covered face. "Only three of them work the shop. The asshole—Mace—he's that one over there getting hosed down. He's at the shop all the damned time. So's his goofy friend Rey, the one Gus is hooked up with. Haven't you been listening to me bitch about them the past few—" Rob clamped his mouth shut before he did any more damage and shook his head with remorse as he leaned across to rub at Lilith's hand. "Fuck. I'm sorry, Lil. I know it's been shitty these past few weeks. Listening to me bitch about the guys in the shop is literally the last thing you want to be dealing with."

"No, it's all good." She returned his squeeze and gave him a crooked smile when she let go of his hand. "It kept my mind off of things. Trust me, hearing you talk about hot guys and ink was a godsend. I just didn't catch the part about the asshole being… that fucking hot. How's he feel about girls? Anything at all? Or is it a lost cause all the way around?"

"Gay." Rob laughed when Lilith threw her hand over her temple and sighed. "Mace is one hundred percent, 'checks guys out of the front window' gay. All the brothers are. Three tattoo artists, a fireman, and whatever the hell Luke does. Something with disadvantaged kids. I'm not sure. And okay, I think Ivo might be bi, but God knows with him."

"I'm not going to say I'd like to change Mace's mind, because we both know that's not how it works." She pulled her legs up and rested her chin on her knees. Her dark eyes turned crafty, and Lilith studied him. "Does he check you out? Was that little emotional land mine a freak thing?"

"I don't know." Rob couldn't take his eyes off of the gleaming red truck and the man crouching next to one of its wheels, vigorously scrubbing at its enormous rim. "No. Maybe. Most of the time, he strolls in and just gets on his brothers' nerves. It was all really fucking… odd."

"Sure doesn't look bothered now," she commented softly.

"No, but…." He paused, caught in the memory of Mace's face draped in the shadows he'd brought in with him. "Last night was… the first time he seemed… *human*, you know? It was like last night he'd come into the shop thinking no one was there, and he left his… person suit outside the door. And for a second—a really short second—it felt like I was seeing him for the first time. Then it was gone, and he was that asshole again."

"Well, just be careful, Robbie," Lilith cautioned, wrinkling her nose at him. "Remember what Ma-Ma used to say—sometimes people only show you the parts of themselves they want you to see, even when you think you've surprised them."

"Babe, I met your Ma-Ma, and every single time, she pinched some guy's ass. There's no way in hell she'd have said that. First time she met me, she told me to only date guys with big dicks," he shot back. "Pretty sure your grandma got more action in one month than both of us in our entire lives."

"Okay, yeah. So she never said that. But she would have if she hadn't been such a broad." She shrugged off his snort. "Or spent most of her Saturday nights playing mah-jongg and drinking everyone under the table. Still, she'd have told you to be careful. Ma-Ma was good that way. She didn't care who you hooked up with, so long as you watched your back and your heart. And kicked him to the curb once you were done with him."

"Yeah. See, I think that's the problem." He turned back to the window and watched Mace hold the water hose over his head to rinse soap out of his slicked-back hair. "The guy I saw last night? The one inside of the asshole? He'd been kicked more than a few times, and there's no way in hell he's going to let anyone else near him again."

THREE

AS MUCH as Mace didn't want to admit it, Rey had been right. He was tired, soaking wet, and a little chilled, but he felt a little better about... last night, or he was okay until his mind drifted back over to the soot-stained memories lying in wait for him.

Guilt grabbed hold of him again, dug its fingers into his chest, and squeezed the air out of his lungs. The little girl was nothing but smoke and death when he worked to get her breathing again. It didn't matter how much coffee or water he drank, he couldn't get the taste of the fire out of his mouth. When Rey suggested he come down to help wash the truck, Mace said no, but his best friend was persuasive.

"You can't just sit in a box and only come out when it's time to live your life, Mace," Rey scolded him lightly over the phone. "Just get down here and help. You'll feel better."

And he had, until he reached his apartment building. Then he remembered the silence waiting for him inside.

There were times when he regretted living so far away from the family, and with Rey pretty much moved in with Gus at the house, he came home to an empty apartment for days on end. Most people wouldn't have liked the place, but there was a busy alleyway beneath his balcony, and a few doors down the street was a tiny bar that served *ika* and *arare* for snacks while people drank and held karaoke contests every Thursday night. The selection ran to old American love songs, Chinese ballads, and K-pop tunes—a far cry from the metal and blues Mace preferred—but from the laughter and clapping he heard, everyone seemed to enjoy it.

Anything to break the silence.

He'd gotten a great deal on the place, mostly because he did most of the renovations himself with the help of his brothers, and it was only a few blocks away from the station. The extra expense of living in Chinatown was defrayed by not having to drive in for every shift. The structure was older. It dated back to the sixties but definitely wasn't as ancient as some of the buildings around the station. There were parts of Chinatown that barely survived the Great Earthquake. He'd done a clandestine tour of the district's buried remains when he was younger, but the quiet pressed in too tightly on him, and he'd been a shaking, sweaty mess by the time it was over.

There hadn't been much to see, but the echoes of the old Chinatown hadn't seemed too much different from where he lived now.

The late-afternoon sun chased him down the street and was heating up the building's vestibule by the time he made it past its heavy metal security door. From the smells and sounds coming down the front hall, someone was frying fish and watching Chinese opera. Mace dug for his keys to grab his mail from the bank of boxes next to the stairs when the door to 1A opened and Mrs. Hwang popped her head out.

It wasn't the first time the old Chinese lady had lain in wait for him, but as tired as he was, Mace had a smile for her.

The old woman hovered somewhere between eighty and eternal, four feet some inches tall, with stooped shoulders and a mop of gray-shot black hair. Her face was as wrinkled as a handful of *li hing mui* plums, and her grin was always broad and sweet when she spotted him. Like many of the Chinatown factory workers, she'd once smoked like a chimney— harsh cigarettes that burnished her teeth and permanently yellowed the skin between her fingers—but she'd sworn off of them when her husband died of cancer decades before. Dressed in a thin pink housecoat over a pair of magenta leggings, she shuffled out of her apartment, her steps making the flowers on top of her plastic house slippers bob in time with the rise and fall of her feet.

She was one of Mace's favorite people.

"*Hǔzǐ*, can you help me?" Her fingers shook as she pointed back toward the open door. "I need the big pot."

"'Course. Not a problem." The mail would have to wait, and he held out his arm for her to lean on. "Are you sure you don't want me to put shelves in your pantry against that one wall? It would give you more storage."

"I do not want to bother you, but if it means you wouldn't have to help me anymore, then yes," she rumbled at him in her raspy voice. "I don't use it all the time, but it only fits on top of the refrigerator."

He knew what she was saying. There was a delicate dance of culture and societal norms they'd done since the moment he moved in. As the only non-Chinese in the building, Mace had to learn very quickly what was meant by certain phrases and how to respond to gifts and questions. He was by no means fluent in the culture or the language, but he knew enough to get by, and he certainly understood the shaky ground he stood on now.

"I will build you the shelves and put the pot on the top one so you still have to come get me if you want it down." Mace kept his tone teasingly light and slowed his pace to match hers. "Mostly, it's so you'll have space on your refrigerator for more lemon jars. That way, you'll need me to help get those down, and I will be right there to eat some when they're ready."

He got the laugh he wanted.

"I can't believe you like sour lemon," she scolded him, falling into Cantonese. "Not even my grandchildren like it."

"That just means more for me," he replied back, not minding her grimace at his accent. "I am trying, Grandmother. I don't think my tongue was built the right way."

"At least you try," Mrs. Hwang agreed and patted his hand. "You get me the pot, and I will make us some tea. The boy brought egg tarts today, so we can have some."

"I'm soaking wet," Mace pointed out. "I don't want to get your—"

"I do not mind. Besides, there is plastic on the couch." She patted him on the back and shuffled past him toward the kitchen. "Close the front door."

Her place was smaller than his—a kitchenette and the dining area to the left of the short front hall and a long shotgun-style living room that faced the street to the right. A small bedroom and bathroom were at the end of the foyer, and the narrow walk's walls were covered with framed photos.

It was like looking into the Chinatown he'd hoped to find underground—faces and lives caught on film and silvered paper. Many were of Mrs. Hwang and her husband in their twenties and thirties, and a progression of children joined them and then aged on trips to Disneyland or at local places Mace was familiar with. He got the pot down from on top of the refrigerator and, with a tape measure he'd left in her junk drawer, measured the back wall of the pantry again just to make sure he had the numbers right.

"I brought you a towel," she said as she shuffled back into the kitchen. "But you are probably dried by now."

"I can sit on it while we have tea," Mace replied and jotted the measurements down on a Post-it note. Then he did what he always did when visiting Mrs. Hwang. He walked to the front hall and took down one of the photos—an image of her laughing in front of a carousel. When he returned to the kitchen, he held it up for her to see while she measured out loose-leaf tea into a porcelain pot. He asked, "Why don't you tell me about what you were doing here? It looks like you're having a lot of fun."

"SHIT, FORGOT the goddamned mail," Mace swore an hour and a half later as he juggled Tupperware containers while he tried to get his front door open. His key turned too easily in the lock, meeting no resistance, and Mace was displeased to discover the stereo he had left playing classic rock was now silent.

Unlike Mrs. Hwang's place, his apartment had been gutted by its previous owner, who tore down its space-consuming front hall. The renovation transformed the once chopped-up area into a single large room with only a marble-topped island with cabinets to separate the kitchen from the living and dining spaces.

So it was easy for Mace to find the source of the turned-off stereo— his youngest brother, Ivo, sprawled over his couch.

Among all of his found siblings, Ivo was both the most perplexing and the one who understood him the best, even more than Bear did. When Ivo came into the house as a deadly quiet, headstrong boy, there'd been friction about everything that surrounded him. The first six months had been the worst of Mace's life outside of the system. He'd butted heads with Bear more times than he could count and pushed his older brother to hold Ivo accountable for his chores and schoolwork.

They all agreed on certain things, and one of them was to raise Ivo into a respectable, independent-thinking adult, but at the time, Mace felt like he was doing more damage than good, especially when Bear countermanded every single thing Mace asked Ivo to do. They fought horribly and had long stretches of silence punched with hot, cutting words. Then Mace threw his hands up and refused to go any further.

He'd been packing his things to leave when Ivo came into his room.

The sullen disregard Ivo wore on his face was gone, replaced by a bone-shaking fear. His eyes were as crystal blue as ever, but they glittered behind a wall of tears Ivo fought to hold back. He'd been wearing one of Mace's T-shirts, something he'd gotten at a concert long before Bear made them a home. It was one of the few things Mace had been able to hold on to during the moves from one foster home to the next, one of the few things he'd been able to call his own at a time in his life when he had nothing but what he could shove into a trash bag to take to the next place he'd sleep for a few months, like a transient ghost visiting families scattered around San Francisco.

It was the shirt theft that drove Mace over the edge, and there Ivo stood, wearing the evidence on his skinny, boyish frame with enough tears in his eyes to fuel a summer rain.

"Don't go," the young boy said, his voice breaking in the echoing emptiness of Mace's spartan room. "Who else is going to be like me if you go?"

They were nothing alike, so Ivo's words jerked Mace's head up, and he stopped packing to stare incredulously at the kid. Clearing his throat gave him time to search through his confused thoughts, but he came up with nothing. Mace cocked his head and asked, "What the hell you talking about?"

"Who else is going to read with me?" Ivo pointed to the bookshelves running under the windows of Mace's room. "It's just you and me. Who else is going to read?"

The books were as hard-won as the shirt. There were a few he'd squirreled away in his things and kept hidden from prying eyes and sticky fingers. For some reason books were a source of mocking amusement whenever he was caught with them before, and even then it was hard for Mace to admit his addiction to the printed word. But he brought home shelves he found in trash bins and garage sales and filled them with paperbacks he haggled people out of, sometimes for as little as a quarter for a box. They were his treasures, pieces of gold and bits of worlds he shared with Ivo only after outlining strict rules against bending spines and dog-earing pages.

He started to unpack his things just as Ivo's first tear wet his cheek.

And despite the years, Ivo still had boundary issues.

"Can we just skip over the conversation about how the key is only to be used for emergencies?" Ivo didn't even glance up from the sheaf of papers he was reading. Pointing in the general direction of the heavy pair of Doc Martens Mace almost tripped over, he shrugged. "I wasn't going to stand out in the hallway wearing those. They're too heavy and new. I just wanted to get them off."

As always, Ivo was a mass of contradictions. Barefoot and wearing a schoolgirl skirt that could have possibly passed as a kilt except for the coin-spangled belly dancer belt slung around his hips, Ivo sat cross-legged on the sofa facing the door. His sparkling blue eyes were rimmed with a heavy layer of kohl, a feminine touch contradicted by the dark scruff on his jaw. An inch or two shorter than Mace, he was mostly leg, but at some point, his shoulders had widened out and he'd gained some muscle along his torso. His thighs and calves were sleek and powerful, probably from wearing the deadly heels he liked to sport once in a while. Mace couldn't remember the last time he'd seen Ivo's natural hair color, and today it was different again, a range of burned reds, yellows, and spots of orange streaked through his ebony-tinted mane.

"If I didn't know better, sometimes I could swear someone stole you from Elfhaine." Mace picked up the offending shoes and placed them on the rack against the wall.

"Yeah, that's me," his brother snorted under his breath. "Ivo, Clan Rogers, Fifth in the House of Bear, Jester of the Ashbury Heights. Pleased to meet you. And since you're up, can you make me some coffee? I didn't want to touch the Transformer you've got living on your countertop. God only knows what would happen if I pressed the wrong button. Last thing I needed was a sentient Pontiac Firebird popping up in your kitchen."

"It's not that complicated. You pull the pot out of the part where… never mind, I'll do it. It'll be easier than having to explain it to you when you obviously don't want to do it yourself." Mace toed off his shoes. "I'll get your coffee going. Then I'm going to take a shower. I'm pretty ripe."

"You're telling me," Ivo sniped. "I can smell you from here."

"Nice. Remind me again why we didn't smother you with a pillow while you were sleeping?" Mace didn't get an answer, but he wasn't expecting one.

He shuffled the Tupperware he'd gotten from Mrs. Hwang into the sparse interior of his refrigerator and quickly checked the expiration date on his creamer. Satisfied it was still good, he got the coffeepot set up and glanced over to the sitting area he'd set up instead of a dining room next to the kitchen. He'd taken off the chair rail, intending to paint before he lined the walls with the floor-to-ceiling cherrywood shelves he'd salvaged from the brothers' house.

The chair rail was still gone, but four feet of the ivory wallpaper he had yet to steam off was now covered with an elaborate underwater scene, complete with mermen and delicate faerie dragons, all done in black marker.

The lines were beautiful, and the stippling ranged from loose to tight, giving the piece dimension. He could clearly see the current moving through the seaweed fronds and amoeba frills, and he noticed a scattering of manta rays in the upper right corner, barely silhouettes in the background. One of them had bunny ears.

Mace took a long, steadying breath. "You were supposed to help me take that down, remember? Not draw all over it."

"If you bothered to notice, it's butcher paper I tacked to the wall. I'm taking it with me. I got bored waiting for you," Ivo remarked. "And then when I was done with that, I went and found what you're working on so I had something to read. You didn't tell me you got up to chapter six. Last I heard, you only had a plot, and that was kind of sketchy."

Another breath did nothing to soothe Mace's rattled nerves. Ivo knew how to push every single one of his buttons, much like their brother Gus. But unlike Gus, Ivo knew exactly what he was doing when he was doing it.

"There are literally boxes of books up against that wall over there," Mace finally said. "None of which involve turning on my laptop, digging through my files, and then printing them out."

"Yeah, sometimes you have to work a little to get something that really satisfies you," Ivo replied unapologetically. "Go take your shower, and when you come back, we can talk about what you did here with chapter two."

THE SHOWER had been long and hot, a welcome respite after a chilled walk down the hill and the cold Mace couldn't seem to shake out of his bones. He'd come back to the living room to find the stereo set to a low murmur—Stevie Ray Vaughan growling about the high waters in Texas—and Ivo accepting a takeout delivery from the Chinese kitchen up the street. The sliding glass door leading to the balcony had been left open a crack, letting the street noise into the apartment, and the rest of Mace's prickliness eased away, soothed by the river of sound that washed over him. They'd settled onto the couches, comfortable in a silence punctured only by their slurping up food and sipping from the cold beer Mace retrieved from the fridge.

"Thanks for ordering." He saluted Ivo with the Tsingtao. "Appreciate it."

"I'm not going to say I'm sick of eating Chinese food, but I'm kind of sick of eating Chinese food," Ivo commented while he picked through his noodles, probably looking for more shrimp. "You should really learn how to cook more than chili, beef stew, and pulled pork."

"I can also make eggs, bacon, and pancakes," Mace corrected, "and waffles, because that's just pretty much pancakes. And if you fuck up the batter, you can fold fruit and shit inside of it, cover it with whipped cream, and call it a crepe."

Ivo looked up at him, judgmentally and skeptically. "That's not how it works. That's not how any of it works. Those things are nothing like—"

"Don't see you complaining when I'm making peanut-butter-and-chocolate-chip crepes on Sunday morning if I'm over there. All those are is pancake batter with too much milk. And don't get me started on the noises you make when I pull out the Nutella." Mace found a shrimp in his house-special chow fun, picked it out with his chopsticks, and put it in Ivo's open Styrofoam container. "You sound like a bad porno from the seventies, where the pizza delivery guy never seems to have a pizza when he knocks on the door."

"Only you would give a shit about the pizza when watching porn." Ivo moved the shrimp aside and began to migrate his pile of discarded mushrooms over to Mace's noodles. "So I've got to ask you, did you happen to notice you wrote Rob, the new guy, into chapter three as your main character's love interest?"

"I did *not*." Mace debated taking back the shrimp, but Ivo would probably stab him with a chopstick in retaliation. "I don't think I even know what the guy really looks like."

"Really?" Again Ivo's voice dripped skepticism. "Because whenever you're in the shop, it seems like he's the only thing that holds your attention. Or haven't you noticed that too?"

"Barking up the wrong tree, kiddo." The lies sat between them like a heavy and bloated tick, drunk on mistruths and deception. Mace knew what Rob looked like. He couldn't help but know. The tattoo artist haunted Mace's dreams, and his hammered-gold gaze and full, ripe mouth fed into every sexual desire Mace's twisted mind could dredge up. But there was no way he was going to let Ivo know that. "He's an employee, remember? We do not sleep with *anyone* who works for us. One of the shop's rules."

"I'm just saying, if you're going to fantasize about someone, you should probably leave him out of your book." Ivo pinched Mace with his toes, something Mace would've thought was impossible considering the distance between them, but he'd forgotten how long Ivo's legs were. "And don't make that face. It didn't hurt. I barely touched you."

"I'm not fantasizing about him. Besides him being one of Bear's artists, I don't do relationships, remember?" He was ready for Ivo's next jab and rubbed at his brother's foot before it hit its mark. Ivo was ticklish, and Mace knew exactly where. A quick slide of his fingers on Ivo's arch and his brother quickly retreated, hissing furiously. Sobering after a quick chuckle, Mace said, "I'm too fucked-up, kid. No one's going to want to wade through my shit for longer than a one-night stand."

"Mace, that's just—"

"It's the truth. Every single guy I hooked up with in the past headed for the door as soon as they got to know me better. I'm not doing it to myself again. I'm not going to give somebody my heart just so they can spit on it like everybody else," Mace interrupted. "Trust me, Ivo, the only love I'm ever going to get in my lifetime is from you and the rest of the family. That's just going to have to be enough."

FOUR

IF THE Craftsman house in Ashbury Heights was a home, the tattoo shop on the edge of Fisherman's Wharf was a sanctuary.

Mace liked the bustle of the crowds around the front door and the ambient rush of voices and footsteps that crept into the shotgun-style shop. There were times when he jogged from his Chinatown apartment to 415 Ink in the middle of the night, touched its locked front door as though to tag himself safe, and then headed back up the hill. Depending on how tired he was, it could take anywhere from minutes to an hour, but the city usually kept him company along the way, even in the dead of night.

But there was nothing like dropping in on the shop in the late hours of the morning, right before 415 Ink opened for business. That was when Mace usually could find a brother or two, and it was better than tagging himself safe on the front door.

The smell of coffee greeted Mace when he approached the back door. The crowds were already thick on the sidewalk—he'd dodged at least five children and two dogs but failed to see the woman dressed in pink from head to toe and carrying her ferret. She went to the left at the same time he did, and the only one to come out of the exchange without a bump on their head was the ferret. He caught up with it before it could disappear, snagged its leash carefully, and then scooped it up to hand the animal back to her.

They did mutual apologies, and she was bold enough to place her business card into his hand after he helped her up from the sidewalk. She was pretty in a way that women were when they were comfortable with themselves, and despite his preference for men, her easy smile brightened the edges of the darkness he carried inside. It only took a moment of hemming and hawing before she rattled off a checklist of reasons why he couldn't date her. She hit on gay at the third try and laughed when he blushed.

"Keep the card," she told him. "I could always use a friend who likes ferrets and drinks coffee."

He kept the card and tucked it into his wallet as he strode to 415 Ink's rear entrance. He hadn't taken more than three steps into the shop when an air-raid siren went off… or at least that's what it sounded like. If the air-raid siren was a little bit taller than knee height, had enormous eyes that took up most of his face, and was a little bit more than three years old.

"Uncle Mace!" The little boy's voice was a shrieking cry, sharp enough to cut through a pack of gulls fighting over french fries, but Mace didn't mind. He caught Chris as the boy launched himself at him and took a knee to his stomach, but that was better than a few inches below—something Mace learned very early in his relationship with the enthusiastic toddler. "Going to the zoo! Want to come?"

"You better ask the adult taking you before you start handing out invitations, kid," Mace laughed. "Unless that's your devious way of getting another adult in on the trip so you can score more goodies."

"You have him confused with Ivo. God knows he looks enough like him, and sometimes I think he opens his mouth and Ivo crawls out," Gus remarked as he came out of the shop's office. "Chris, dude, what did we talk about? About jumping on people? If Earl doesn't get to do it, you don't get to do it."

"That's a pretty low bar to set for parenting," Mace teased. "He just has to behave better than the dog? Earl will eat cat shit or any dead squirrel he finds on a walk."

"Look, that's my baseline." His younger brother shrugged and then took his son out of Mace's arms. "Earl's rules are simple—no bringing dead things inside, no eating dead things you find outside, and no jumping on people. If I can get Chris to master that, we can move on to things like not eating crayons or paste."

"Really?" He crooked an eyebrow at Gus. "Pretty sure you were still eating crayons just last week."

"Yeah, fu—damn it." Mace saw Gus catch himself as he lifted his hand up and folded his fingers down, but he shook off the gesture before Chris saw him. Gus slid Chris around onto his hip and kept a tight hold on his wiggling kid. "Bear's setting up. He's got a twelve thirty coming in, and I'm on this evening, after I drop off the monster here."

The grin Chris exchanged with Gus was heartbreakingly sweet. It was the kind of moment Mace could never admit he longed for. Father and son were nearly two peas in a pod, but Chris's eyes were nearly Ivo's in shape and color, a darker blue than Gus's silvery sky hue. It was easy to see the little boy Gus had been in the toddler he held now. Their smiles were both off-kilter, and even though Gus's hair was a darker blond and much more golden than Chris's wheaten locks, the strands fell in the same way—a tousled mane around their attractive faces.

They would probably eventually share the same body frame, broad shoulders and long legs, just like Ivo, and Chris's dimples were hints on his cheeks, but his facial structure was pure Gus, a cherubic version of his father's roguish features. They even laughed the same way, starting off with a small chuckle and building up to a full-throttle guffaw.

But it was the sheer joy in Chris's expression that Mace one day hoped Gus would share. None of the other brothers carried their shadows as close to their soul as Gus, and if there was anything Mace wished for most, it wasn't to exorcise his own ghosts, but rather to put Gus's to rest—anything to see him smile with as much unabashed pleasure as his son did.

"He's probably going to be taller than you," Mace poked at Gus. "Give it a couple years and the only person you're going to be standing over will be Luke."

"Dude, why don't you go find your uncle Bear and say goodbye," Gus muttered as he set Chris down, "so I can kick your uncle Mace in the—"

"Remember the Rule of Earl." Mace *tsk*ed and brought his knee in to block Gus in case his brother decided against common sense and hit him. "Make sure your kid has better manners than the dog... or in your case, you should have better manners than the kid."

"One day...." Gus shook his finger under Mace's nose. "One day someone is going to come along and kick your ass, and I only hope that I'm there to see it."

"Well that day isn't today, and that someone isn't you," he shot back and lightly punched his brother on the arm. "You guys go have fun at the zoo. Bear said there was mail for me up at the house that he brought down. And if you should happen to see the guy who used to live with me sometime today, tell him to swing by and let me know what he wants to do with the storage space in the garage. I don't want to put anything in front of his stuff if he's going to run away and join the circus, but I need to build out a couple of shelving units, and I want to store lumber down there for a while."

"Got it," Gus grunted when Chris came barreling back into him. "I'm going to go pick him up from the station. He should just be getting off shift. I told him he should go home and crash, but he wants to come to the zoo with us."

"Rey?" Chris asked, cocking his head. "I like Rey. He shares his fries."

"Ivo is never going to be forgiven for that." Gus slapped Mace on the shoulder, leaving a slight sting. "If you don't have Bear take care of that touchup for you, come by later and I'll do it."

"I can do a touchup if Bear can't and you don't want to wait." Rob, the bane of Mace's existence, came out of the employees' lounge, one hand wrapped around a steaming mug and the other raking through his blue-tipped black hair. "I don't have anything until three. I'm just doing walk-ins." He caught the look the brothers exchanged, and then he grimaced. "Okay, *Barrett*. I don't know why you guys are such hardasses about that. It's his *fucking* nickname."

"And with that swearword in front of my kid, I'm out of here," Gus said with a nod toward Mace. "Hit me up later."

"Later. Don't forget to tag Rey for me." Mace forced himself not to look in Rob's direction. He waved Gus and Chris off and turned, only to find Rob standing in front of him. "What?"

They needed the space between them. *He* needed space between them. Rob was becoming an itch Mace knew he couldn't afford to scratch.

The shop had rules. *Bear* had rules. And no matter how many years Mace spent calling Bear his brother, he wasn't willing to risk being tossed out by crossing a line clearly drawn in the sand. He didn't have to look deeply to know he didn't have… faith in being loved unconditionally. There'd been too many infractions in the past, both real and imagined, with his father and then the families he'd been handed to. He loved his brothers too much to risk even the taste of Rob's mouth.

But God, at that moment, the thought of getting his first hit of coffee off of Rob's lips was something Mace couldn't shake.

He couldn't figure it out. Rob was nothing like any of the men he sought out to hook up with. He didn't want complications. He didn't want to know somebody's phone number beyond a couple of weeks or get a text at three o'clock in the afternoon wondering if he wanted to try a new restaurant at the piers. Even as much as he avoided the vivacious artist, he knew Rob was a social creature who squeezed every last bit out of the day and then licked its remains off of his hands. There were no boundaries Rob respected. He was in everyone's space, asking questions or prying out secrets.

He talked with his hands—his graceful and strong fingers sketched out flurries of ideas in the air as his words danced in and out of Mace's thoughts. Rob couldn't stop moving, even when tattooing. He tapped at the floor with his free foot as he rattled on to his clients about everything under the sun.

And damn it if Mace didn't want to shut him up with a kiss.

Rob's mouth wasn't moving now. Instead he was chewing on his lower lip and tilting his chin up slightly, his intense gaze fixed on Mace's face. The summer had left its burnished kiss on Rob's body and deepened his golden skin, and there was a faint spray of freckles across his nose and cheeks. Under the shop's bright lights, his lashes threw down long shadows when he blinked and were so thick and black they looked fake. Mace knew better. He'd seen Rob bolting past the shop's front door after a downpour, rubbing at his face to sluice away the dribbles of water that ran down from his hair.

He was the kind of guy who needed taking care of, someone who liked to wake up on Sunday mornings to a blueberry-pancake breakfast, then a leisurely walk down to a coffee shop to meet up with friends. Despite his bohemian nature, Rob was a seeker of domestic bliss, with occasional stops at a club or two just to dance off his nervous energy.

The wicked parts of Mace's brain had more than one suggestion on how to work off Rob's energy.

"What do you want?" Mace didn't care much for society's games. One of them was a form of chicken, the question of who was going to move to get by in a narrow hallway. He was bigger and taller than Rob, but ducking around the inker meant giving way, and Mace wasn't willing to do that. "Do you need something?"

"I need a lot of things, but the first thing that comes to mind is maybe you trying to be a little nicer to me." Rob couldn't help but purr when he spoke. His voice had a hint of a lingual influence Mace couldn't identify, but whatever it was, it rolled Rob's consonants around his vowels in an erratic river of sound that ran over the jagged rocks lodged in Mace's belly. "I was serious when I offered to do your touchup. Your brother doesn't hire shitty artists. I wouldn't be here if I didn't deserve it."

"Bear put it on me. Bear touches it up." Mace gave Rob a little smile and hoped the conversation would be over soon. Rob had some muscle on him, a denseness that came with whatever ethnic blend went into creating a golden-skinned, amber-eyed, pretty-mouthed artist, but

Mace figured he had enough power in his body to pin Rob up against the wall and do things to him until Rob was breathless and couldn't think. Since that way led to madness and Bear kicking his ass, Mace shoved his hands into his pockets and forced himself to concentrate on getting past the man he wanted to fuck every time he saw him. "If he doesn't have time today, it can wait. I just caught my shoulder on some gear. Scratch went down deep, so it just needs a little saturation."

Mace figured it was time to toss his ego aside and say to hell with the chicken game, so he nudged past Rob to get to the front of the shop before he lost whatever willpower he had left. He hated feeling drunk and out of control every time he got close to Rob, and he didn't know what was worse, the frustration of not having him or knowing that even if he lost his mind and gave in to his desire, it would be a one-way street and a ticket to heartbreak.

Rob's hand burned on his bare arm, and Mace sucked in a sharp breath and forced down the raging fire that Rob's touch stoked in the embers Mace had banked not a moment before. He'd worn a thin T-shirt, thinking he could roll up the short sleeves to give Bear access to the spot he needed re-inked. But once he felt Rob's fingers—imagined those fingers elsewhere on his body—Mace wondered if he shouldn't have worn a suit of armor so he could survive the battle brewing inside of him.

"Tell me what I did to piss you off, because I have to work here, and like you really love to remind me, you're one of the owners." He tightened his fingers, and Mace choked on the hot air he was holding in. "Every time you see me, you act like I'm a piece of shit you have to scrape off your shoe. I just—"

"Did you ever think the reason I keep reminding you I'm one of the owners is because we're not allowed to hook up with anyone who works here?" Mace growled as he reluctantly pulled himself free of Rob's grip. "So maybe—*just fucking maybe*—I'm not reminding you. I'm fucking reminding *me*."

MACE STILL felt Rob's fingers on his skin even five minutes after he'd pulled free. He sat in Bear's chair, cautious of its wonky wheel and mindful of Earl's tail, not more than a foot away. The dog looked up when he came in, and his ears perked up enough to say hello, but the shaggy mutt didn't move from his sprawl, and his long legs were hooked over a pillow Ivo normally used to support his back. Technically Earl should have been on his dog bed in the reception area, but the shop wasn't open yet, and Bear let Earl have the run of the place right up until the first client walked through the door.

"I sent Rob to the store to get some creamer." Bear came down the hall from the back room holding a plastic bin full of ink bottles and wrapped needles. "Behind you over there. That's the letter I told you about."

If there was anyone Mace revered more than the firemen who pulled him out of his old life, it was Barrett Jackson. The couple who gave Bear shelter had decided they could take in one more child at the exact same moment when Mace's foster family was done with him. Whoever was manning the karmic wheel that morning was a god in Mace's eyes. He'd spent six months being shoved and beaten for every little slight, caught between two adults who should've known better than to stay married and their children who were pawns in a battlefield they had no control over. Mace couldn't even remember their names, but he knew the man's face in his nightmares. He was a florid, spitting scarecrow with iron fists and a hair-trigger temper.

It had gotten so bad that Mace slipped up. His brain short-circuited, and the echoes of violence were so familiar, he'd called the man *Dad*.

Mace was dropped off at CPS within the hour, gripping a paper bag filled with only the meager things he could grab in the few minutes he was given.

Coerced by his social worker, a tired woman with a smoker's cough and a sad smile, the Johnsons took him in. That was where he met Bear, a long-lost brother he didn't know he had.

They weren't related, but something between them clicked. Bear understood Mace's needs before he tipped over into frustrated rage, and he was willing to share a cramped room with a clock radio set at an empty AM number. He was the one to shatter the brittle silence around Mace, the one to stoke Mace's interest in homework, and then the first one to promise Mace he would have a family to call his own.

Bear left the Johnsons first, but he remained a firm presence in Mace's life. It didn't take long for Mace to emancipate himself from the system and move into the ramshackle Craftsman Bear purchased so they could make it a home.

There was always another project, and the house seemed more Winchester with its never-ending list of broken things, but Mace wouldn't trade it for the largest mansion in the world—any more than he would ever give up any of the men who'd become the family Bear promised him.

"Did you see Gus and Chris before they left?" Bear began refilling Ivo's stall, probably preparing for their younger brother's appointments later in the day. "They were going to the zoo."

"Yeah, he told me. I've got to get the storage room cleaned out a bit to make room for some lumber." Mace wrinkled his nose at the thought of digging through what Rey brought with him. "I can't wait for Rey to tell Gus about the house. I know it's not a done deal yet, but it's kind of hard to wait."

"I know he's going to be just over the hill, but is it stupid to be sad that he won't be crashing at the house anymore?" Bear looked up with a wistful expression on his bearded face.

It wasn't strange for Bear to grow sentimental. Of all of them, he was the gentlest. He was a large man who looked as though he could fell a forest with a few swings of an ax or punch through a mountain to get to the other side. There was a steadiness to his demeanor, a rumble to his deep voice, and a bit of silver in his dark brown hair, but the light in his deep blue eyes sometimes bordered on mischievous, and a bit of his enthusiasm for life shone through.

Usually that meant Mace or one of the others would find themselves being volunteered for something they didn't want to do, but if it was Bear who asked, they wouldn't complain.

Or at least none muttered where anyone else could hear.

"I'd think you'd be glad to get rid of them." Mace leaned over to scratch the dog's belly when Earl rolled over and looked up at him with mournful eyes. "I can hear them from across the hall, and God knows my walls are thicker than yours."

"They're not so bad," his brother replied with a grin. "Rey does dishes. I like coming home to a clean kitchen. Ivo is like a tsunami and can't even drink water without dirtying every glass in the cupboards. All he has to do is put them in the dishwasher."

"If you recall, I was the one who had to go through the house on the great cup hunt two years ago. I know exactly how he is." As he reached for the envelope, Mace endured a grumbling sigh from the dog at his feet. "Get over yourself, Earl. I've got human things to do now."

When he turned over the letter, Mace understood why Bear had him come in. He'd had other envelopes emblazoned with official seals and embossed letters, just like the one he held now and none of which he wanted to see. Someone had gone to the trouble of handwriting his name and the address of the brothers' house in a flowing cursive that wouldn't have been out of place on a wedding invitation.

It *was* an invitation of sorts, just not to a party Mace ever wanted to attend. But he forced himself to go every time he got one of the letters.

Bear's shadow filtered out some of the light, but Mace welcomed his brother's presence. He tried to tell himself his fingers were only shaking because he hadn't had enough coffee, but the lie didn't sit well in his stomach.

"These fucking things are always hard to open," Mace joked when he couldn't get his thumb under the corner of the flap.

"You want me to help you?" Bear laid a large hand on Mace's shoulder, anchoring Mace before he spun into the terrors that lurked in his mind.

He appreciated Bear asking. It would've been an easy way out of everything to let Bear handle what lay inside of the envelope, but Mace didn't want to admit he wasn't strong enough this time around. The flap gave, and he felt the bite of paper slicing the tender flesh under the edge of his thumbnail. He hissed and sucked at it for a moment and then blew on his hand to ease the burn as he shook the letter's contents onto his lap.

His brother took the envelope from him, letting Mace unfold the paper that had fallen out. It took him nearly a full minute to realize the words he'd expected to read weren't there. There would be no party this time. It was an invitation to dance with words and broken hearts and horrific memories. This time he was being invited to a nightmare.

"What's wrong, Mason?" Bear filled the space in front of Mace, crouching at his knee, and rubbed Mace's back. "Are you okay? Do they want you to go in?"

"Never." Mace swallowed around the sick rising from his belly, but it kept coming in a sea of panic and disbelief.

Bear stilled his hand and drew even closer, until his warmth was all Mace could feel... other than the spreading cold that gripped his spine and heart. "What do you mean never? Are they saying you don't have to go back anymore?"

"No. They're…," Mace whispered, and suddenly the nightmare became real. "They're letting my father out of prison, Bear. Fucking hell. After everything he's done, they're just letting him *go*."

FIVE

MACE DIDN'T come back.

And neither did Bear after he finished up his noon-thirty appointment, told Ivo to watch the shop, and took off with Earl without giving so much as a backward glance.

Something was going on, and it was driving Rob nuts.

"Just… grab anyone who walks in," Ivo told him when he asked about Bear. "Let's just get through the day and see how it goes."

Walk-ins were hot and heavy and nearly overwhelmed them until Gus dropped by with his kid and spent an hour knocking out bits and pieces of flash that a group of middle-aged women picked out from the books. Rob ended up doing a butterfly and then a spray of shooting stars while Gus took care of most of the others in the couple of hours he could spare. Then he had a phone call from Bear, made his apologies, and left. Assuring his brother he would take care of the rest, Ivo wrapped up an appointment and moved on to a pair of redheaded twins who asked for a delicate filigree compass to be put on their hips.

"God, I hate it when we get groups like that," Dave, the shop's apprentice, groused not more than five minutes after the group laughed and chattered their way out of the door, every single one of them sporting a clear covering of breathable film to protect their new tattoos while they healed. "They always make a mess, and it's not like they're serious about the ink. It's shitty they spotted a tattoo shop and think it's cool to just drop in and get something done. We shouldn't even agree to ink them. It just makes us look bad. Like we'll slap a tattoo on anyone."

Rob braced for Ivo's lecture.

When he first met the youngest of 415 Ink's brothers, Rob learned to throw out any preconceptions about gender or masculinity where Ivo Rogers was concerned. His introduction to the mercurial wild child of the bunch was colored by the talk among other tattoo artists. Ivo had a reputation for being a diva, slightly arrogant about his art and his skills and with a flagrant disregard for social niceties. Rob's only reservations about working in 415 Ink stemmed from having to work shoulder to shoulder with Ivo. He was torn between how much he could learn from someone who'd grown up in a tattoo shop and his fear of setting off a hot-tempered, unstable young owner.

Rob quickly discovered that any diva behavior Ivo might throw would've been deserved. Despite being younger than most shop apprentices, Ivo could blow away most artists in the business with what he could do with some ink and a machine.

The only thing Rob really had to adjust to was getting used to seeing a gorgeous, masculine, six-foot-one man with long, powerful legs stride confidently across the shop in deadly three-inch heels.

Ivo was fearless, wore what he wanted to when he wanted to, and boldly mingled gender roles with his wardrobe and look. Some days were T-shirt, jeans, and Converses, while others were kilts, thigh-high stiletto boots, and a smoky eye makeup Lilith ached to learn how to do. Ivo was… experimental. He wasn't androgynous per se—there was always a defined maleness about him, a leonine presence in the way he moved and walked. He wrapped a shimmer of femininity around himself, picked and chose bits he liked, usually eyeliner or a flare of glitter nail polish on his fingers, and more than a few times, he gave Rob advice on how to get the most vibrant colors from a particular brand of hair dye.

But the rumors were right about one thing. Ivo had no time for bullshit or social head games, and judging by the quick jerk of Ivo's head and the narrowing of his ocean-blue eyes, he'd definitely heard Dave's complaint and was not pleased.

"Didn't Bear talk to you about that before?" Ivo didn't stop cleaning his machine, but his gaze was fixed on Dave. "We're here to ink. Not judge."

"It's not like we're going to see them again. They come in because they think it's some kind of rebellion on their part. A chick gets a small little heart or daisy on her ankle, and suddenly she's a badass." From the look of things, Dave didn't realize he was cutting the carrots for the hot water he was in, adding to the stew Ivo was about to make out of him. "I mean, we get, what? A couple hundred dollars? Maybe three? We should just get one of those machines that make temporary tattoos on paper for those kinds of people to pick up instead of wasting our time inking them. They can pick out what they want, you can charge them ten bucks extra for the sponge and water, and then they're gone."

Ivo's gaze flicked toward Rob, and the hard fire he saw in their depths made Rob flinch. There were moments when lines were drawn, and where someone stood, what side they were on, meant everything. It seemed silly to be caught in one of those moments over little dots of ink and a group of laughing women, but in that particular moment, that's where he was.

"Nuh-uh." Rob shook his head at Ivo and gathered up the used plastic pots of ink he had on his station. "Day one of working here, Bear told me exactly where he stood and said if I didn't like it, I could walk. Notice I still work here."

"Yeah, but Dave doesn't," Ivo replied softly. "Grab your stuff out of the back room and go. I hate to do this, dude, but we can't have you here if you don't respect everyone who comes through the door."

"You can't tell me to leave. I'm Bear's apprentice, not yours." Dave dropped the broom he'd been using, outrage churning on his face with a red flush. "They're just a bunch of stupid bitches—"

"That's your problem. *That*, right there." This time Ivo put down his half-cleaned machine and walked out to the middle of the floor where Dave stood with his fists on his hips. There was about three feet between them, and Rob didn't like the twitch of Dave's nostrils when Ivo drew near. "Bear might be your mentor, but this is *our* shop. You are *everyone's* responsibility. If you can't understand the shop's—*this family's*—fundamental philosophy, then you need to find someplace else to be.

"Those women came in here looking for something to wear for the rest of their lives," Ivo said softly and pointed at the front door. "Just like everybody else. It doesn't matter if it's small or large or if it's the only tattoo they'll ever get in their entire life. It's for *them*, and it's *special*. A good inker isn't just about being able to tattoo or be a great artist. You also have to respect the person who's going to walk out with what you've done. They've got to be happy with it, and they deserve to have a good experience while getting inked. You're not understanding that. You're not getting that those women are as important to the shop as that guy who's going to come in next week for a full back piece. And that's why I'm telling you to get the fuck out. If you want to call Bear tomorrow to talk about it, go ahead, but he's going to back me on this. Because you just don't get it."

It was really the most he'd ever heard Ivo say. Most of the time, Ivo spent his hours at the shop with his headphones on or bent over someone's body or working on sketches in the art room by the back door. There were always brief floods of discussion between the brothers and their clients, but speeches were few and far between.

Dave didn't seem to like this one, and he stepped closer, his fists pulled back. He was a gangly knit of elbows and knees, with about twenty pounds less muscle than Ivo, but there was a coiled rage in his stance. Rob dropped the pots into the trash can and waited for Dave to respond.

"You think you're just hot shit, don't you?" Dave growled up into Ivo's face, his chin jutted forward. "You wouldn't be here if you weren't Bear's cousin. And no matter how much you guys call each other brother, you're not. Shit, I wouldn't be surprised if the only reason Bear took you out of foster care is so his hump buddy Mason had someone new to fuck because Gus was getting too old."

No matter how fast Rob could cross the tattoo shop's floor, he wasn't as quick as Ivo's fist.

There was blood—lots of it—and Rob hesitated, unsure if he could get involved without getting his head knocked off. But when Ivo dodged Dave's flailing strike and dipped his shoulder to punch up into Dave's chin, Rob knew he couldn't stand by and do nothing. A few quick strides and he was in the middle of the skirmish, taking a glancing blow on his cheek from Dave's fist as he tried to get between the men.

Rob's idea of fighting pretty much started and stopped at sarcastic rejoinders. Dave seemed more like a drunken brawler, uncoordinated and unsure of why or who started the fight, but he was all in. Ivo—complicated, surprising Ivo—fought like he was going in for the kill. Rob knew who he had to stop, and it sure as hell wasn't Dave.

"Not in here, man," Rob pleaded as he pushed his shoulder against Ivo's muscular chest. "Not in the shop."

It was the only leverage he had, especially since he was pretty sure none of the brothers were going to drop by and magically calm him down. Ivo shuddered, took a step back, and shook his hands as he walked in a tight circle, his attention fixed on Dave's bleeding face.

"*Get the fuck out,*" Ivo growled, a razor edge of dangerous riding his voice. "If you've got any shit in the back room, you come by when

Bear is here and get it. You're not fit to be inside of the shop, much less fucking working in it."

Holding Ivo back wasn't easy. He pushed with every word and moved Rob back an inch or two with his powerful legs. But Rob held firm and prayed Dave would gather up what little sense he had and leave. Turned halfway, he could see Dave seriously think about not going, but then he spat a mouthful of blood and spit onto the shop's concrete floor.

"Fuck you. You're still just a piece of shit Bear lets scar up people with your crappy ink." Dave wiped at the blood pouring out of his nose. It was beginning to swell, and his words were garbled, a numb drone of sound that echoed through the shop. "I hope somebody comes in here and kicks your ass."

"Jesus Christ, Dave," Rob screamed at him and wrapped his arms around Ivo's waist to hold him still. "Will you just get the fuck out?"

Dave was gone with the rattle of the bell against the door and a brief burst of cold air that he let into the heated shop. Ivo was fairly panting, and Rob could feel the anger thrumming in his body. He slowly let Ivo go and carefully stepped back, unsure if Ivo would strike out at him since Rob was the only one left in the place.

"You good?" he asked cautiously and gave Ivo some room to breathe. "Because I don't want to get punched in the face."

"I'm not going to hit you." Ivo sucked at one of his knuckles and then grimaced. "You can say anything you want about Mason, because he can be a dick sometimes, but he would never hurt a kid, not in a million years and especially not me. Not after what his father did to him. So fuck Dave for saying that. Fuck him and anyone else who thinks we're not brothers. Lock up. We're done for the night."

IF THERE was one thing that kept Mace sane, it was running. Bear had started him on it, more of a way to get Mace some exercise, but then it dawned on Mace that running gave him a sense of freedom, a way of pushing his body to its limits and reminding his obsessive, anxious mind he was no longer trapped in a box. Eventually it evolved into a game of tag, a sprint toward a building or object along the running path, a slalom of landmarks with a set destination and bragging rights. When he introduced the game to Rey, Mace knew he'd found his lifelong running partner, someone as competitive and driven to win as he was but without any ego if he lost. As much as Mace hated losing, he hated winning against a sore loser.

This time, as he pounded up the hill toward the brothers' house, he wasn't playing tag against anyone. Rather, he was running to remind himself he was free.

Rey was somewhere behind him, probably more than a little bit exhausted, having done a circuit at the zoo with Gus and Chris, but he'd been willing to tie on his sneakers when Mace's pacing around the living room finally drove Bear over the edge. He needed to burn off energy, to drive himself into the ground until he was too tired to think. There were too many ghosts and too much anger brewing in his belly and mind, so running it off seemed sensible.

This time it felt less like a race to beat Rey back to the house and more like he was being chased by a monster with his father's face.

"Behind you," Rey shouted up the hill. The desperate yell was weak, punctuated by a short huff of breath, and Mace couldn't hold back his chuckle when Rey swore a few seconds later. "Fuck, I'm tired."

Mace turned around and paced down his run to a slow jog. The slant got easier, pulled on his thighs less, and he let the distance between them diminish. Rey looked worn out. He'd come off a long shift and then rolled into a prolonged visit with a three-year-old. It left bags under his liquid brown eyes, and his dark hair stuck to his forehead, tamped down with sweat. Mace had a few inches on Rey and a bit more width in his shoulders, but Rey had great stamina. Stockier in build, he could take flights of stairs for days without stopping, something Mace envied, especially in the labyrinthine architecture of most Chinatown buildings. But put Rey on a hill and Mace could usually win, especially when he needed to.

"Shouldn't have had that corn dog at the zoo," Mace called back, "or the cotton candy."

"Kid only wanted a mouthful of the hot dog," Rey panted. He quickened his step to catch up with Mace, but it was hard going. "And if he ate all the cotton candy by himself, he would've been buzzing. With the kind of prices they charge over there, you think I was going to throw it all out?"

"Yeah, probably would've been a good idea." Mace lengthened his stride and threw a quick glance backward in anticipation of a bump in the sidewalk that had been there for more than a decade. His heel hit it, and he almost lost his footing, but he recovered before Rey could take advantage of the bobble. "Can you hurry up? There's a shower waiting for me at the house I want to take."

"Fuck you, Crawford," Rey spat halfheartedly. "I know how that house is, and as soon as you get into that shower, I'm going to turn on every single faucet and flush all of the toilets until your nuts freeze off."

REY WAS gone by the time Mace finished his shower, leaving his excuses in a nearly illegible cursive on a piece of paper taped to the main second-floor bathroom. Bear was somewhere in the house, but Mace didn't go looking for him. He felt like an imposition. He'd moved his things into the smallest bedroom of the Craftsman and left only a few jeans and lounging clothes tucked inside a scavenged dresser. There was barely enough room to walk around the queen-size bed shoved up against the wall, and during the winter, cold air seeped in around one of the window frames and made it impossible to sleep comfortably without a mound of quilts. It was meant to be a nursery or maybe even a walk-in closet, but Mace assured the others it was good enough for him.

He hated it. It reminded him of every closet he'd been shoved into, every cramped space he'd been imprisoned in, but asking for more room seemed… he told himself it would make no sense to take up a bedroom someone else could use, especially since he lived elsewhere.

The reality was that Mace was kind of afraid to hear those exact words come from Bear's mouth. He didn't want to ask for more than what was given. If he didn't ask, he would never be told no. And he never wanted to risk his friendship… his brotherhood… with the others over something as inconsequential as a bedroom he'd rarely use.

With a towel slung around his hips, Mace tucked his clothes into a bundle under his arm and padded to the tiny room tucked in next to the stairs. The floorboards creaked a bit under his feet, and the old runner they'd laid down on the landing felt a bit rough and was probably in need of a carpet sweeping. There was evidence of Earl everywhere—a bit of fur caught on the rug's burgundy edge and the flattened remains of a once-yellow stuffed duck left in front of Ivo's closed bedroom door. He opened the door to his room and stood in shock at the sight of heavily packed bookcases lining the walls and a pair of enormous armchairs standing where his bed used to be.

Mace wanted to throw up on his own feet. He'd been in his room only a few days before, straightening the bed linens until they were practically creased over the mattress and falling straight. There hadn't been anything out of place. His things were put away out of sight and everything left in an orderly fashion. There was never anything left out, nothing to be held under his nose as an example of his slovenly nature or evidence of the trash he'd come from. There was no reason to *erase* him.

"This was supposed to be a surprise, but I told Ivo it was a bad idea to do it without telling you." Luke's quiet voice startled Mace, and he almost dropped the towel he held clenched at his waist. "They moved you into Ivo's old room because it's bigger and warmer."

Mace shook his head but shivered when a brush of cold air hit his still-damp chest. "I don't live here. I don't need—"

"None of us were happy you moved in there. We voted. Ivo went back up into the attic, and once Gus and Rey figure out where they're going to be, he'll probably still be in his old room sometimes. Or we can use it for Chris when he comes over." Luke opened the other bedroom door. "But this was something they wanted to do for you, and you better like it, because I had to take a day off to get all of the wallpaper down. I don't know how Ivo could stand it, but I knew you didn't want to wake up to 1950s fruit baskets."

Mace didn't trust himself to look through the cracked-open door. He was caught in the emotional upheaval of his brothers' surprising regard and their stubborn, willful care of him. "Where's Bear? Did he call you to come over? I'm *fine*."

"You are about as far from fine as you ever have been, brother," Luke said as he swung the door open the rest of the way. "Go in. Bear went to go pick up some cheesesteak sandwiches, but traffic got a little thick, so he's running late. And of course he called me. That's what we do. We call each other when shit hits the fan. Now get inside of your damned room and tell me the paint I picked out is nice, because Ivo and Gus wanted green and I want to rub it in their faces that you prefer blue."

Luke was like him, connected through friendship rather than blood, but he'd been brought in by Gus, and people instinctively loved Gus despite his roguish nature. Luke was a slender, quiet Hispanic kid with a lisp and accented English when he moved into the house. He was still entangled in the system's red tape, but they eagerly handed him off to Bear, and he'd been shuffled through so many foster homes that he'd been held back a grade.

They'd all had burdens put on them, but Luke's seemed to drag at the edges of any happiness he'd found. There was a sadness in his enormous cinnamon-brown eyes, a wistful longing on his sweet-featured face every time Gus and Ivo wrestled and ended up in a laughing clutch of hugs when Bear jumped them. For the longest time, Mace felt like he and Luke were always on the outside looking in, but at some point, Luke was enveloped into that laughter and Mace was alone again.

Or at least that's how it felt.

Bear assured him that wasn't the case, and Ivo more than a few times declared Mace was crazy, but whenever he met Luke's sad eyes, Mace knew he was understood. It was hard to let go of his fear. He'd beaten it into shape until it was a set of armor, wrapping him in a steeled distance, something impenetrable to keep him safe. But the brothers seemed to know exactly how to get inside without even trying.

Like a freshly painted bedroom to remind Mace where he belonged.

"I like the blue," he whispered as he hesitantly stepped into the room. It was bright, a cheery sky color rarely seen on most San Francisco mornings, and it reminded him of Gus's eyes when he smiled. "My books...?"

"Those are in the small room. We made that your library. Bear said that we would fix that window casing, but let's face it, that's been on the to-do list for years now. It was just a hell of a lot easier to give you more space and paint this one than to fix the damn window." Luke made himself comfortable on the old iron bed that Gus paid five dollars for at a swap meet. They'd coated it with a fresh layer of glossy black, and somehow his two pillows had multiplied into what looked like fifteen. "The dresser was shot. I don't even know how you could open up a drawer without it falling apart. So you're going to have to make do with that armoire and those cubes until we can get a new one."

"I see Gus has made me a nest." Mace inspected the stacks of wooden cubes on either side of the art deco armoire and then pulled out a pair of underwear, cotton pants, and an SFFD T-shirt. Changing was easier since he was in a room large enough for him to move without hitting a wall with his elbow, but he wrinkled his nose at the tall wicker hamper set in one corner. "*That* is too big. There's no way I'm ever going to fill it. I don't like letting dirty clothes sit."

"Consider that a challenge," his brother offered. "When was the last time you worked on changing your habits?"

"See, that's what I hate about you. I'm not one of your kids that's got to be fixed," Mace muttered as he pulled the shirt on. "I wouldn't put it past you to do all of this *just* to make me use that hamper. I can't deal with that kind of thing right now. I'm not...."

"You don't have to use it now, but maybe soon." He leaned back against the bank of pillows, pulled his leg up, and rested his bare foot on the quilt covering the bed. "And I know you're not one of my kids, but that doesn't mean you can't take advantage of the years of my schooling you all helped pay for. I've got the degrees. Might as well use them. Do you want to talk about why you needed to run today? Or do you want to continue to pretend like nothing's happened and bottle it up inside until you pop?"

"I don't...." Mace wanted to deny needing to let off steam, but Luke knew him too well. Luke knew them *all* too well.

"Do you want to tell me to fuck off?" His brother's nearly black hair fell forward across his cheek when he tilted his head. "You can if you want to, but it's not going to make that letter any less real or make you any less angry."

"It might make me feel better."

"That it might." Luke chuckled. "I can tell you it won't threaten our relationship. You can tell me to fuck off and mind my own business, and I'll still love you. I'm not the hamper, Mace. I'm not a challenge. I'm your brother, and I want you to know that if you need to yell or cry or just say you're angry, I'm here to take that."

Mace studied Luke through his lashes. They'd taken different paths out of their pain—Mace chose to turn his back on his while Luke confronted his anguish head-on. On the surface it appeared that Luke survived his battles while Mace floundered, but he knew better. They were both still embroiled in emotional skirmishes every day, fighting to get past another hour without taking a step backward and sometimes losing momentum as well as whatever scrap of humanity they'd earned.

He could talk to Luke and Bear if only he were willing to risk it. They would listen. They always listened. After years of struggling and sublimation, Mace knew his brothers were there for him, but his heart was broken, torn apart, and whispering of past betrayals.

Luke was wrong. He was a challenge, but Mace was more than willing to take him on.

"And what if I tell you I'm not angry?" His whisper cracked under the weight of the emotion he was trying to hold in. "I'm afraid, Luke. For some stupid reason, the idea of that fucking asshole being outside of those walls turns me into the little kid again, and I am so *damn fucking* scared. I wish he'd died in there. I wish he'd die now. Anything so I don't have to feel or think about him ever again."

Luke crossed the room quickly and folded Mace into a hug as soon as he reached his side. For a slender man, Luke had a fierce grip and an even fiercer resolve. Clutching tightly as Mace refused to let his father bring him to tears, Luke whispered, "We can do that. We can make that happen so he'll never make you afraid again."

SIX

"REALLY?" BEAR looked up from behind the kitchen peninsula, twisted the cap off a second beer bottle, and handed it over to Mace. "He offered to kill your father? Did he mean it?"

"How can you tell?" Mace took a sip of the chocolate stout his brother had picked up from Finnegan's Pub. "This is Luke we're talking about. I'm never sure if he's serious or being… I don't know, flippant?"

"Me neither." His brother scratched at the thick scruff he'd grown over his jaw. "He's good for looking at everyone's problems but his own. That's something he's going to have to face someday, and soon."

"I'll let you tell him that," he said and gave Bear a mock salute with his stout. "Any time I bring it up, he loops it back to me. It's his superpower—obfuscation and deflection."

"Good words." Bear leaned on the counter, nodded at Mace, and then took a long draw off his bottle. Mace followed Bear into the living room, and they each settled into their respective spots on the enormous sectional Mace usually fell asleep on when he came to visit. Bear let a moment of silence pass between them and then reached for the stereo remote before Mace could. He turned it to a classic rock station and dropped the volume down until it became a murmur in the room. "Speaking of deflection, what are you going to do about your father?"

If it was any other person, Mace would have sidestepped the question, but Bear had raised four headstrong teens to adulthood, and he knew more tricks than Luke could ever dream up. There would be no avoiding his older brother, at least not without dropping off the face of the earth or becoming a Tibetan monk under a vow of silence. Even then, Bear could hunt him down.

He avoided Bear's gaze under the guise of collecting his thoughts.

The old Craftsman existed in a constant state of noise. It sang and chirped, warming its bones in the afternoon sun and shrinking back in on itself when the night air cooled it. The house's constant murmurs were what Mace missed the most after moving out. There were many nights at his place when even throwing all the windows open to let in the street noise didn't help, but after a half-hour drive over to Ashbury, he found the sounds he needed to lull him to sleep—cradled in the odd song of the house he used to call home.

It was never silent in the brothers' home. Even in the dead of night, the house whispered to him and reminded him he was alive.

As thankful as Mace was for the bedroom his brothers made for him, the family room was still his favorite space in the house.

In the beginning of their renovating adventures, they tried to set up a formal parlor, but it soon proved to be a room no one spent any time in. Everything they knew about creating a home was knitted together from a variety of television shows that featured smiling parents and mischievous but well-meaning offspring. There'd always been a sacred adult space, a parlor where people visited and where there was no sign of television or children.

It didn't take the brothers long to realize that wasn't going to be their life. They needed space, not just to live in but also from each other— safe havens from the storm of forging relationships between problematic personalities and quiet places to nurse deep-seated traumas. Bear, who normally asked for opinions about what to do with the house, made an executive decision and carved individual spaces out for each of them.

The front parlor became Luke's bedroom, and they knocked down a couple of walls and expanded the family area into a giant space to fit the five of them.

In no way was the family area magazine-pretty. None of the house was, but it felt comfortable around Mace. When he walked through the back door, he didn't feel as though he were intruding into a place he didn't belong—not like every single time he'd come into a foster home and slunk off into the room they put him in so he would create as small a ripple in their lives as possible.

Ripples meant being kicked out. Conflict of any kind meant taking another trip escorted by a hard-faced social worker and losing half of his things in the process.

The space was a patchwork of electronics, a humongous pit that held the sectional, and bookshelves lining the wall that separated the area from Luke's bedroom. The opposite wall had windows overlooking the tiered backyard—another endless project of patio-building and landscaping with a few vigorous attempts at vegetable-growing, something they finally mastered once Luke figured out where things should be planted and what drainage meant. Heavy blackout curtains hung from sturdy wrought iron rods and were easily pulled shut for the days when Mace or one of the others fell asleep on the U-shaped couch and wanted to keep the day at bay.

It was in the family room where they argued and made decisions, sometimes screaming themselves hoarse to be heard over the chaos. But it was also where they forged the bonds of their patchwork clan.

Scattered around the room were definite signs that Chris had joined the family. There was a basket of toys, and Mace couldn't identify whether they belonged to Earl or the kid. Then he recalled how his nephew interacted with the family mutt and realized there wasn't much difference. They shared and gnawed on the ears of their stuffed animals indiscriminately. A short plastic basketball hoop sat in the corner where a fake plant once took up residence, and it took Mace a moment to realize the silk dieffenbachia now resided in the library his brothers had created for him. At some point they were going to have to teach Chris about boundaries and private areas, but for the life of him, Mace didn't know how to bring it up. None of them had had the luxury of being an only child with two handfuls of adults raising them.

He almost asked Bear how they were going to teach Chris things like sharing and privacy, but the sharp look he got told him his older brother wasn't going to be diverted.

"Mace, dial it back in," Bear scolded softly. "How do you want to deal with him?"

"I don't know what I'm going to do about him, because I don't have a clue about where he is or anything else." The stout turned sour in his mouth, but Mace swallowed anyway and welcomed the numbness on his tongue. "He's got a probation officer he has to check in with, but you know how that goes. Luke thinks I should get a restraining order, but I don't have anything to put behind it. What am I going to say to the judge? 'Yes, I am a firefighter, and I can lift people up over my shoulder to cart them downstairs, but I'm afraid of an old man who hurt me when I was a kid, so can you please give me a piece of paper to tell him to stay away from me?' How do you think that's going to go?"

Mace could almost feel the exasperation pouring out when Bear sighed.

"They might not give you a restraining order, but you never know." Bear grunted when Earl joined him on the couch and the dog's massive paws dimpled the cushions between them. Bear waited for him to settle down and then scratched at a spot between Earl's shoulder blades. "At the very least, we can have Luke make a few discreet inquiries and find out where he is."

Mace made a face at Bear. "Do you really want Luke to know where he lives? Even if what he said was off the cuff, do you really want to chance it?"

"I am ninety-nine percent sure he says that kind of shit just to keep a sense of humor about it," Bear replied. Then he sipped his stout and mumbled around the glass rim, "It's a sick sense of humor and kind of dark, but that's Luke."

"Let's just say the one percent isn't small enough to comfort me where Luke is concerned." Mace moved his hand so Earl could rest his head on his thigh. The dog shuddered and then seemed to ooze as every muscle in his gangly body relaxed. It was time for Mace to face the truths he'd been ignoring. The man who'd spent most of Mace's teen and adult years locked up behind bars was now out, and Mace had no idea what he could do about it.

"Fair enough," his brother replied softly. "I'm not asking you to make any decisions about him. Whatever you want to do, we'll support you. I just need to know where your head's at right now."

"I know I don't want to see him. And it's not like my mother...." He couldn't bring himself to talk about the woman who'd.... Mace couldn't even think about her, not without losing what little grip he had on his emotions. "I don't want him anywhere near the family. And I sure as hell don't want him ever to get close to Chris. I'm going to be honest and say I wish to fuck that one percent of Luke was one hundred percent, because that way he'd... never hurt me again."

"He can't hurt you anymore," Bear assured him as he reached across the space and squeezed Mace's thigh. "We'll do everything we can to protect you. And yeah, you aren't that little kid anymore on the outside, but there's still a lot of him left in you—enough for your father to terrorize just by being around you. You don't have to take that from him. You don't have to let him in. And if we're on the honesty train, I don't want you to let him in. What he did to you was... fucked-up, and you've worked hard to get through a lot of it. I love you, brother. And if I have to help that one percent in Luke to protect you, I'll do that. We all would."

"I appreciate it, but I'd rather not spend my lifetime trying to get you guys out of prison when I spent most my life trying to keep him in one. How about if we just agree to see where things go. He's not welcome in my life, and if he tries to force his way in, we'll deal with it." Mace glanced toward the kitchen as the back door opened and its telltale creak echoed through the house. Frowning at Bear, he asked, "Is that Gus? I thought he and Rey were going to spend the night down in Chinatown."

"Can't be Ivo." Bear glanced at the clock and then stood and set his beer down on the coffee table in front of him. "Shop's not supposed to close for another hour."

"Is there food?" Their youngest brother's voice rang through the house. "Oh, never mind. Found some. Can I eat the Chinese?"

"Definitely Ivo and his stomach," Bear muttered. "Think I should tell him we're in here?"

"Pretty sure he could find us." Mace finished his beer and shouted toward the kitchen, "Bring us the wontons and a couple of beers."

"I'm not your fucking maid… oh. Who picked up Finnegan's?" Ivo yelled back. "I'm taking the last of the shrimp."

Bear creased his brow. "Was there a lot of shrimp left?"

"No, but at least he told us he was taking the rest of it." When Ivo walked into the room, Mace reached up for one of the bottles he had tucked under his arm. "Did you throw away the empty Styrofoam containers? Or did you leave them on the counter?"

"I'll throw them away later." Ivo scowled at him, baring his teeth. "Right now I'm hungry, and just so you know, I fired Dave. I tried to grab In-N-Out with Rob, but some old bearded guy cornered us by the parking structure and told me to give Mason a message for him."

The food in Mace's stomach threatened to come up, and he swallowed hard against the sour at the back of his tongue. Trying to keep his voice steady, he croaked, "What did he say?"

"Dave?" Ivo let out a terse snort and picked a shrimp out of the scoop of fried rice he'd heaped onto his plate. "He—"

"No, you idiot," Bear growled, "the guy down by parking."

"I didn't give him a chance to say anything. I knew who that fucker was," Ivo said around a mouthful of noodles as he simultaneously lifted his elbow to drop a second bottle of beer in Bear's lap and stepped over their legs to get to his spot on the couch. "If you wanted that asshole in your life, you wouldn't have gone to all of those damned hearings to keep him locked up. So, we can either talk about Dave or about how we get Mace's dad to understand that if he comes anywhere near us, he's going to wish he was back in prison."

HAVING A kid in their lives changed things. The day off from the fire station was sometimes stolen and the hours given to the shop because one thing or another cropped up. An early-morning phone call from Gus brought the news that Jules, Chris's mother, had woken up with a bad case of the flu and needed Gus to step in and take care of his son for a few days. His response was swift, but it meant putting aside plans—everyone's plans. If there was one thing the brothers agreed on without hesitation, it was that Chris's care and well-being came first. They'd each grown up without that, and to a man, they refused to let Chris have a moment where he didn't feel loved and protected.

So for Mace, that meant driving down to the shop to pick up the opening shift and cover reception until Ivo got out of his classes for the day, hopefully by late afternoon. Bear would be in at six to pick up the evening shift. The workload was projected to be slim, with only a few appointments scattered about the schedule, and while Mace couldn't tattoo to save his life, he could handle the walk-in traffic, help set up the stalls for the artists, and handle the money.

"Times like this, I wish I could at least ink flash, but you all wear the only piece of art I will ever do." Mace tapped at the 415 Ink logo silkscreened on a clean shop T-shirt he'd pulled from the laundry.

The points of the nautical star between the numbers and the letters had been divided up and drawn by each of the brothers. There was no mistaking the lack of talent on two of the points—specifically the contributions by Mace and Luke. Somehow, even using a ruler and the same pens, their sides of the star were wonky. The other three insisted it lent character to the logo, but Gus visibly winced when it was suggested they all wear the star on their bodies. Still, he'd gamely agreed to put it on his wrist, and Mace tucked it into the knight inked on his upper arm.

The star represented not just the shop but the family itself—slightly fucked-up, made up of five pieces, and something they all would die fighting for if they needed to.

Chris was now a part of that star, so the storage room in Mace's garage was going to have to wait, and Gus would spend the day riding herd on a three-year-old little boy with an endless amount of questions and a mischievous streak as long as the Golden Gate Bridge.

And as much as he loved the kid, Mace was glad to leave the chaos and mayhem behind for the relative sanity of a tattoo shop that faced the San Francisco piers—that is, until he parked his car and looked out at the deluge pouring down on the city. It was as though the sky had ripped open its belly and was bleeding out, its death throes punctuated by rolls of thunder and metallic clashes of lightning. He was trying to ignore the persistent whispers of his father's presence creeping over his life, but he still hurried past the corner where Ivo said he'd seen the man.

"Last thing I need is to see him," Mace muttered to himself as he hurried across the street, surrendering any hope of dryness when the wind picked up and slashed the rain sideways. It wasn't far, but the downpour was intense, and the sky was dark with its fury. "Bad enough I've got to deal with Rob for a few hours."

He'd agreed to take over the shift before he knew Rob was the artist on duty that day. There was no backpedaling, not once a brother made a promise. Mace wanted to, but he couldn't, not without drawing suspicion. He'd already sensed Bear's eyes on him when Ivo read off the schedule for the day and Rob's name sent a shiver through Mace's spine.

The lock on the front door was difficult, as usual, and by the time Mace got it open, the rain was coming down hard enough that he wondered if he would have to go back out and get sandbags to keep the front door clear of rising water. The sidewalk dipped at the corner, and the champagne lounge next door always seemed to have a plumbing backup during a storm.

"I'll cover the shop," Mace grumbled as he finally got the key into the lock. "But I'm not going to spend the day shoveling through somebody else's shit, especially since Ivo fired our apprentice."

Firing Dave had been necessary. Mace understood that. He was still leery about the time-honored tradition of taking on a young tattoo artist and making them do all of the shit work in the shop. He'd seen Bear work through his time as an unpaid apprentice just to learn the ropes while he held down two side jobs, and then he watched Gus and Ivo take their turns to earn dirt wages as they struggled to master skillsets and machines. It was hard, grueling work with a lot of emotional turmoil. When Bear opened the doors to 415 Ink, he swore that any apprentice working under him would earn a living wage and be treated with respect. All they had to do was follow the shop's rules.

"Fucking Dave. I really didn't want to spend the morning getting ink all over myself, but fuck, I'd probably be down here anyway with the sandbags." The front door was stuck, swollen by the rain, and Mace put his shoulder to it and pushed it open. The glass insert and the blinds rattled, mimicking a pissed-off snake. He took two steps into the shop and had just reached for the switch on the wall when the lights flared to life. Mace shoved his keys between his fingers, made a fist, and then called out, "That better be Rob or Missy, because I swear to God, if it's you, Dave, I am in no mood."

He recognized the silhouette of the man at the end of the hall, and another flick of the light switch illuminated Rob's sweet face. Holding up a set of keys, Rob called out, "It's me. Dave never had keys, and Missy's in San Jose today visiting her mom, but she's working later. What are you doing here?"

"Gus had to call out," Mace replied, raising his voice so he could be heard over the rain.

Staring through the shop at Rob, Mace asked himself the same thing—what the hell *was* he doing there? If he'd been smart, he would have conned Luke into taking the day off to cover the shop. Hell, he would've recruited somebody from the firehouse or even pulled in somebody off the street to avoid working that morning, because the image of Rob in a rain-drenched thin white T-shirt plastered to his trim chest and flat belly would forever be burned into his memory.

Rob might as well be shirtless... or maybe not. There was something subliminally erotic and beautiful about a man secure in his own body and unconsciously displayed behind a veil of transparent fabric. There was no artifice to Rob's stalk toward the open shelf of supplies near the back door or the brusque grace of his shoulders rolling in as he ducked his head to dry his hair off with one of the shop towels. His jeans were splattered with dark splotches from the rain that had soaked through the blue denim fabric, and he got a good peek at Rob's muscular thighs through the various tears in his pant legs. And when Rob bent over, Mace bit the inside of his cheek and cut off his involuntary moan at the sight of Rob's tight ass filling out the seat of his jeans.

It wasn't just that Rob was beautiful in a way heavy with dangerous promise and broken hearts, Mace couldn't handle the artist's easy smile and sweet golden eyes. Rob was proof God was a mean prankster who'd molded a man out of caramels and cockiness. From the hard curves of his Filipino German features to the soft plump of his full mouth, Rob was trouble, a compact, muscular wet dream with a cutting tongue and a flirtatious nature.

And he seemed to slither around Mace's defenses without even trying too hard.

"This was a really bad idea," Mace muttered to himself as he closed and secured the front door. "Maybe it's just been too long since I've had sex. There just hasn't been time."

Even before the words left his mouth, Mace knew they were a lie. He'd gone out with Ivo a few weeks before and hit up a club his younger brother wanted to check out. It was loud and pulsating, a colorful splash of warm bodies and neon lights with enough shadows in the corners to hide anything nasty a couple wanted to get into. He'd grown bored within an hour, and when Ivo stumbled off the dance floor, slick with sweat and followed by a group of casual friends, Mace made his excuses before he was trapped at the table between a set of pretty-faced twins who made it quite clear they would give him a good time.

It was stupid to leave, especially since they'd promised everything he normally went for—long, sweaty bouts of pleasure and no obligation for anything in the morning except perhaps a cup of coffee before he left.

He'd been wondering how Rob tasted after his first sip of coffee the entire night and for the life of him, Mace couldn't even remember how the twins looked.

Standing behind the reception desk, Mace was thankful for its protective cover because, while his cock didn't respond to the young men who cupped his crotch under the table that night, it thickened when his mind wandered to how the faint blue rivulet of hair-dye-tinted rainwater running down Rob's neck would taste on his tongue.

"God… *really* fucking bad idea." Mace huffed out the breath he'd been holding in. Intent on making coffee, he shook his head lightly to rattle some sense into himself and forced his feet to carry him back toward the lounge. "Okay, it's just a couple of hours. As soon as Ivo shows up, I'm gone."

MACE WAS the last person Rob expected to see coming through 415 Ink's front door an hour before opening, but there was no mistaking his broad shoulders and chiseled face. Dressed in worn jeans and one of the shop's T-shirts stretched to its limits across his torso, Mace looked… damned good, and not for the first time since he'd begun working at the shop, Rob closed his eyes and begged God to stop torturing him.

When he cracked one eye open, Rob saw God hadn't quite gotten the message because Mace was staring curiously at him, framed by the opening at the end of the hall. Rob tugged on the handle of the back door to make sure it clicked shut and locked, and then gave Mace what he hoped was a welcoming smile.

Mace smiled back… sort of, and Rob felt his heart trip in his chest.

Jesus. The man was sex on legs. He kicked in every single instinct Rob had to push the man down to the floor and use up the ninety minutes they had before Rob's first appointment. Mace made his teeth ache, and Rob wanted nothing more than to kiss him senseless until his dark eyes turned black with desire.

If that wasn't frightening enough, he'd also scared the shit out of Rob when he called out in a gruff, dominating voice that got Rob to thinking about wrought iron bed posts and the twenty-five or so ties he had stashed in his closet, left over from school uniforms and formal suits he'd worn for family functions.

If he'd known Mace was going to be on the breakfast menu that morning, Rob would've dressed a little more carefully, or at least he thought he would have until he reminded himself that in no way shape or form was Mace *ever* on the menu. The brothers didn't date staff, and he was pretty sure Mace hated him. Still, he was a delicious sight after running full tilt from his parking spot to the shop as the sky poured its guts out.

Rob's hoodie was soaking wet, and it made squishy noises when he peeled it off. His jeans had large dark patches on his thighs and were drenched from his ankles to his knees. He grabbed one of the shop towels from the cabinet by the back door and attempted to get most of the water out of his hair. He winced at the blue streaks he left on the white terrycloth.

"*Shit.*" There wasn't enough bleach to get out the stains his hair left behind, but he didn't have much of a choice. It was either the towel or his neck, and Rob had no intention of spending the day looking like he'd painted himself with woad in preparation for battle with the Wild Hunt.

When he stole a glance, he was startled to find Mace walking toward him. Rob held the towel up and said ruefully, "I'll replace this."

"Have you met my baby brother?" Mace's chuckle was a splash of light against the dark tones in his voice. "Most of the towels in our house look like they were used to mop up a My Little Pony slaughter. Don't worry about it."

"Is Gus okay?" Remembering what happened on the shift before, Rob's mouth went dry. "He's not sick, right? Shit, I drank out of his coffee cup accidentally yesterday. Thought it was mine."

"No, you're fine. Gus was supposed to open, but Jules woke up with the flu, so he's watching Chris. Ivo's coming in at three to help with any walk-ins so Bear doesn't have to do a double shift." Mace nodded toward the employee lounge. "How about if you make coffee, and I'll get the cash box set up. We can open the doors whenever you want. Bear told me you had a client first thing so you'd need backup. I'm just here to handle the front and make appointments if anyone comes in. Do you need help setting up your table?"

"Normally Dave does it, but since he got quitted… I'll take care of it." Rob was struggling. He knew what he had to do to get going that morning, but Mace seemed to take up most of the space in the shop's hallway. His feet refused to move, and Rob wasn't sure his knees were up to holding his weight if he had to squeeze past Mace to get to the main room. "Ivo told you about Dave, right? Oh, and some guy stopped us before we—"

"I know about the guy. Don't worry about him. If you see him again, just walk away," Mace growled at him. "And yeah, Ivo told us about Dave last night. Bear's going to see if we can't get an assistant in. I know running an apprentice is better, but usually that comes with an ego and an attitude. Right now I think we would rather just pay somebody to help with appointments and setup and breakdown, but Bear has the final say in that."

There *definitely* was something up with Mace, and it didn't take a rocket scientist to realize the bearded older man who'd come out of the shadows when Ivo approached the restaurant's front door had something to do with his agitated state. It was a quick encounter, but Ivo's heated shutdown of the man bordered on violent. There'd been an edge in the air, and Ivo quickly excused himself from grabbing a burger, shoved a twenty into Rob's hand, and told him to grab a meal on the shop.

Rob had bought food for himself and Lilith. He'd noted the crazy in the man's face and the similarity of his eyes to Mace's and contemplated what to say to Mace the next time he saw him. He just didn't realize it was going to be the next morning.

He was given a bit of a reprieve when Mace went to set up the register for the day, and Rob hustled to get his ink palette arranged before his client came in. It was hard to ignore the rattle of Mace moving around the shop and the heat of his presence on Rob's back even though he was yards away. He took out the sketch he'd done for the stained-glass peacock he was going to wrap around an ex-nun's thigh, smoothed out the wrinkles on the tracing paper, and tried to get his racing thoughts under control.

"You've got shit to do today, dude," he scolded himself as he spun around on his stool to get his machines from their cases. "So he's here. Big deal. He comes here all the time. He owns a part of the fucking shop. He's just—"

"Here's some coffee." Mace reached over Rob's shoulder and put a mug down on his worktable. "What do you need me to do?"

What he really needed him to do was step away. If even the thought of Mace in the shop muddled Rob's senses, the sear of Mace's hip on his back wiped away any grip Rob had on his sanity. He didn't have to imagine the strength in Mace's body, because he felt it when Mace's leg muscles bunched and gave when Mace stepped back. He didn't go far, or at least not far enough for Rob to breathe easily. No, his every intake of breath was overwhelmed with the musky deliciousness of Rob's wet dream and the woodsy, clean scent Mace wore on his skin.

"Nothing that I—" Rob stammered on his own tongue.

And then the world fell apart.

There was never any warning when California woke up to turn over. If there were, Rob probably would have stayed in bed that day. If there was one thing he hated, it was feeling helpless, and nothing made him feel more helpless than an earthquake.

This one struck hard, rolled in waves, and knocked him off of his stool. The floor moved underneath him, an endless second of tumbling he couldn't seem to stop. He cried out or maybe even shouted in fear, because everything went Wonderland and folded in around him in accordion creases of walls and lights. Something snapped and popped, and then the shop was drenched in an inky black. But before Rob could fall into a panic, he felt someone strong and warm gather him up—a fearless and steady someone who murmured as he wrapped his arms around Rob and pulled them under the worktable to ride out the earthen storm.

"I've got you," Mace whispered with a sensual heat molten enough to chase away the cold lingering in Rob's bones. "Don't worry. Nothing's going to happen to you. I won't *let* anything happen to you. Just hold on to me and don't let go."

SEVEN

IT WAS stupid to get aroused. Rob was pressed down into the painted cement floor, half sprawled on the spongy floor mat he'd put under his stool to cushion his feet, his right cheek slightly gouged by the sharp corner of the padded square. The ground wasn't shaking anymore, but the old building swayed and creaked as it tried to settle back in on itself. Outside, the rain continued its furious screaming, almost as though the sky were enraged at the earth's hubris of interrupting the storm.

The earth might have stopped shaking, but he sure as hell hadn't.

Rob could feel every inch of Mace's long body against his. The heat of his breath on Rob's ear tickled, and then Rob's mind seized at the idea of Mace's tongue there instead. The press of Mace's hand into his side was warm through the fabric of Rob's shirt, and he longed to explore how much hotter those tapered fingers could get if they could find their way to Rob's bare skin.

He felt… safe and horny at the same time, a confusing and conflicting set of emotions Rob didn't have time to parse out before Mace rolled over and slid off of Rob's back. He didn't just miss the heat. He missed… Mace, missed *knowing* it was Mace holding him, lying on top of him, filling up all of his senses, because the air tasted of him, and Rob only knew he wanted— *needed*—more.

There were a million and one reasons why kissing Mace was a bad idea. Every single one of them flipped through Rob's brain, starting from Mace being one of the shop's owners to there was no future in it. The rational half of his brain screamed that it was a bad idea, and his stomach twisted into proverbial knots at the thought of what would happen afterward.

He did it anyway.

Rob didn't think beyond *no, this is a bad idea*. He hooked his fingers into Mace's waistband before his brain could register an objection. His knuckles brushed against a silken line of dark downy hair, and Rob lost what little wits he had left. Clutching at the rough denim, he yanked Mace toward him, fought to get his arm loose, and then cupped the back of Mace's head once his hand was free. The space between their mouths was lean, and all Rob had to do was tilt forward to close the gap.

He parted his lips and leaned in for a kiss.

Mason Crawford tasted as good as he smelled.

The feel of skin against his fingers was as much a part of the job as art, ink, and needles. He intimately knew the sensation of sleek muscle under his palm, the tensile strength of a tendon as it flexed, and the rigid firmness of bone beneath his thumb. Still, Mace's jaw in the cup of his hand, the rough scratch of his unshaven cheek, was different.

All of it was different.

The taste of coffee on Mace's lips was familiar, but the sweetness of something primal lingered beneath it, something dark and alluring that simmered with a hint of heady intoxication. Rob feared he would get drunk on it if given half the chance. He flicked his tongue across Mace's pressed-together lips and was elated when they parted. The hands he'd wanted on his skin were quick to find the hem of his shirt, and Rob gasped when Mace skimmed his long fingers up his rib cage. Time slipped away, or at least that's what it felt like, because Rob didn't have enough of Mace in his mouth when the kiss intensified and stole away the last bit of Rob's sanity, and he found himself on his back, the floor mat giving beneath his shoulder blades.

"We shouldn't be doing this," Mace growled into Rob's mouth. The rumble of Mace's deep voice echoed against Rob's teeth, and he smiled through the kiss. "Aw, *fuck it*. Bear's just going to have to kill me."

That was exactly what Rob wanted to hear.

"I won't tell him if you don't," he muttered into Mace's ear. Then he nipped lightly at the tempting lobe. "This is stupid. I don't even like you. And you can't stand me."

Rob's T-shirt was caught over his chin when Mace stopped pulling on it. His view of the shop was filtered through the thin fabric, and then Mace wrestled it free and hooked it behind Rob's neck. Mace was on his knees, hunkered over Rob's torso, supporting his weight with his hands flat on the floor. His gaze flickered across Rob's features, and then their eyes met, and Rob wondered at the strong emotions that roiled across Mace's beautiful face.

"What makes you think I don't like you?" Mace drew his fingers up Rob's side with a slow, erotic sear of a touch. "I can't stand to be near you without wanting you. Yeah, this pisses me off, because underneath that fake toughness is a spoiled little boy. I know guys like you. People are disposable, but it's not like I'm looking for anything other than a couple of hookups. I can't touch you because you're Bear's—the shop's—and as much as you make my teeth ache, you're bad news. All the way around."

There were times in a man's life when he had to grab what was in front of him. Mace Crawford offering sex in the shadowy confines of a darkened, closed-up tattoo shop after a heart-pounding earthquake was something Rob knew he had to grab before it slipped away. Mace was an itch he had to scratch, a guy he had to experience at least once in his life, let the man blow his brains out so he could move on to saner and better things.

Or at least that's what Rob told himself when he grabbed at Mace's short dirty-blond hair and yanked him down for another kiss.

"I've got a couple of condoms in my wallet, and we have about half an hour before someone comes knocking on the door." Rob tried to dig into his back pocket for the leather wallet his mother gave him when he was sixteen. "Make it worth my while, Crawford. Make it worth getting fired over."

It took less than a minute of scrambling and heavy panting, and then Rob's ass was resting on a pile of clothes and Mace's hands were everywhere. The man knew what he was doing. There was no doubting that. It was as though he'd read a manual about where and what Rob needed from a lover, because Mace's mouth and fingers were a sublime dip of heaven.

Rob gasped when Mace slowed down after the quick strip of jeans and shirts. They didn't have a lot of time, but Mace was going to use every second of it. His teeth clipped at the edge of one of Rob's nipples, and he gasped and arched into Mace's narrow hips. His own hands were busy, one filled with the hard, thick cock jutting up from between Mace's powerful legs, and it was all Rob could do to hold on.

Mace found the tender skin along his throat where Rob loved to be kissed and nibbled. He heard a little chuckle from his clandestine lover when Mace discovered Rob hadn't been circumcised. A moment later his smile grew wicked and fierce while Rob gasped and nearly lost himself to his release as Mace shucked back his foreskin and exposed his sensitive tip. The press of Mace's callused thumb on him was almost too much to bear, a bright, brittle sensation that rippled up his cock with every stroke.

But if Mace's thumb was too much for Rob, it was his mouth that took him over the edge.

"God, we don't have time," Rob ground out, his mind folding in on itself in an origami puzzle of pleasure. His thoughts couldn't work past the tight shock waves brought on by Mace's mouth around his cock. "I need—"

"*I* need to taste you," Mace mumbled. Then the back of his throat closed around Rob's cockhead. He swallowed once or maybe three times. Rob wasn't sure because he simply couldn't think anymore. "We have time. And if I don't get inside of you now, I promise I'll have you flying so you won't regret it."

Any other time Rob would've mocked his arrogance, but Mace dragged over the jar of Vaseline that had fallen from Rob's tattoo station, dipped his fingers into it, and then pressed into the crest of Rob's ass. His balls grew tight, and the ring of muscle gave way beneath Mace's explorations. The tip of an index finger sliding into his heat tingled every nerve under Rob's skin, and he lifted his hips and silently begged for more, even as Mace swallowed him down again.

What they were doing was wrong—unsanitary at the very least and professionally dangerous at the far end of the spectrum of bad ideas. Guilt edged in only enough for Rob to hesitate and press the heel of his hand against Mace's shoulder, but the last thing he wanted to do was push him away. Mace *needed* him. A hitch in Mace's voice resonated in Rob's mind, a desperate longing that surged up from Mace's murmurs, something empty inside of a man Rob believed possessed everything in the world.

"Let me," Rob whispered, his words probably carried away by the slashing of the rain that pounded the sidewalk outside. Mace's cock throbbed in Rob's hand, and he gripped tightly and slid his palm down its length. "I want you inside of me so I can watch you lose control. Let me give you that, Mace. Let *me* take care of *you*."

SEX WAS something Mace was good at. God knows, he'd started at an early age. It was a way of earning emotional coin, using the one thing he couldn't lose in the shuffle of houses and the sea of apathetic faces—his body. He'd propositioned Bear the first night they shared a room together. By then it'd become instinct, a way of ensuring some kind of bond with a larger, more forceful boy in the house or block. He always looked for an alliance, because there would always be somebody bigger and faster, someone willing to take what he could give on his own terms.

Forging those connections was a key to surviving the system and its labyrinth of turmoil and pain. It was one of the first lessons Mace learned and something he'd mastered by the time he ran into Bear. So it came as a shock to his system when the thickly muscled, frighteningly strong young man turned him down but protected him anyway.

It'd been a revelation to be wanted for nothing other than himself. Months had gone by before Bear's faith in him worked its way into his subconscious, but even now, Mace questioned his own worth. He worked so hard to be perfect, dependable, and steady—an unwavering monolith of strength and guidance for his younger brothers.

But the entire time, every single damned waking moment of the day, there was a niggle of fear his family would turn around and discard him, just like his mother had when they'd finally wrested him from his father's grasp.

Now here was Rob begging Mace to let him take the lead, to let him bring Mace pleasure. It was uncomfortable and unfamiliar but… *sincere*. And it went against everything Mace had laid out for himself to be. He got pleasure from giving, satisfaction from being able to get his lover to the brink of release, and he reveled when they shook apart in his arms.

"Roll over," Rob commanded and pushed at Mace's shoulder. "Give me the condom to put on you. I want to ride you until you can't think."

The line was cheesy, and Rob looked like he knew it. He wiggled his eyebrows and grinned. His smile was a playful curl of white against his golden skin. Sex wasn't playful, or at least not the kind Mace had. Still, he let himself be pushed onto his back and grunted when he landed on the Vaseline jar and felt its plastic case give beneath his weight.

It seemed that Rob wasn't going to let a silly thing like a handful of smeared lubricant and plastic bits stop them.

The condom went on tightly and snapped at his base when Rob rolled it down Mace's length. His hands were sticky, still coated with Vaseline, and Mace left a sheen over Rob's forearm when he brushed away a piece of foil from the condom wrapper. He'd forgotten to ask how long Rob had the packet in his wallet, and he wasn't sure if he'd even care if it'd been there for years, not when Rob rested his ass on Mace's belly, leaned over to seal their mouths together in a kiss, and then reached back to guide himself down onto Mace's aching cock.

Mace was *never* on the bottom. It was a position where he had to give up control, to let someone else push the event, and more importantly, it trapped Mace against a hard surface. Being beneath someone closed in the space, folding shadows and heat around Mace's face and shoulders and pinning down his hips. He had a momentary flutter of panic as his brain threw up other memories of walls and darkness, of silence and hunger.

And then Rob moved his hips… and Mace found himself swept away on a rising tide of pleasure, cradled by the fury of the storm outside.

Sex was never quiet. It was often loud and messy, a dance of heated skin and slick sweat. Mace spent most of his time focused on the man he was with, watching for little cues of what he needed to do. There was always something remote in it, a detachment Mace kept in front of him. He was unwilling to let someone else have control, or worse, and scared to fall fully into the connection he was having.

Rob took that away from him.

Every lift of Rob's hips drove Mace further from the corner he hid in. The tight grip of Rob's body around his cock seized at the rational part of Mace's mind and shattered its steely hold. The stroke down across his length slammed at the wall Mace struggled to keep between them, and then Rob delivered his most deadly blow.

He dipped into the cracked Vaseline jar and pushed the tip of his index finger into Mace's entrance.

The sensation of being entered while encased in Rob's heat overloaded Mace's senses. He grabbed at Rob's hips, thrust up into him, and bathed in the animalistic mewls that poured from Rob's sinful mouth. Mace found a spot with his cock and triggered a shiver through Rob every time he pulled the man off of him and buried himself balls-deep into Rob's hole.

They found a rhythm of sorts.

They'd definitely found a beat. The slap of their bodies was loud, a percussive roll punctuated by the cymbal crashes of thunder. Mace caught flashes of Rob's face when the lights flickered on, but he lost Rob's beauty when the sienna wash of shadows returned. There was a mounting pressure in his belly, his nerves tightening and twisting around his spine, and Mace felt Rob's body tense around him. Neither one of them was going to survive the afternoon, or at least not with all their wits, and Mace wasn't sure if he was even going to make it with all of his limbs attached.

As Rob rode him hard, Mace felt himself tearing apart. He loved the long kisses they shared between them, the lingering stretches of their tongues touching and then the brief bursts of air as they caught their breath. For a brief second, or maybe even a minute, Mace risked tangling his fingers into Rob's when he slid his hand up Mace's heaving chest. Their eyes met, and Mace, enraptured by Rob's impossibly golden gaze, couldn't breathe. The connection fell apart when Rob tilted his head back, and Mace drove his cock in deep, nearly lifting Rob's knees off the ground.

"*Jesus!*" Rob gasped. He bit at his lower lip as he pressed his hands on Mace's chest and steadied himself for the ride. "Fuck, your cock is…. Mace, I can't hold on."

Rob came hard. Mace could barely get a grip on his lover's jerking shaft before Rob climaxed. The first shot of hot, musky fluid hit Mace's chest, and the second smeared over his hand, its flow caught by Mace's thumb. Rob squeezed down, and his fingers slid in and brushed at the edge of Mace's nerves.

Rob was flexible. Mace couldn't deny that, especially when Rob twisted and worked Mace's body, tensed the skin along his rim, and then undulated his hips to push Mace over the edge.

He surrendered as lightning cracked open the sky, bleached the shop's darkness, and muted the colors of its graffiti-decorated walls. The maelstrom outside paled in comparison to the erotic turmoil exploding inside of him. There were anchor points in his awareness—the firmness of Rob's ass in his clenched fingers and the press of the floor across his shoulders when he lifted his hips to shove his cock into Rob and let himself be brought to release.

His cock was reluctant to slacken, still eager for the velvety sensation of Rob's clench around his flesh. He was softening slowly, and Rob seated himself down and rocked back and forth with tiny rolls of his hips to prolong their connection. Mace eased his fingers out of their tight grip and followed the planes of Rob's thighs with his hands until he reached his knees. He cupped the curves of the bones along the joint and then continued, feathering a light touch down Rob's calves.

Rob's fingers slid out of him, and Mace mourned the emptiness they left behind. He'd never liked being penetrated, didn't like the feel of someone else inside of him, but Rob felt *good*. All of it felt… mind-ending and amazing.

Then the rattle of the front door jerked them both to the present.

"*Shit*." Rob fought to unfold his legs. "My client's going to be here in ten minutes. *Fuck and shit*."

It hurt a little to pull loose, but the panic was rising between them, and the shop was out of power. Mace couldn't see much through the murky grayness inside of Rob's stall, but there was enough light coming from the front windows to illuminate the waiting area. The street was nearly invisible behind sheets of rain, but he knew a simple storm wasn't going to be enough to stop someone from getting a piece of ink they'd wanted for years.

It was also hard to let Rob go.

"You and I…," Rob said, catching Mace's chin in his hand. "We're not done. Now grab those baby wipes over there and let's clean ourselves off. And once I'm off shift, you and I are going to talk."

EIGHT

THE HOT and dirty sex on 415 Ink's hard floor did not ease Mace's aching want.

It *should* have. He'd poured all of himself into Rob—not simply by reaching his satisfaction but also by giving Rob as much as he could to reach his. His elbows hurt where he'd rested them against the cement floor, and there was a bit of rug burn on his knees from the mat in Rob's station. His cock was sleepy for about ten minutes, but as they scrambled to clean up and put the stall back in order, Mace brushed up against Rob's back and he was at square one again, hard and aching to put his hands on Rob and slake the unquenchable thirst in him.

The hours until Ivo showed up were the longest, most agonizing stretch of time Mace had ever experienced.

It should've been easy. One of the other tattoo artists, Missy, carved out some time to work the shop, and Mace thought he was cut a reprieve, only to be flooded by walk-ins and clients who came in for one thing or another. The reception desk was three deep at times, and he nearly called Bear to ask if there was a word-of-mouth special going on, because the foot traffic was insane. Either the rain drove people inside the shop or the full moon was affecting their moods, but either way, he didn't have a chance to do more than breathe from the moment he unlocked the front door.

Yet every time he turned around, he found himself seeking Rob out, watching as the man he'd just had screaming and writhing on top of him worked on an outline for an elaborate peacock tattoo. His client was talkative, boisterous, and laughing despite the variety of needles, and for the most part, Rob was attentive and engaging.

Except for the times when he looked up and met Mace's gaze.

The heat between them was still palpable and thick enough to kiss if only Mace leaned forward and puckered up. His desire built up momentum and energized the air until it crackled every time he glanced behind him, anticipating Rob's soulful gaze. He shouldn't have had enough time for contemplation or regret, not with the bell over the door ringing and the phone going off every fifteen minutes or having to break down a station for cleanup and running ink over to Missy, who always seemed to forget to get enough black or blue.

Mace couldn't go near Rob. He didn't trust himself, and the one time Rob called out for something, it was to replace the jar of Vaseline they'd broken. Mace's hip rubbed against Rob's arm when he edged past the artist to put the open container within Rob's reach, and he heard Rob catch his breath before he muttered a strangled thank-you.

When Ivo walked in the door, Mace handed him the shop's wireless phone, grabbed his jacket, and was out the door before Ivo had the chance to put his things down.

Having sex in the shop was a mistake, but making love to Rob was a disaster. He'd downed at least four cups of coffee and two bottles of water to get the taste of the other man off of his tongue, but Rob lingered, an aromatic musk Mace couldn't shake.

"A run in the rain never killed anyone," he told himself. "Go home, change, and just run it off, dude. You're just too tightly wound."

The storm raged on. There were brief stretches of drizzle and mist, but when Mace pushed out of the shop, the downpour began anew. He flipped up the hoodie he'd put on under his leather jacket, shoved his hands into his pockets, and ducked his head to sprint across the street.

Despite the heavy traffic at the shop, the sidewalk was fairly empty. In the middle of the afternoon, the pier was usually a jostle-and-dodge game to get to the parking structure a few blocks away from 415 Ink. There were clusters of tourists wandering in and out of the stores and protected by the wide veranda spanning most of the old buildings. But there was a stretch of unprotected sidewalk, and Mace was glad for his jacket because he made it about halfway down the cement ribbon and his hoodie was drenched through.

The bracing cold felt good… right and cleansing, even as it stripped the warmth from his flesh and made his feet and hands feel as though they were encased in ice. It chilled him down to the bones and numbed his face and his chest until he could no longer feel the ache for Rob under his skin. A few more steps and Mace reached the cement overhang of the multistory parking structure with its collection of restaurants and shops that faced the street.

As tempting as the scents of broiled burgers and fresh-cut fries were, Mace just wanted to go home. He didn't know which home he needed at the moment. Heading over to the Ashbury house would probably lead to questions about the shop, and Mace didn't think he could look into Bear's face and lie about his involvement with Rob.

Lying to Bear was inconceivable, but breaking a promise was worse.

"Jesus, what am I going to do? I know better. It's just… fuck, it was *crazy*. I've got to tell Rob we can't do that again. We just fucking *can't*."

Either the ground had been too dry to absorb the downpour or just couldn't take any more, because the wide streams along the road were packed with floating soil, and a dirty film capped the rivulet Mace avoided as he headed toward the stairs. The sidewalk and the lower landing of the parking structure were nearly empty, an unusual sight for a midafternoon on the pier. The morning had been busier, and the first floor was packed with cars, so he'd parked on the next level. When he hit the stairs, Mace was caught in an updraft of cold wind, and the puddles on the cement steps were massive unavoidable lakes he was forced to step through.

His shoes squelched with each step, and he couldn't stop shaking from the cold. The icy rain made his fingertips numb, and Mace fumbled with the hoodie's zipper and struggled to keep his jacket tucked under his arm while he unhooked the bottom stop. He didn't see the man lurking at the top of the second-floor stairwell until he hit the top step. Then a chill hit him and the prickle of uneasiness filled him.

His father was waiting for him in the shadows.

It was one thing to dream of the man who'd done everything in his power to make Mace as small and insignificant as possible.

It was quite another thing to find that man waiting to step back into his life.

The numbness from the cold had nothing on the dead quiet of Mace's brain as it shut down.

The mind often does funny things with memory. Most of the time, it softens the blow of past events or dulls the edges of sharp pain, making it possible for a person to move past traumatic events or push forward through adversity. But when confronted with the reality of a memory, the brain often glitches, caught between accepting the hard truth standing right before it or clinging to the illusion of survival and healing.

One look into his father's rigidly stern face and Mace's new life tumbled down like a house of cards.

Mace expected his father to look old. From the description Ivo gave him and the warped twisting of his mind, the man should have been a decrepit wrinkle of flesh and bone barely held together by spit, anger, and a couple of pieces of gum.

Instead he looked exactly like he did the last time Mace saw him, when he shut and bolted the closet door and sealed Mace away in the silence and the dark.

He was still muscular, his brawny frame nearly hidden by layers of clothes, and his face was obscured by an overlong dark beard shot through with silver. There was an eerie familiarity about him, more than something pulled up from memory. Seeing his father was like looking at his own face cast into the future and ridden hard by years in prison. As he stared at his father, Mace saw himself, a little older and meaner, but they shared the same eyes and mouth. Then his father smiled, and Mace was forced to swallow back a wave of sick that rushed up from his stomach.

There was no way he could turn away, even if he wanted to, because showing his father any bit of weakness would be like opening a floodgate, and he would drown in its aftermath.

Mace would have to talk with Ivo about his perception of *old*.

"I was just about to head down to that tattoo shop to see if any of those assholes over there would tell me where you lived." His father's sickening smile grew. "How are you, Johnny?"

There it was, the name he'd been hidden behind for years. *Johnny.* It was an echo from the past, the creak of a closet door opening and the darkness inside pouring out to consume him. Mace took the last few steps up the stairs but jerked back when his father crossed the landing toward him.

If he hadn't been fighting his instinctive fear, Mace would've laughed at how conditioned he was. It was like playing fetch with Earl and pretending to throw a ball, simply to watch the dog bolt forward and then glance back in confusion when he couldn't find his toy.

Mace wanted to cower, to duck his head down and sweep his gaze to the side so he wouldn't make eye contact. He fought the urge to fold his shoulders in, bend his spine, and make himself small so as not to challenge the dominant man in the house. Hearing his father's voice, its harsh tones thickened with a suppressed rage and deluded superiority, kicked off long-buried fears, and Mace felt the muscles in his face twist into a flinch before he could stop himself.

There was no conflict. There was no question. In the space of a few words, Mace nearly lost everything he'd worked hard to achieve and became that scared little boy again, trapped behind a locked door.

He *couldn't* go back to that. He *wouldn't* go back to that. This time no one would come and save him. No one would come to pull him out of the darkness. If he stepped toward the invisible door his father held open for him, Mace knew he would be lost.

"That's not my name." It was the first shot he could fire in a battle for his identity—a battle he'd intended never to fight again. "That's who you tried to make me. That's not who I am."

"That's what *I* named you. That's who you are." His father jabbed at the air with his finger and brushed Mace's chest. "You're my son. She should have named you after me. Just like I was named after my father. You should be thankful for that name. I fixed what *she* fucked up. I made you, and she tried to take that away from me."

The brief contact felt like a bullet going through him, and Mace couldn't stop himself from taking a step back to give himself distance from the anger boiling up in his father's face. He choked back the words of apology his brain threw up in defense, following long-scabbed-over routes of behavior.

"Everything that I am, I made myself." Mace heard the shaking in his own voice, but he squared his shoulders and presented an attitude he didn't feel. "Anything that you did to me, I scraped off. There's nothing of you left. And I don't even know why you're here. You and I are done."

"We are *never* going to be done. You're my kid. I brought you into this world, and I can fucking take you out if I need to." His father leaned in with spittle on his lips as he nearly shouted into Mace's face. His hate and anger echoed through the stairwell, and his words bounced before they whispered off around the smatter of parked cars behind Mace. "Did you forget where you came from? Did you buy into the lies those people sold you? That's what I was protecting you against. That's the reason I took you, because your mother—"

"You took me because you wanted to hurt her. You took me and the dog," Mace shot back. "Then you killed him and left him on our front porch so I would know how little I meant to you and to tell her what you would do to me. You spent years making sure I knew I was shit. So don't come around me now and tell me you made me, because you didn't make me, you *destroyed* me."

"I made you strong." His father crowded in, and Mace steeled himself not to move. The smell of cigarette smoke clinging to his father's baggy clothes drowned out the scent of the rain, and his breath reeked of onions and decay, but still Mace locked himself in place. "Do you think you'd be as big and tough as you think you are right now if I hadn't made you that way? Your mother would have turned you into a pussy. I made you a man. I made you a man who could hold his head up and walk through a crowd of people, knowing he's superior to them. I made you proud to be a strong white man. I gave you a legacy, and you spit in my face for it?"

Mace waited for the other shoe to drop, and when it did, the sick rode over him again. He stared into the face of a madman—his own face worn around the edges with the filth of a personality his father once hoped to instill in Mace. He'd heard those whisperings all through his childhood—slithering tidbits of hatred and dominance that crept under the closed doors he lived behind. They were at odds with the memories of his life before the day his father shattered his childhood. The people in his mother's circle, who were a rainbow of skin tones and languages, a welcoming kaleidoscope of different foods and unfamiliar customs.

It wasn't just his best friend his father killed that day. He'd also killed Mace's chance for a normal life and extinguished the love his mother once had for him.

"I don't want you in my life." Mace kept his arms down and his fists clenched around his jacket. "I didn't want you then. I don't want you now."

"I'm the only family you have. Remember?" his father countered. "Did you think word wouldn't get back to me about her? About how she refused to come get you after they took you from me? Did you forget that? Did she even look you in the face when she decided you weren't good enough for her anymore?"

"You don't know fuck about that day," he growled back menacingly, but doubt was creeping in along the edges of his confidence. The pain of that afternoon resonated and rippled up from the sticky darkness he had on his soul. "She hadn't seen me in years, and after you were done with me—"

"After I fixed what she did do you. Our kind has a rightful place in this world—"

"Don't start that shit with me. I don't buy into that crap. Despite everything you tried to make me believe, I didn't buy it, and I'm not going to start now," Mace snapped through his father's words. "You broke her. Just like you broke me. So no, she can't stand to look at me because I remind her of you. I have you to thank for that. And you're not the only family I have. You're just the family I don't want."

"Don't hold your breath about your mother ever wanting you back." His father pushed forward and cornered Mace against a concrete pylon meant to keep cars from driving onto the stairwell. Its rounded cap dug into Mace's lower back, but the sharp glimpse of pain gave him focus. He held his ground and brought his chin up as his father sneered at him. "You think you're so tough now? You don't think I can take you? If I wanted to, I could break you with one hand. That was always your problem; you're too fucking weak to do what has to be done. That's why you needed me to make you a man. You've got too much of your mother in you."

"I wouldn't know," he replied. When he realized he'd angled his body to present as little of himself to his father as possible, he shifted his weight forward to his other foot and pulled his shoulder back. "I don't know her. You took care of *that* for me. I'm going to ask you this just once—what the hell did you think was going to happen today? Did you think I was going to throw away everything in my life for you? To follow whatever crazy thing you're doing? Because I can tell you right here and right now, that's not going to happen."

It was probably a psychosomatic response to his father's presence, but that didn't make the throbbing twinge on his shoulder blade any less painful. The scarification his father did to him one night in a dirty hotel room thankfully hadn't produced the symbol he wanted, but it was close enough to make one of the doctors who'd examined Mace nearly refuse to treat him that night. A series of injections were meant to minimize the keloid, but they left the area stretched out in places and bumpy in others. Years later Bear took a needle to Mace's back and set down Mace's first tattoo, erasing his father's repulsive marking from his skin.

"You owe me." His father jabbed at Mace's chest again and dug his nail into the wet fabric. The bright bitter terror in Mace's throat thickened. "I took you—"

Someone cleared their throat at the top of the stairwell. Rob's sneakers splashed through a small puddle and sent rippling rings out over the shallow water. He was slightly winded, as though he'd run to catch up with Mace, and his T-shirt was as soaked through as it had been earlier that morning.

Rob's attention flicked once toward Mace's father and then settled back on him. Concern clouded his expression. "Is there a problem? You okay, Mace?"

Mace had never been good at lying. He didn't know if it was a genetic deficiency or just something he couldn't properly do, because he sucked at it. His father wasn't any better, or maybe he just didn't give a shit who knew how monstrous he was inside.

"I'm good," Mace replied, but even as the words left his mouth, he knew Rob didn't believe him. "You should go back to the shop. Take my jacket so you don't get wetter and head back before—"

It was a stupid mistake. Mace should've known, but he'd come so far to becoming a normal human being that he'd forgotten how depraved and malevolent his father was. Mace caught the exact moment his father realized Rob was gay and then his sickening delight at the near desolation of the garage.

"Shit, you're the faggot I saw the other day. You were with that other kid from the shop," his father practically purred. "Did you come chasing after my son? Looking for something from him?"

"And if he is, he's probably going to find it," Mace growled as he pushed his father away and stepped in front of Rob. "Leave him the fuck alone. Actually, leave us both the fuck alone."

The buildup of violence was quick, surging up from the bowels of his father's constantly simmering rage. It struck as hard and fast as the lightning that arced over the angry sky and left a trail of crackling electrical stink in its wake. Mace could taste his father's hatred in the air, its spit of iron nails and rotted morals, foul enough to drown any decency lurking in the recesses of his father's soul. The fist came in hot, a wild swing fueled by powerful muscles and an insanity Mace hoped he would never understand.

For the first time in forever, Mace ducked to avoid his father's blow.

He'd stupidly never done it when he was a child. His mother never struck him, so his father's first punch to his four-year-old temple had left Mace's ears ringing and his mouth filled with blood where he'd bitten his cheek. It happened too quickly for him to experience anything other than a mind-blowing pain, and then another punch followed and led to a string of concussive strikes that Mace could only avoid by curling up into a ball.

His father had peeled him open, knelt on Mace's hips and thighs to hold him down, and then punched him again. Mace thought he was going to die. Betrayed and hurt by a man he'd thought loved him, he'd been unable to do anything to protect himself, other than scream his apologies.

This time Mace was not going to apologize.

This time he wasn't going to curl up and pray—and certainly not when it looked as though his father intended to teach Rob a lesson by beating him simply because he existed.

Ducking the first punch left him open for the second, but it landed wide and glanced off of Mace's ribs. He grunted under the impact and absorbed the shock wave of pain as he lashed out and connected with his father's jaw. The man staggered back, his eyes wide with shock and wild with rage. Stumbling into the stairwell railing, his father grabbed at the metal pipe and touched his now-bleeding lip.

Mace shoved Rob toward the cars and circled around to keep himself as a barrier. He felt Rob at his back, edging in closer, but Mace warned him off and held out his hand. "Stay there. You don't need to be in between us, Rob."

"So that's how it is, Johnny? You making friends with… *them*?" Panting heavily, he grinned at Mace with a bloodstained row of yellowed teeth. "You should stick to people like you. Not that kind of—"

"Shut up." Mace cut him off before he could go any further. "I'm going to tell you this again, and maybe this time you'll hear me. I don't want you around me. I don't want you in my life. I am *nothing* like you. I will *never* be like you. I don't want you around my family. I don't want you around the shop. And I sure as fuck don't want you around Rob or anyone else I know. So crawl back into whatever hole you found after they let you out and stay there. Because if I see you again, we're going to finish this, and you're not going to like how it ends."

NINE

ROB STILL wore the pricks on his heart from his own father's thorny words—sarcastic, cutting, demeaning sneers meant to make him feel small, and he bled a little bit every time he thought of the battles they'd waged. They'd been merciless, especially once Rob turned his back on the path his father decided for him, and more than a few times, Rob's mother became an emotional hostage in their war, forced to choose between her husband and her son. He had regrets—deep ones—and doubt constantly ate at him, especially after a long, hard day with no clients and an empty wallet.

But he couldn't imagine dealing with the hand Mace had been dealt.

"I'm a little short of cash." The bearded man shifted his shoulders and tilted his chin back, his narrowed eyes fixed on Rob's face. "How much do you have on you, Johnny?"

"I'm not giving you any money." Mace's honeyed baritone dropped to a raspy growl and layered a veneer of menace over his words. "You're not going to get anything out of me, so you might as well just go."

Tension threaded through the air, a tapestry woven from a past Rob didn't share but that wasn't hard to guess at. He would have to be senseless not to see or hear the trouble between Mace and his father. The man who only a few hours ago broke Rob's mind with a seemingly endless patience and passionate lovemaking lay buried beneath a lock-jawed granite barrier, his rigid, strong body shielding Rob from harm.

And there was definitely harm. Rob didn't need to know exactly what had passed between Mace and his father, and he wasn't sure he wanted to, at least not firsthand. There was malevolence in the man's body language, an unspoken promise to peel Rob's skin from his flesh so he could use it as a mat to wipe his feet on. The derision Rob had reaped from his own family was always subtle, a minimizing of his intelligence and capabilities, but this was something more than the casual dismissal he'd encountered before.

The man staring over Mace's shoulder left Rob with no doubt that he would take his time breaking Rob's body and enjoy every second of pain he could inflict.

Father and son stood only a few feet apart, but the distance between them was vast. Rob wasn't imagining the tremble in Mace's fingers when he clenched them into hard fists, his knuckles already bloodied from striking his father moments before. Something passed over his father's face, and the smirk he gave Rob was a promise of future violence if their paths ever crossed again.

"I'll leave you to your friend." The man shrugged and stepped sideways down into the stairwell but kept his shoulders turned and his attention fixed on Mace. "See about trying to help your old man out. I'll talk to you later."

The only sound fighting the rain was the man's heavy boots as their thick soles scraped at the cement stairs. Rob didn't realize he'd been holding his breath until his lungs began to shake in his chest and stabbing pain shot through his ribs. He gasped at about the same time Mace did and trembled in both relief and suppressed terror.

They stood in the cold until a VW Rabbit rattled its way onto their level, its body doing a metallic salsa, shimmying and shaking until it finally came to a shuddering rest in a parking spot a few feet away. Its driver, a young girl with blond dreads, flung herself out of the vehicle and slammed the door behind her. Muttering to herself, she looked shocked when she slammed into Rob and then stepped on Mace's discarded jacket. She apologized in a stream of words Rob couldn't make sense out of and then hurried toward the stairs as she awkwardly tied an apron branded with the name of a nearby restaurant around her slender waist. A few steps later, she nearly knocked into Mace, and she muttered another garbled apology as she took the stairs at a full run.

"Jesus, she's... lost in her own brain there." Rob shook his head at the woman's pinball bounce past them and then said, "Are you al—"

Mace turned, and the look of fear and disgust on his face stole Rob's breath.

He watched as Mace fell hard and dropped to his hands and knees. Wracked by spasms, Mace gagged, and his back arched as his taut stomach struggled to push up its contents. Mace retched and dry heaved a few times. Then he sat back on his haunches, and his throat rippled as he stared up at the ceiling.

The sick hit Mace in the few steps it took for Rob to reach his side.

It was as violent as the encounter with Mace's father, a twisting of flesh and bitter fluids, and it was all Rob could do to get Mace to let him help. Mace strong-armed Rob and pushed him away with a hard shove as he scrambled to his feet to get to a nearby trash can. Partially open to the sky, the landing edge was wet. Mace's shoulders were quickly drenched, but the cold rain didn't seem to have any effect on him or the shock waves that coursed through him.

Mace's fingers were cold and clammy when Rob grabbed at them to pull Mace out of the downpour, but he shook him off. Trembling, he continued to empty his stomach, and his shoulders quaked with the effort to stop, but his body refused.

"I'm going to call Ivo. He'll—" Rob had already hit the shop's number on his phone when Mace shot a hand out and knocked the device down. Its protective case hit the cement, and the phone bounced and landed facedown a few feet away. "Fuck, Mace… you need some help."

"He's… got a client he's working on. I'm not worth pulling him out of that," Mace grumbled as he turned his head slightly to look up at Rob with wild blue eyes. His hair was nearly black from the rain, and the edges of his mouth were tinged with blue. His lips quivered as he spoke. "I… just need to get… home."

"Let me get one of your brothers," Rob insisted, and he swallowed a scream when Mace shook his head. "I can't leave you like this. At least let me help you get back to your place. Jesus, what kind of asshole do you think I am? That I'll just dump you after you went through that shit?"

"That?" His snort was as bitter as the smell of his sick in the trash can. "That was nothing. And why should you be any different from my mother?"

LETTING ROB take him home was a mistake. It was one of a long line of mistakes, but as he stumbled into the living room, partially blinded from the cold and the shock of seeing his father, Mace knew it was the blunder of a lifetime. He didn't take anyone he had sex with home, and he refused to show any bit of his life to anyone he shared his body with. But there was Rob, in the middle of his living room, arm around Mace's sore ribs and straining to get Mace to a shower.

If there was one thing Mace learned that afternoon, it was that Rob was a stubborn, hardheaded fucking asshole who didn't take *go away* seriously. Or at least that's how he felt once his ass hit the bed and the warm air of his apartment started him shivering again.

"I'm going to help you get undressed," Rob muttered. He crouched down in front of Mace and parted Mace's knees with his shoulders to get at his shoelaces. "You're turning into a snowman in front of my eyes, and I didn't even get to sing a song about it."

"That doesn't make any sense." Mace struggled to find a connection to Rob's words. "What the hell are you talking about?"

"Oh, I forget Chris is new to the family. I used to babysit for my neighbors' daughters. There's no such thing as watching a cartoon movie just once. It has to be on repeat for five to six weeks until you start hearing it in your sleep. Then you realize that you're not crazy, because the walls are thin and the damned television is on the other side, wailing away about snowmen or rats that can cook pasta." Rob shuddered, evidently unable to forget his first reaction to the idea of a rodent handling his spaghetti. "While you're in the shower, I'll make you some tea. Or coffee. Something to warm you up."

The apartment was eerily silent and draped in a milky dimness much too familiar for Mace's liking. He leaned over to turn on the bedside lamp, but Rob was in his way, tugging at his shirt. The neck grabbed at his ear, rubbing his lobe raw, and Mace swore and slapped his right hand over the burning skin. His fingers brushed the pull chain of the bedside lamp, the bulb flared on with a bright flash, and the darkness receded.

Or at least it had in Mace's mind, but a piece of it was lodged on his shoulder, and he heard Rob draw in a sharp breath.

"What the fuck happened to you?" Rob's whisper was a thread of white noise in the rush of blood that carried Mace's panic through his veins. He brushed his fingers over one of the larger keloids under Mace's skin, and Mace flinched at the memories of hot knives and sharp fingers ripping at his flesh. "Seriously, dude, who did this to you?"

He was naked in more ways than one. Stripped of his T-shirt and his dignity, Mace's humiliation only grew with every inch of skin Rob explored with his fingertips. His stomach, wrung dry of everything but the tears he'd swallowed on the ride over, threatened to turn itself inside out. There was too much silence and way too many shadows, and the bedroom door swinging partially closed on its well-oiled hinges ratcheted up his anxiety. He would take the damned thing off its frame if he could, but Rey occupied the other bedroom—however infrequently now that he and Gus were back together—and he still needed a bit of privacy.

There was no simple way to explain the terrors that lurked at the edges of every room, the nightmares of every door latch that clicked into place. Normal people weren't supposed to be afraid of silence. They outgrew their fear of darkness and the imaginary monsters living there, but Mace didn't think he ever would. Those monsters wore the faces of ordinary men, including his own father, and as hard as he searched through the world's whisperings, he never heard his mother calling out for him. He had been consigned to his fate.

When Rob's hand ghosted across the massive scar over his shoulder blade, Mace closed his eyes and once again wished for something to take away the pain that lived in his tangled tissues.

"Did your dad do this?" Rob rasped. Emotion ran hot through his voice, and Mace couldn't bear to look at the judgment he knew would be in Rob's gaze. "Dude, I get that you probably don't want to talk about this, but what happened today was pretty fucked-up, and right now you're scaring me, because… as long as I've known you, you and your brothers have been tight, so talk to me. Tell me why you don't want me to call one of them."

Mace closed his eyes and then dug the heels of his hands into them and scrubbed out the crust of salt on his lashes. He'd handed Rob the keys and somehow mumbled directions or maybe an address, but he didn't remember being driven home or even the elevator ride up to his place. There'd been tears. Mace was sure of it because his eyes hurt and his nose was stuffy, slightly swollen, and hurting from the ugliness of his afternoon. He wanted nothing more than to crawl under his blankets and hide away from the world, maybe even drag Rob in with him so he could pretend someone cared about his broken heart and torn-up soul.

He knew better. Seeing his father in the stairwell brought everything back in full living color. And as he stared out across the spartan bedroom he slept in between shifts, Mace finally saw that Rob was standing in front of him, waiting for an explanation Mace didn't know if he had it in him to give.

"That's it, I'm calling Bear," Rob muttered, and Mace grabbed at his wrist and captured him before he could slide away. "Dude, you need help. And if it's not going to be me—"

"Let me… take a shower and… I don't know," Mace stumbled around his own tongue. "I don't know if I can talk to them right now, because… my father… the things he did to me were evil, but the things he had me do were… far fucking worse, and if I tell my brothers about them… about what I've done, they'll throw me out of the family and…." He screwed his eyes shut and willed away the fear choking him, but it wouldn't dislodge from his throat. "They're all I've got. I can't lose them. And that's exactly what will happen if they ever found out about… everything."

THE SHOWER turned lukewarm, but Mace was reluctant to get out. Slipping out from behind the glass door meant having to face Rob and scrape off every scab he had inside of him. But no matter how much hot water poured over him, Mace couldn't warm up the chill in the center of his chest. He'd run from the truth of himself for far too long, and it didn't seem like the marathon was going to be over anytime soon.

He was too tired and too sick to keep pushing himself past all of the walls he'd built up to keep his nightmares at bay. No matter how many bricks he ordered into place, they kept crumbling beneath him, and his memories slithered and wove out to find him, sink their poisonous fangs into his psyche, and suck him dry of any confidence he had.

It was all he could do to get dressed in a pair of sweats, but he gave one last longing glance at his bed, put on a T-shirt, and headed out to the living room to face his fate.

And as he expected, there was Rob, waiting for him with a large cup of tea, concern written all over a face Mace had kissed only a few hours before. What he didn't expect was the lights on low and the sound of the muted thunderstorm rolling out of his stereo speakers. The tea was probably one of the breakfast blends Ivo kept stashed in the kitchen for the mornings when he couldn't make it home and crashed on Mace's couch. Somewhere Rob had found a tray and arranged it neatly on the coffee table. A bowl of sugar cubes and a plate of lemon wedges kept company with a pair of mugs, and the teakettle was wrapped in a towel for warmth.

It was oddly domestic and unexpected from a man who was just now drying his hair and marbling an old beach towel with streaks of cast-off blue dye. There was even a stack of cheap paper napkins, folded in half and held down by one of the spoons, to complete the tray's oddly delicate arrangement of old cutlery and utilitarian mugs.

"Sit down and tell me what you want in your tea." Rob tossed the towel onto the counter that separated the living room from the kitchen. He sat down, reached for the kettle, and lifted it from its nest to pour hot water over the teabags in each mug. "I can never keep track of how you like coffee. You're like Gus. His shit changes up with his mood."

"Sugar's fine. I like my tea sweet. What did you tell Ivo about leaving the shop?" Mace grabbed the mug when Rob held it out and put his hand underneath it to support its weight. "Do I need to call him and tell him it's okay?"

He could maybe talk to Ivo, but Mace wasn't going to bet on it. Ivo liked to pick apart things and dig into any sign of weakness or trouble, intent on rooting out its cause. One wrong word and Ivo would be charging up the hill, ready to do battle against any of Mason's demons. Problem was, the phantoms Mace carried with him were real, and the last person in the world Mace wanted his father to interact with was Ivo. It was bad enough the man spoke once with the baby of the family. Luckily—and as much as Mace hated to say it—it was on a day when Ivo looked relatively normal.

Mace didn't want his father to ever see Ivo in stilettos and a kilt. He knew what happened to people—to men—who crossed the societal lines his father had drawn in the sand. Any deviation from the norm was an affront to him and God, and in his sick mind, he would be forgiven any violence he used to bring the world back into order.

He was scared shitless and numb with fright, and the cold solidified in Mace's gut. Burning buildings and explosive fires fed by gas lines were nothing compared to the damage his father could do to Mace's life. He would probably start with Ivo or Gus, snatch them off the street or lure them into an alley, where he and a few of his friends could work them over. He did it with a sense of perverted justice, or at least that's what he'd always told Mace, but there was sexual sadism beneath it all, and Mace knew where that sometimes led.

Suddenly Luke's horrific offer—even if given in jest—seemed like a good idea.

"He knew I was chasing after you, actually left me a text asking if I was still alive, because he was pretty sure you killed me when I didn't come back. I told him you weren't feeling well, so I wanted to make sure you came home, but he said that was bullshit because there's no way you'd ever admit to being sick. So he thinks we got into it." Rob paused, probably because he caught Mace's wince. "Then he told me there was enough coverage if you and I need to hash out a few things, because Bear's not going to put up with any shit and to remind us to work it out. For some reason, he thinks you hate me, and to be honest, despite you fucking my brains out today, I'm not sure he's wrong."

"Jesus, you have no fucking idea how wrong he is," Mace ground out between his clenched teeth. "I'm okay. You can go—"

"I'm not going anywhere." Rob pursed his lips and blew at the steam coming up from his cup. "I think I've got you figured out now. You've got crap going on in your head, and it scares you, so you shove everybody away, including your brothers. But I'm not going to let you do that to me, because for some damned reason, while I was making tea, I found out I actually gave a shit about what happened to you. So fuck me, right?

"Tell me what I walked into today. This afternoon was a scary as all hell, and I didn't know what to do," he confessed softly. Then he took a sip of his tea and let his gaze slide up to Mace's face. "If you won't talk to your brothers, then talk to me. You're insane if you believe they'll turn their backs on you. I mean, *shit*, Gus went out and came home with a surprise baby and no one blinked an eye. You don't think they'd be willing to kick your racist father's ass?"

Mace turned the cup around in his hands. His knuckles were swollen, the skin raw from punching his father. It'd been a reflex, but the guilt lingered. His thoughts were muddied, too thick to see sense through, but Mace understood that he couldn't wallow in the filth he'd been dragged through, not anymore. Ignoring who he'd been only worked if the man who shaped him sat behind concrete walls and iron bars. There was no running from the truth anymore, no hiding in the light to keep the shadows from wrapping around him, and no amount of street noise and loud stereos could drown out the subaural murmuring of his awakened consciousness, the sly whispers that dredged up every little memory of his time before Bear called him brother.

He was just so sick of running.

"It's not my father's racism I'm worried about." Mace put his mug down and flexed his hand, welcoming the stretch of skin and the faint pain it brought. "It's going to come out anyway. What I've done, what

I helped my father do, and what I let him do to me. And you're wrong about what it takes to get people to walk away from you.

"My mom did." Closing his eyes didn't stop the tears, but oddly enough, it helped to fold in, keep his head down, and let his tears fall into his lap. He didn't have to look at Rob that way, didn't have to see the disgust that would eventually be on his face, much like his brothers would look at him. "When they got me away from my dad… he took me from her, and once they told her about… everything, she left me there. She couldn't even look at me. I'm her kid. She's supposed to love me. But in the end, what I was… who I am… she couldn't love."

"Weren't you a kid?" Rob slid across the couch, his cup left on the table so he could cover Mace's hands with his own. They were nearly burning with heat, and Mace flinched, shocked by the need to bury his face into the crook of Rob's neck and hug him until the world stopped spinning out of control. Rob ducked his head, his cheek nearly against Mace's, and he whispered, "No matter what happened, you were just a little boy. Nobody can blame you for what happened."

"I blame myself," he confessed around the rush of sick threatening at the back of his throat. Mace swallowed and surrendered to the growing burden of truth pressing down on him. "I might've been a kid, but we were doing wrong. I was maybe seven the first time and I was scared and sick as hell afterwards, but I still did it because he was my dad and I loved him. Or at least I thought I loved him. It got worse, so much fucking worse. He was my whole fucking world, Rob, and a couple of years later, he told me to help them beat a man almost to death with a baseball bat. So I did."

TEN

OF ALL the regrets Mace had, the worst was the one he carried with him in a cracked case of memories he wasn't even sure were real. It'd been nearly twenty years since he'd been given a baseball bat and told what to do, but his hands still burned with the echo of the wood against his chafed palms, and he woke up in the middle of the night trying to wipe away the hot smears of blood off his face.

His face never felt clean, and he'd never picked up a baseball bat again. That night became a long, filthy string of rusted metal links, anchoring Mace down to drown in the sewage of his actions, and he didn't know how to sever himself from the chain, especially since he seemed to be forging new links every time he closed his eyes to sleep.

And now Rob sat next to him, asking Mace to tear down the flimsy membrane he pulled up over his mind every morning to protect himself from the past that lurked in the darkness.

He didn't dare look at Rob. He didn't deserve any sympathy or empathy, but even knowing his life would be over once he spoke the truth about what happened to him and what he'd done, Mace knew the time had come to put his lies down. The burden was too great, and he just couldn't do it anymore. So he hunkered forward on the couch cushion, stared at his hands, and picked at his thumbnail while he tore his world down.

"I was playing with my dog in the field behind my house when my dad took me. I was six… maybe almost seven, I think. He'd just won the court case to get visitation rights, but my mom was still fighting him. I knew who he was. My grandmother—his mom—would come visit me and tell me about my dad because the court said she could have contact with me." Mace snorted. He tried to dredge up the face of the woman who'd smelled like lavender and who pinched his thigh every time his attention drifted away from the photos she shoved at him. "He told me he was going to take me to see my mom because she'd been in an accident. But I wasn't that far from the house, so I began running home, and he grabbed my dog and screamed at me to stop, but I was too scared.

"I don't know where he got the knife or even if it was in his hand the whole time, but all I remember was how much blood there was, and then my dog went limp and silent. That's when he told me if I didn't listen to him, he would do the same thing to me." He didn't have anything left in his belly but a few sips of tea, but it felt like a quarry of rocks was lodged in his gut. "The stupid thing is I don't even remember my dog's name. I was just so fucking overwhelmed and scared. And I *never* stopped being scared."

Rob moved closer, and the sour churn in Mace's stomach began anew. When Rob slid his arm around his back, Mace wanted to scream that he didn't deserve to be touched and held, not with as filthy as he was inside. But then Rob leaned into him and rested his cheek on Mace's shoulder, and the simple, intimate touch chased off the cold in Mace's spine that the hot tea hadn't even touched.

"Whatever you tell me stays between us." Rob slid his hand down to rest on Mace's thigh. There was nothing sexual in the contact, simply a connection of one person to another, but it was more than enough to bring a new sting of tears to Mace's eyes. "But I really hope you've talked to somebody about this, or at least you're thinking about telling someone about what this does to you."

"Talking to someone about this made it too… everything, and by the time I could even look at it, Bear had taken me in, and I didn't want him to know about it because… it's that fucking ugly."

Rob murmured a soothing sound into Mace's ear and then asked, "How long did he have you?"

"He had me for… I was eleven… maybe about five years. He had to hide me from anyone who'd come over, because he'd stolen me. I figured that out later, but at the time he told me… first he took me to keep me safe, and then it was because my mother really didn't want me. The story kept changing, but every time it did, he would convince me it was because he didn't want to hurt me so he would lie," Mace mumbled and kept his head down. Then he choked back his disgust as Rob ghosted his fingers over the scar on his shoulder blade. "Don't… touch me there. That's where he—*Jesus*, I don't even know where to start."

"What is it?" Rob ignored Mace's rebuke, but as much as he wanted to pull Rob's hand away, it was the first time he'd been touched there for a long time. A fingertip trace along the edges of the scar knotted Mace's nerves, and he exhaled hard to force the hot air in his lungs out. "I can't tell what this is."

"It's… it was supposed to be some Viking rune they use to…." Mace couldn't bring himself to admit what his father was. "It didn't go well, and it scarred funny, which I'm glad for but… I know what they were trying to do, and every time I think about it… about him…. I spent so much of my life trying to forget what happened when I was with him. Then he shows back up and it starts all over again."

"What does?" Rob stroked up and down Mace's thigh with his graceful fingers, a comforting touch he probably didn't even realize he was doing, but it was an intimate gesture, something a man would do to show his lover he was listening. "Start wherever you want to start, but dude, this shit is tearing you apart, and no one's going to be able to help you if you don't talk about it."

Mace finally looked up and drowned in the golden gaze of a man with a pretty mouth and apparently a beautiful soul. The itch he had for Rob was threatening to blossom into something bigger and deeper, a tantalizing will-o'-the-wisp of an emotion, but Mace feared he would be doomed if he followed.

God, he *ached* to be loved. He wanted nothing more than to fill the emptiness inside. No matter how hard he fought to secure a place among the brothers, he knew their affection was built on a lie, a construct of the person he'd thrown up to shield their eyes from the monster he'd been. There couldn't be any forgiveness for him, not with what stained his past, but the festering decay of his memories needed to be cut out, even if it left gaping holes in who he was.

He would begin to strip away the lies starting with Rob, and then he would stand before the four men he loved more than anything else in the world and beg for them not to throw him out. But no matter what happened, it was time for him to break free of those chains.

"We were driving around in a van, one that didn't have any windows on the sides. It was my father and three of his friends. I was about nine, I think. It's fuzzy because… you see, he would lock me in a closet or bathroom when people would come over, because he couldn't show my face. If I did anything wrong, he would put me into the darkness and leave me there." Mace went back to picking at his thumbnail, comforted by the *click-click*. The ever-present hunger was back in his mind, and the hollow pressure built in his belly and stretched back toward his spine. "I could never tell how long, but there were times when I was so hungry I scraped paint off the walls to eat. I would piss myself, and then when he let me out, he would beat me because a dog knew better than to go to the bathroom inside the house.

"I could hear them talking but then there would be long stretches of silence, and sometimes I wondered if he forgot me. He started going out for longer periods of time, locking me in there with Gatorade bottles and those neon-orange peanut-butter-and-cheese-cracker packets. I'd have to make them last, but I never knew how long he'd be, so sometimes I ran out, and I'd get so thirsty," Mace confessed with a chuckle. "It's stupid, but now I always have a water bottle on me, and I can't stand the fucking silence or the dark. I hate closing my bedroom door. I hate the sound of the lock on the front door, but it's not like I can leave it open. If there's noise, then I know I'm alive. There were quite a few times when I wondered if I was actually dead, because it never ended."

"What were you saying about the van?" Rob pressed against the spot. There was something in Rob's voice, something thick and dark, but Mace still couldn't meet his eyes. "What does that have to do with the scar?"

"The scar… he put that there because I needed to learn a lesson. Because I…." Mace moved forward and pulled away from Rob's touch. He wouldn't be able to speak if Rob continued to touch him. It was hard enough not to wrap his arms around Rob and hold him until the sound of the rain sluiced away the stickiness left over from that horrible night. "He told me we were going to go out and get something to eat, but instead, we drove around for… I don't know how long, but it was like the city got quieter and quieter as we went. One time we stopped for gas, and they started in about going in to have a talk with the guy behind the counter, but my father said it was too… open. Too many people. I didn't know what he meant then, but later on…. He didn't want anyone to see what they were doing, because they'd already made up their minds to kill someone. They just didn't know who."

Rob sucked in a breath and clenched his fingers, digging into Mace's thigh. "Fuck. Mace…."

"I fell asleep in the back of the van. It didn't have any seats, so I was on the floor, leaning against some carpet. I woke up when the van suddenly stopped, because I hit my head on the side." Mace grimaced and rubbed at a spot on the back of his skull. "I gashed it open, and I started to sniffle, but my dad told me to shut up. Then everything… kind of went to shit."

That night, the van's doors had opened up to a deluge not unlike the one pounding at the apartment's windows. It was as though even the storm was frightened of the past, flogged on by the whipping frenzy of Mace's shrouded memories. He'd cowered against the cold steel of the van's bare metal walls, his legs cramped and twisted from being curled up in a ball.

"I don't know who the guy was. I think he was Hispanic. I don't know." His breath was hot, but a chilling numbness spread through Mace's limbs. "It had to be two or three in the morning, because nobody was around. And maybe this guy missed the bus or he just walked but… they pulled the van in close to him, and my dad pushed open the side door before it even came to a full stop. I remember crying out, thinking he was going to fall and hurt himself. Then I wondered if they were stopping to pick up this guy because he was their friend and it was raining.

"It's kind of stupid what your brain does when you're a kid. It tries to make sense out of things even when you know in your gut something's wrong. Your brain tries to make it okay. And it was okay until my dad caught the baseball bat one of his friends tossed at him and swung it against the guy's back." The crack of wood on bone resonated in Mace's mind. It became a drumbeat, an uneven roll of percussive strikes with the occasional slap of the bat on the concrete stretch separating the two buildings the man had cut in between. "They wouldn't stop hitting him. And I didn't understand what he was saying, but he was begging, there was no mistaking that. He was begging for his life and maybe his family. I don't know.

"I started screaming, and my dad looked up. I wanted them to stop, but when he did, his face was… he was splattered with blood, and you would've thought he was bathed in chocolate, because he was ecstatic, like he'd seen God." Mace bit his lower lip hard enough to cut it, and Rob made a worried sound and slid his thumb across Mace's mouth.

"Don't do that," Rob admonished. "You didn't have anything to do with that. You've got to stop beating yourself up over it. That's your father—"

"He grabbed me from the van," Mace said. He shook his head as he grabbed Rob's hand, kissed his fingers, and let it drop. "He rushed at the open doors and grabbed me by my shirt, holding the bat in his other hand. He dragged me across the ground. He didn't care that I wasn't walking or that he was tearing open the skin on my legs because my sweatpants were too big and they were getting pulled off. We got close to where the others were, and he threw me down on the ground. Then he grabbed my hair and held the bat out, and when I wouldn't take it, he bent my fingers open and wrapped them around the grip.

"That's when he told me I had to prove to him that I loved him, that I'd do anything for him." He choked on his words as he forced the barbed truth to leave his throat. The smell of blood was in his nose, a constant metallic aroma he always associated with rain, but Mace pushed on. "He punched my face and told me if I didn't do it, if I didn't help them beat this man, he would use the bat on me and leave me there."

He paused to catch his breath, then said, "So I began swinging."

IT WAS painful to hear and even more agonizing to watch, but Rob knew he couldn't turn away from Mace. Too many people had. And those who'd reached out to him had done so only to inflict unimaginable trauma. His dark lashes were matted with still-damp tears, and speckles of dried blood dotted his lip where Mace had worried at his flesh with his teeth.

Seeing Mace relive that night was like watching an angel being condemned for crimes he didn't commit and then plummet from the heavens as he fell from grace.

One thing was certain—the only one who felt guilty about that night was the man who sat next to him on the couch, broken and torn apart by a father who should've loved him, who should've protected him. For the first time in his life, Rob was grateful for his father's apathy. Despite all of the subtle slurs and jabs he'd suffered through growing up, his family had never tried to turn him into a monster.

He was also damn sure Mace's father had failed to do that to his son.

"You aren't responsible for any of that," Rob assured him, but it seemed as though he was speaking to a shadow, because Mace only stared off into the distance, his attention fixed on something Rob couldn't see. "I need you to hear me. You've got to know that—"

"My mother turned me back over to CPS," Mace whispered. He ran his hands through his hair. It was too short to tangle but long enough to stick up, and Rob resisted the urge to stroke the bristly locks back down because he wanted to give Mace some kind of order in his life, no matter how small. "When they finally found me, she couldn't stand to look at me. She saw the scar on my shoulder and told me she couldn't take me home. He'd had his friends hold me down, and they carved that into me that night because I'd become one of them. I didn't understand what it meant, but I found out soon enough once they found me.

"She fell in love and married a guy while I was gone. Had a couple of kids, and then all of a sudden, I show back up with this thing on my back and my soul twisted up. I was all ready to go home. I didn't even care that there were other kids or that I had to share her. I just wanted to go to someplace he wasn't." Mace closed his eyes and turned his face away from Rob. "I only saw her long enough for her to tell me I wasn't going with her. And that night I had the crazy idea that if I could somehow get that mark off of me, she would take me home. So I tried to dig it out with a fork I got from the cafeteria. That's why it looks the way it does, because... I just wanted to go home."

It was the final bit of truth that broke Mace. One moment he was as pale and stiff as a piece of marble, a beautiful statue carved by a master hand, a thing of beauty with hairline cracks barely noticeable to the naked eye, and then a moment later, he was flesh and bone, curled up into a ball and weeping uncontrollably.

Rob wept with him.

He grieved with Mace and sobbed for a little boy who'd had his entire life stolen from him and then was left to pick up its shattered pieces. In the moments between crying jags, Rob sent rusty prayers to a God he'd turned his back on years before and gave thanks to fate for bringing Mace to Bear's family.

"I can't ever get clean," Mace confessed through a barrage of hiccups. "And there's things that I do that I can't stop, like needing the stereo or TV on or having a nightlight in the bathroom. It took me five years to stop stashing food in my stuff, and I fucking hate the taste of those goddamned crackers, but I still buy them because... you just don't know... it's like a safety net. I'm never going to eat them, but I know they're there, so I have something to fall back on. And they get bugs. After a fucking year, they get these little bugs, and I have to throw them away, and I keep promising myself I'll never buy them again, but I fucking *do*.

"I'm too fucked-up to have somebody in my life, and now that my dad is out, I'm scared shitless he's going to hurt somebody I love. I can't risk Bear and the others." Mace pulled Rob's hand toward him and cradled it against his hard abdomen. "You drive me crazy, and I've been wanting to see what you tasted like for… *shit*, since the day you first walked into the shop."

"If you want the truth, you kind of make me insane." Rob made a face, caught between comforting Mace and confessing something he hadn't even been willing to admit to himself. "I kind of… like you. Even when you're an asshole and bossy, you turn me on, and I think you're crazy if you believe no one will love you. Yeah, your dad fucked you up good, but your brothers… man, I wish they were my family, because I know they're going to be here for you. *I'm* going to be here for you. After what happened today—*everything* that happened today—there's no way in hell I'm going to walk away from you, not when you've shown me that you're the strongest and best person I've ever known."

ELEVEN

EVERYTHING WAS too raw, abraded past the skin of Mace's emotions and in the midst of Mace's breakdown. Rob felt himself swept away by the sorrow pouring out of the man sitting next to him. Rob held Mace until he couldn't cry anymore and then bundled him in a blanket and put him to bed. He left a white-noise machine on and cracked the bathroom door open so the nightlight would spill into the bedroom.

When he closed the front door, he promised himself he'd circle back, dig back into the pain festering in Mace, and do whatever it took to break through the mask Mace wore to keep the broken pieces of his heart safe from hurt.

FIVE DAYS later they still hadn't talked about what happened between them, and Rob was pretty sure Mace hadn't said jack shit to his brothers about Mace's father approaching him in the parking garage.

If Rob was being fair, Mace seemed to constantly be at the fire station, pulling extra shifts and covering for Rey as Gus's custody case came to an end. He'd had to reschedule a couple of clients around the celebration party the brothers would be holding in an hour, and his invitation to the festivities came with a subtle hint from Ivo that his help setting up would be greatly appreciated.

And by *subtle*, Ivo pretty much looked at him and said, "It's free beer and food. Show up at four and help me get the tables set up. I'll make sure you get the first hamburgers off the grill."

Hamburgers were the least of Rob's worries, but it was as good of an excuse as any to corner Mace that evening.

By the time Rob returned with a rolling steel chest he'd filled with ice at the burrito place a few doors down, the shop had gone from empty to packed with familiar faces that Rob had only seen in videos or on CD cases. It seemed like the brothers were hooked into a social circle that included rock stars, police officers, and the occasional performance artist, one of whom showed up with a bag full of long balloons and was currently twisting his way into making a googly-eyed walrus.

He found Mace in the crowd as soon as he came through the front door.

Even worn down around the edges and bone tired, Mace in old jeans and a thin T-shirt was enough to make Rob's mouth water.

"Jesus, why the fuck do you have to be so damned hot?" Rob grumbled as he dragged the ice chest across the reception floor. "Just you breathing messes up my brain."

It didn't help to know how Mace's stomach muscles rippled when Rob licked at his nipple or the delicious, slightly stinging pleasure of Mace's fingers when they tugged through his hair, pulled Rob's chin up, and exposed his throat to Mace's teeth, or how Mace's eyes seemed to darken and his jawline grew hard when he met Rob's eyes from across the shop's floor.

"You better wipe that expression off your face before one of the other owners sees it," Lilith whispered into his ear, "because right now you look like you're starving to death and he's the biggest piece of macadamia nut brittle cheesecake you've ever seen."

"*Shut up!*" Rob glanced around him, hoping no one overheard her. "I like this job. I like this shop, and the brothers not only know their shit, they share it, so I'd kind of like to not get fired. I've also got bills."

"Well, since I'm your landlord, we can take rent off the table. That'll cut things down." Lilith eyed Mace and murmured in appreciation. "He looks a hell of a lot better up close than he does washing down that fire truck. That *is* the one, right?"

"Once again, zip it, Lil," he muttered. "Help me get this—"

"Hey, let me grab that." Bear had cut through the crowd, and gave Rob a welcoming nod. "Why don't you guys grab some food and mingle? Thanks for helping out, and don't let Ivo con you into doing anything else. He shouldn't have drafted you to begin with, but I really appreciate it. Means a lot to me and the guys."

Bear grabbed the heavy steel ice chest by the handles and hefted it up as though it was empty and made of Styrofoam. The man was pure muscle, his 415 Ink T-shirt strained across the bulge of his biceps, and Lilith growled somewhere deep in her throat. Either Bear didn't hear her or he politely ignored her sensual moan.

"Down, girl," Rob muttered back at Lilith. "Besides, he's gay. And when did you start going for the 'one blue ox away from lumberjack'?"

"That bit of lovely is more stevedore than lumberjack." She hooked her arm into his as she teetered on her high heels and leaned against him for support as they began to work their way through the crowd. "And that's the best part about being omnisexual—I can have lots of types. As my Ma-Ma said, don't limit your choices."

"She said that about dim sum, not men." Rob snagged a Finnegan's special brew from one of the steel washtubs filled with ice, popped the cap off, and handed it to Lilith. "She also said that about sushi-boat restaurants. And taco shops. Actually, I think that was pretty much her standard opinion about anything with a limited menu. It's why you had to lie to her about where you got her burgers, remember?"

"It applies to men." She shrugged and rustled the curls of her dusky-rose wig. Then she tugged the hem of her short black bandage dress, and Rob watched as Lilith put on what he called her game face. "I'm going to see if I can talk to one of the Crossroads guys. Maybe I'll get lucky and—"

"Don't corner anybody." He rolled his eyes when she sighed dramatically. "I can't believe I'm the one who's the adult here. I asked if you wanted to come because I thought you might like talking to some of the other artists or to just grab some free food. So, new rules." Rob dropped his voice down to a whisper. "One, no hitting on any of the musicians, especially Miki St. John. I don't want to have to pull your face out from between his teeth. Two, don't hit on any of the brothers. Yes, a couple of them are bisexual, but I don't want to be coming out of my bedroom and see one of my bosses naked in the living room. Which leads me to three, no mentioning anything about me and Mace, because if I'm going to find one of my bosses naked in the living room, it's going to be because he's there for me. Can we agree on that?"

"Fine." Her eye roll was much more impressive, enhanced by her thick sweep of fake eyelashes and her bloodred lipstick pout. "Do you mind if I pet the dog?"

"So long as any tonguing is only one-sided and on *his* end." Rob chuckled and dodged Lilith's punch. "Just go have fun and try not to get either one of us in trouble."

It was risky letting Lilith run free through the crowd, but Rob spotted Mace going out of the back door with a pair of tongs in his hands.

The shop was packed with people, but no one interested him as much as the firefighter who'd gotten under his skin. He gave Gus a quick smile when Gus's little boy ran into his leg. Then he turned Chris around gently to aim him back toward his father.

"Behind you," Luke said as he pressed his fingers into the small of Rob's back. The crowd shifted and jostled Rob into Luke's hand. "Here, step back. We'll make you some room."

"I was just—" Rob's brain short-circuited when he turned around and found himself staring up into the long-lashed hazel eyes and beautiful mouth of a musician who'd pretty much provided the soundtrack for Rob's coming out. "Shit. Um, hi."

He'd seen Miki before, mostly side-eye glances Rob caught in between his appointments when the singer came to visit Ichiro Tokugawa or accompanied someone else to the shop for work. He'd fallen into some of the teasing conversations, but never anything truly one-on-one. To suddenly find himself face-to-face with the singer almost made him forget he'd been trying to get to Mace.

"Hey. You're Rob, right?" The honeyed-whiskey voice Rob would recognize anywhere sounded amazing up close and live. "You were working in the spot next to Gus the last time we were here. I think you were doing a New School piece."

"Yeah, it was... the Monty Python rabbit." His feverish brain slapped up the image of the tattoo he'd been working on at the time. "Um... I was just heading to the back to help... Mace with a couple of things."

"Probably a good idea," Luke said with a chuckle. "Mace likes a layer of charcoal on anything he grills. I think he just spends too much time walking through smoke, so something doesn't taste right unless it's slightly burned. You driving? Damien brought a bottle of fireball whiskey, and I'm going around giving people shots so we can get rid of it. Want one?"

"Lilith and I took a taxi over because I figured neither one of us wanted to fight through traffic when this was over. And that way if one of us gets a little bit tipsy, we don't have to worry about a car." Rob grimaced. A dose of liquid courage seemed like a good idea, especially since Miki St. John had rattled him and he still had to go poke Bear's little brother with a very sharp stick. "A small one, though."

"That's easy," Luke replied, his dark eyes sparkling as he poured out a glug of whiskey into a plastic shot glass. "These don't hold a lot, but it saves washing glasses."

The liquid burned going down, and the sensation of red-hot cinnamon candies lingered on Rob's tongue. It warmed up his skin, much like Mace's hands did during sex, and it was tempting to take another, but if he didn't move fast, Mace would be back inside and he would lose his chance to talk to him.

"God, that's...." Rob gasped. "That's... *strong*."

"Yeah, none of the Morgans will touch that kind of shit... or at least admit they drink it," Miki purred in his feral-cat drawl. "It offends their Irish sensibilities. I think Damie buys it just to piss them off a little bit. I love him, but he's an asshole."

"You should go find Mace. You know, because he needs help." Luke spun a bit of humor in his voice, and Rob wondered what exactly he knew. Of the five brothers, Luke was the most opaque. His visits to the shop were few and far between, normally nearer to closing time when his arrival wouldn't disrupt the work. He said something in Spanish under his breath, and Miki laughed. It caught Rob off guard, but the sly smile Luke gave him did little to reassure Rob that the teasing was innocent. "We'll be around if you come back. Probably going to be a long time before we can get this bottle empty. Miki's not helping at all."

"Shit no." The singer grimaced. "I puked that stuff up once. Not going near it. Oh, and tell Mace hey for me."

Rob's mouth was still burning when he brushed past Ivo and caught a snippet of conversation the leggy inker was having with a short curly-haired redhead with a thick Irish accent and wearing stilettos that resembled Ivo's favorite pair of heels. Ivo's attention snagged on Rob momentarily, and he narrowed his eyes, but he didn't break from the conversation. Slowing his weave through the crowd, Rob tried to make his path look random, and when Ivo's back was to him, he made a break for the back door.

As soon as he was past the heavy steel door, Rob kicked out the doorstop and let it close behind him.

All of the brothers were attractive in their own way. Bear had cornered the market on "slightly scruffy muscular with a heart of gold," while Luke was an odd blend of quirky, deadly serious, and simmering hot. Gus and Ivo shared many of the same characteristics—they were brash and reckless pretty men with an air of vulnerability that Ivo spiced up with a healthy dose of sarcasm and teasing. Still, it was Mace's avenging-angel face and tight body that made Rob's heart pound in his chest and sent a fire through his veins.

It was just a pity Mace spent his childhood being raised by someone intent on sawing his wings off and hearing about how he'd never fly. Rob was going to have a fight on his hands, battling against ghosts and a steady drip of poisonous thoughts, if he hoped to get Mace to see he was worth all the love given to him.

Reality sometimes hit hard—a powerful sucker punch straight to the balls—and Rob felt its sting as his heart whispered sweet murmurs about waking up on Sunday mornings with Mace next to him. Then his wicked brain chimed in with how nice it would be if only Rob could sink his teeth into Mace's tight ass, even if he had to tear his way through the old jeans Mace wore low on his hips.

"Jesus, I'm falling in love with this asshole," he whispered to himself. "Well, *fuck me*."

The back door finally shut and clanged loudly when the lock's heavy strike plate hit the frame, but Mace didn't look up. Instead he fiddled with something on the barbecue Randy brought over and said, "These are going to be about ten minutes more, Bear. The flame was turned off, so I need to let it heat up again. You might want to put the cheese—"

"Bear's inside talking to a couple of cops, so the cheese is probably going to have to wait anyway," Rob stammered out when Mace twisted around to stare at him. "And I think I kind of locked the door behind me. I didn't throw the latch to hold it open."

Rob got a suspicious look from Mace, but then it changed and went smoky and hot. The shot of cinnamon whiskey in his belly was a block of ice compared to the smoldering perusal Mace gave him.

"You shouldn't have followed me out here," Mace whispered over the crackle of fire and the murmur of street noise from the pier. "You should go back inside before I—"

"I'm pretty sure I can handle anything you can dish out," Rob cut in. He was tired of chasing after Mace, weary of dodging the sexual tension between them, and most of all, sick of seeing the hints of doubt peek out from behind Mace's hard mask of a face. "In fact, maybe you should get it all out of your system, and then we can talk about how much you get under my fucking skin."

THE ALLEY behind the tattoo shop was dark, a shadowy sliver of space blocked off by their cars and the cooling grill that Randy had brought over from his house, so the chances of them being discovered with their pants down around their ankles was slim, but there still was a chance... especially since his entire too-damned-nosy family was only a door away.

"Jesus.... God, what you can do with your fingers," Rob gasped. "Fuck... me."

"Not only do I not have time, but if Bear finds us, we're dead." Mace reluctantly let Rob go, light-headed after losing himself in Rob's kisses. He wanted more, but Rob deserved better. "We've got to stop doing this. It's... nuts. I don't even like you."

"Yeah, you're no fucking treat either," he grumbled back. Rob tried to straighten his hair, but the shock wave of blue-tipped ebony strands wasn't willing to be subdued. "I was crazy for doing this once, much less—"

"Don't count. I don't want to know." Mace tried not to think about the incredible sex they'd shared on the shop's floor that day—that *one* day—and Mace hadn't been able to get Rob off his mind ever since. It'd been a mad scramble of sweat and stinging skin, fueled by the excitement of knowing someone would be by to catch them if they tarried and having to be inventive because they only had a couple of condoms between them. He needed Rob to move on. Life would be better, he told himself, once Rob walked away from him. "That's it. Tonight's... we're done. No more."

Mace couldn't afford to have Rob attached to him. He didn't trust himself, not knowing where he'd come from—the cruelty his father raised him in and the emptiness his mother left when she turned her back on him. He had his own rage to worry about and his concern that he would lash out and hurt like his father had done in the past. It would start small, with a bit of anger at something done wrong, and the next thing he knew, his hands would be painted with hot blood and he'd be standing over Rob's broken body. It was too much of a risk. He had too much to lose—his family, his job, and his sanity.

Walking away now was the best thing for both of them. He knew that, so why did it hurt so much when Rob's gaze dropped away and his raspy voice finally whispered, "Yeah, you're right. This is nothing but a quick fuck we like because we shouldn't be doing it. So yeah, from right now, you and I are done.

"And if you believe that, you haven't been fucking listening," Rob growled. "Let go of me. Just for now, so we can get our heads on straight and get our shit together. We need to work out what we're doing, because I know that was a bunch of lies we just told each other. I'm not walking away from you any more than you're walking away from me."

TWELVE

FRANKIE'S DINER was a throwback slop house tucked away in a corner of the city where only locals roamed. It was built in the early days of mass transportation, nestled up against what had once been an old bus yard and a set of train tracks that now went nowhere. It was within walking distance of the trolley station and a city parking lot where transit drivers and city employees left their cars for the day and rode BART into work. The original Frankie was a steel-jawed woman rumored to be the granddaughter of an aging New York prostitute who'd come out to try her luck in the last days of California's Gold Rush. A photograph of Frankie and her grandmother standing in front of the diner held a place of prominence behind the cash register—a black-and-white snapshot of hard living and gritty determination.

A couple of generations later, another Frankie worked the kitchen—a sharp-tongued, brassy-haired woman with a jawline much like her grandmother's and armed with the attitude of a badger with a sore tooth.

There were too many years on the diner's red vinyl booths and seats for its retro feel to be anything but authentic. Set in a lower quadrant of a brick building, the diner's exterior was deceptive and hid much of its roomy interior. Its outer walls were lined with banquettes, and its kitchen was hidden behind a pass-through window set into a wall behind its L-shaped lunch counter.

Delivering the last of the burgers to the shop's buffet table, Mace pulled Rey aside and told him to cover for him. He didn't wait for Rob to shoot a few quick words to Lilith while he slipped out the back door to wait. A few seconds later, Rob stumbled out to tell Mace Lilith hadn't even blinked an eye when Rob told her he was leaving.

"She's got musicians to talk to. Pretty ones," he chuckled. "I'm the last thing on her mind right now."

They'd arrived in the middle of the dinner rush and waded through a small cluster of people to get to the counter. The clang of utensils scraping across thick, heavy white plates battled for dominance against the stream of chatter that poured out from the full dining room. The air was thick with the smell of burgers and gravy and punctuated by the crackle of fries hitting hot oil. The servers did a fierce dance around their tables, refilling coffee cups, dropping off checks, and then stopping at the next gathering of diners to see if they needed anything else.

The diner was loud, fragrant with common, hearty food, and ripe with the promise of leftovers and possibly heartburn.

It was also one of Mace's favorite places to eat.

A slender Chinese man whose name Mace never caught was working the cash register. He chirruped a sweet hello when they walked through the door, and there was a quick spit of shouting until a corner table set aside for the staff was hastily cleared for them to sit at.

Mace thanked the teenage girl who led them to the table, slapped a couple of menus down, and promised their waitress would be by in a few minutes. Rob slid into the seat next to him, both of them angled toward the door because the table's location meant only two people could sit there at one time or it would block the flow of servers to and from the kitchen.

"When you said you knew the perfect place we could talk, I figured you meant your apartment, where it's kind of quiet," Rob muttered as he shrugged off his jacket.

Mace didn't hold back his short laugh. "Do you really think we can trust each other if we're alone and there's a bed nearby?"

"No, probably not." He hung the garment off the back of his chair and glanced around the dining room. "How the hell do you stay in shape if you eat here all the time? I'm getting fatter just breathing in the air."

"I do a lot of running," Mace reminded him. "Also, our equipment is pretty heavy. You try lugging fifty pounds of gear up and down flights of stairs and see how much a salad satisfies you. And you're not fat. Why do you—"

Rob lifted up his T-shirt, pinched at his side, and rolled a bit of his flesh out for Mace to see. "Look. You see this? I inherited my mom's metabolism… and kind of her face. I was a chunky kid. It took a lot to get rid of it. Okay, mostly quitting college, my dad kicking me out and not supporting me anymore, then a steady diet of veggies and ramen noodles. Combine that with not having a car and using a bike to get to work for two years? Took off enough, and I don't want to gain it back."

"If you inherited your mom's face, she must be stunning," Mace replied. "And if you gained it back, you'd still be gorgeous. Anybody who tells you otherwise should fuck off. Sit down, have a salad or a burger, whatever you like. Just...."

Rob's poured-whiskey-over-ice gaze flicked up and snared Mace into a trap he hadn't seen coming. There was a lot about the irreverent tattoo artist Mace hadn't planned on knowing. In the back of his mind, he knew people were flawed. Just Gus alone was proof in that pudding. But Rob... he hadn't imagined the folds of self-doubt hidden beneath his brash confidence.

Maybe they weren't so different after all.

"I'm going to guess they don't have a grilled-chicken-and-salad plate." Rob leaned back in his chair and studied the menu. "Or do I live dangerously and have a double bacon cheeseburger with a side of poutine in the hope we'll work it off later?"

"Well, since I have my car, I wasn't planning on taking a run up the hills, but if that's what you want to do, I'm willing."

"As attractive as that sounds, I haven't bought my cemetery plot yet, so I'll have to pass." That time the glance Mace got was accompanied by a nibble on Rob's lower lip. "Besides, I think we should talk about you first."

Their waitress was an old hand at taking orders, delivering drinks, and leaving her customers with the impression that they'd only see her again if it was time for them to cash out or die of a heart attack brought on by the triple-layer cheesecake that was seducing Mace from its place in the refrigerator case a few feet away. Her nonchalant attitude was a lie, because the ironically named Marge worked the floor like a master, and there were quite a few times when Mace reached for his half-empty glass of iced tea, only to find it filled to the brim and a fresh slice of lemon floating among the crushed ice.

He did smile when Rob opted for the cheeseburger, slightly egged on by Marge and her promise that the gravy was calorie-free and his salted-caramel-and-coffee malt didn't count, because it was a special of the day.

"Are you working or are you off?" The pink-haired older woman poked at Mace's shoulder with her pencil. "Because if you're working, I don't know what kind of fish we have in the back. But if you're off, I'll have the cook drop some of that buttermilk-and-bacon-battered chicken into the fryer for you."

"Was that on the menu?" Rob shuffled through the pages. "Because I didn't see that on the menu."

"It's something Frankie made up for him." She winked at Rob. "He saved her dog's life."

"So now she's trying to kill me by giving me clogged arteries. Chicken's fine, but mashed potatoes instead of fries." Mace handed her his menu. "And a side of greens."

"Smothered?" Marge tucked both menus under her arm. "I'll put an extra piece of chicken on your plate for your guy here."

"Smothered's great." Mace smiled up at her. "And an—"

"Iced tea. And for you, I'll bring you a glass too, because the malt's kind of thick. I'll give you boys a little time to talk. Kitchen's a bit in the weeds, so it's going to be a while. I'll send one of the boys around with a mess of jalapeno onions to tide you over. Unless this one doesn't do hot."

"I came in with him," Rob shot back to Marge's delight. "I think I can handle any heat you throw at me."

"You better keep this one," she said as she tucked her pencil behind her ear. "Might just be the kick in the pants you need to get your life in order. If you need anything, scream for one of the boys."

Rob watched her leave and then gave Mace a blinding grin. "I like her. She gives you shit."

"A lot of people give me shit. I have four brothers, remember?" Mace pointed out. "You don't leave that house unless you get a cupful of shit with your breakfast every morning. Two if you have to eat it with Ivo."

They sat in silence as their drinks were dropped off, and then a moment later, a basket of onion petals and deep-fried jalapeno slices was placed on the table with a tub of sriracha-ranch dressing. Mace picked at the steaming clump to find a thick pepper, popped it into his mouth, and savored the crunchy heat. His eyes watered, and when he blinked them clear, he found Rob studying him.

"Are we just going to sit here and pretend like… we didn't just fuck behind the shop?" Rob kept his voice low and glanced behind him when the kitchen door swung open and a tide of servers poured out, their trays piled high with dishes of steaming food. He pulled out a chunk of onion, dipped it into the dressing, and bit into it. Murmuring a happy noise, Rob waved the bitten onion back and forth. "Never mind. I'm just going to act like we're on a date and eat all of this. Fuck the pressure to look hot in skinny jeans. I'm going to eat this and then harass you into talking to your brothers."

DINNER WAS an odd affair with an undercurrent of frustration, sexual tension, and oddly enough, laughter. The emotions Mace locked down early that evening crept out from the boxes he'd put them in. Rob did most of the talking, but it was nice to sit back in his chair, pick off the skin of his fried chicken, and listen to stories about crazy clients and bad tattoos. He heard enough of those things from his brothers, but it was different from Rob, a perspective not tied to the family business. After half an hour, Rob felt comfortable enough to share how he saw Bear, Gus, and Ivo, as well as the shop he owned but wasn't really a part of.

"Every place kind of has its own feel," Rob said between slurps of his malt. "The shop I worked in before I came to 415 Ink was a shit hole. I mean, the work was good, and it was steady, but a lot of my time was spent trying to *keep* appointments, because the owner was okay with other artists sniping your clients. So I get a call telling me my one o'clock canceled, and I go in later thinking I don't have to cover the shift, and when I get there, somebody else is working on the guy I'd booked."

"Bear would tear apart somebody's ass if they did that." Mace shook his head. "I don't even work there, and I know that. I gotta give you credit for working with Gus and Ivo, because they're pains in the ass."

"I was kind of intimidated by Ivo when I first started, because he's got a rep for not taking any bullshit, but he's a really good artist, and he's serious about work. That's hard to find sometimes." Rob pushed his plate away and picked up his water to take a sip. "I didn't know what to think about Gus because—and don't take this wrong—but I've wanted him to give me a sleeve for a really long time. The shit he does with shadows and light is incredible, and it's weird because he's a little bit more aloof than Ivo, but when he's with you guys, he's kind of a goof.

"And Bear is just...." Rob let out a soft whistle. "The man's just a fucking legend with Neo-Traditional. I've learned more about black ink and skin types from him in the time I've been there than I have my entire career of doing tattoos. It's like God said, 'Let there be this one family who knows everything about tattooing and put them someplace Rob Claussen can learn from them and be humbled by them.' Because every single one of them can kick my ass nine ways to Sunday, and I will come back every single time to find out why."

The passion in Rob's face was breathtaking. It was cliché and cheesy to say, but as he began to talk about his craft, he literally glowed. The play of the diner's bright lights over his skin gilded the sweep of his cheekbones and played with the cognac streaks in his eyes. His hands were animated, a murmuration of delicate gestures combined with staccato stabs of his fingers in the air to make his point.

Rob had just begun to wax poetic about the joys of derma film instead of old-school meatpacking strips and gauze tape when he stopped midsentence and snorted.

"What? It's interesting to hear this, because I sat through the same conversation a couple of years ago with the three idiots back at the house, and by the end of it, they were all arguing *for it* but *with* each other, for some reason." Mace organized his utensils next to his plate and moved his elbow out of the way as a server collected everything to box up their leftovers. He murmured his thanks and then turned his attention back to Rob. "Really, I used to spend a lot of time buying supplies for the shop when it first started, so I can tell you all about the pros and cons of the film. For one, it might be more expensive, but in the long run it's a hell of a lot cheaper. Do you have any idea how much those pads cost?"

"I was supposed to spend this time trying to get you to talk to your brothers about your dad, remember?" Rob set his water glass down, and Mace saw the tease of a smile that touched the edges of his lips. "I always thought you were an asshole because you ragged on Ivo and the others. But now I think it's because you're backing Bear up."

"Most of the time, yeah." He shrugged as he remembered the days of runny oatmeal and dragging teenage boys out of bed so they wouldn't miss the bus to school. "He and I kind of divided up the adult shit between us. I was going to school and doing training while he was working through his apprenticeship and tattooing at night. The house was crappy, but the roof didn't leak once we figured out how to fix it, and over the years, we just sorta tackled projects on the weekends… with a *lot* of fighting."

"Ivo looks like he would fight dirty." Laughing, Rob shook his head. "They give me shit about calling Bear by his nickname."

"It's important to them. But that's Ivo's thing. His story to tell." Thanking the server for the packaged-up leftovers, Mace handed her the check folder and the cash he'd tucked into it. "I've got to stop at my place to pick up a tricycle that Rey got for Chris. I'll be heading over to Ashbury afterward, but do you want me to drop you off at home or back at the shop?"

"Are you going to talk to your brothers? About your dad and the crap he pulled?" The skepticism in Rob's voice was as thick as the malt he'd sucked down.

"Probably not tonight, because it's kind of shitty to follow a party up with that, but I promise I'll sit down and have a talk with them. It just... Jesus, I really don't want to. There's a lot of shit smeared on me, and it's going to be hard to let them see it." The idea of facing his brothers turned the greasy food he'd eaten into a sour mess in his stomach, but Mace knew Rob was right. He had to tell them what had happened when he was a kid and hope for the best. Luke's reaction worried him, but it would kill him if Ivo looked at him with disappointment in his eyes. "Come on. I'll stop at the garage first to grab the tricycle out of my storage and then take you home. You live in Chinatown, right? What street are you on?"

"Funny you should bring that up." Rob's chair screeched when he backed it up across the linoleum floor. "I seem to live right across of this fire station where a bunch of guys come out every once in a while and wash their truck."

"I CAN'T believe you sit in your living room and watch me wash the truck," Mace repeated for what was probably the fifth time since they'd left the diner. "That's—"

"Don't take this wrong, but you're not the only guy out there in a wet T-shirt and shorts. And Lilith swings all ways, so it's kind of like a buffet for her," Rob corrected him. "But I'm not going to lie and say I don't like how you have to squat on the roof to scrub it. And it's nice when you guys have a water fight and your shirt gets soaked through so you take it off and wring it out. I had to talk Lilith out of recording it so we could watch it at night over and over as we ate ice cream. You should thank me for that."

Mace glanced at Rob in the passenger seat and narrowed his eyes. "So I should thank you for not turning me into soft porn that you fantasize over while you eat mint chocolate chip ice cream?"

"Mint chocolate chip? Please. Rocky road with caramel Magic Shell. Only plebeians eat mint chocolate chip. It's either rocky road or rum raisin. Double *R*s all the way."

"I happen to like mint chocolate chip," Mace grumbled back as he eased the SUV into the parking level of his building.

"I will have to teach you the error of your ways and bring you over to the rum-raisin side of the Force. Not strong enough for rocky road yet but soon...." Rob *tsk*ed. "You will be, just not tonight. Tonight you're going to be a good little fireman, grab your nephew's toy, drop me off at home, and then head out to the family estate, where you will masterfully assemble said toy for a three-year-old who would probably rather play with the box."

"So, I see you've met Chris. You're not far from wrong. The kid does like a good box."

Even though it wasn't quite midnight, Mace was fairly certain most of the tenants in the building were already asleep. His headlights flashed across the small dumpster the residents used for their trash, and as he pulled into his parking space, the fluorescents next to the stairs flickered erratically. Barred half-moon openings ran around the perimeter of the level and pulled in some illumination from the streetlamps, but for the most part, the level was lit by pale yellow bulbs, barely strong enough to turn the shadows milky. Only a few of the other residents had cars. Most lived a walking existence, which was easy to do in Chinatown.

"It's kind of spooky down here." Rob peered out at the deserted level. "And just so you know, I'm really resisting the urge to ask you to take me upstairs. Not because I don't think I'll have a good time, but because I think you and I need something more than just a good time."

Mace turned off the SUV's engine and shifted in his seat to face Rob. There were so many things he wanted to say—*needed* to say—and the words came to him too quickly to sort out. Swallowing the garbled sounds he knew lingered in his throat, Mace nodded. "You're easy to talk to. And that's not something I've ever really looked for. You make me hot, and there are times when I just want to pull you down to the floor and make you scream my name.

"And then—especially now—I just want to see what it's like to sit on the couch with you and watch a movie or read a book." Mace raked his hand through his short hair. "I like how you're noisy even when you're not saying anything, because I kind of need that. You also don't...

you're not scared of me. You give me my shit right back, and that's something, in my books. So yeah, I think you and I deserve something more than just a good time."

"Okay." Rob flashed him a quick, rueful grin. "Let's go get the tricycle box into the SUV so you can take me home, and I'll fall asleep on the couch with ice cream on my face instead of partying with rock stars."

"Well, if it makes you feel any better, at least you know Lilith won't be bringing one home with her tonight," he pointed out with a laugh. "Actually, your help would be great. Rey just tosses the stuff in there sometimes, and I usually have to dig things out."

The ground was a little wet under their sneakers, and the weak light made opening the lock on his storage unit a little difficult. He'd just gotten the latch popped open when Rob made a startled sound, jerking Mace's attention up. A shuffling noise echoed through the parking level, the *click-click-click* of something being dragged slowly down the open staircase.

Moments after Rob seemed to catch his breath, a long shadow lumbered from side to side, thrown against the retaining wall at different angles from the various light sources in the garage. A form emerged from the faded brown darkness, armored with a helmet of tightly wound pink curlers and clothed in a floral housecoat bright enough to burn Mace's retinas. A pair of yellow plastic slippers embellished with rainbow-hued vinyl flowers caught the light at the bottom of the stairs, and a single red dot flared up, glowed bright, then faded back down as a stream of smoke ghosted over the person's face.

"Mrs. Hwang, I thought you quit smoking. The doctor told you to stop." Mace let the lock drop, and its heavy weight slapped the storage door. "And what are you doing taking out the trash this late? I would have gotten it for you in the morning."

"Hush. Just don't tell the doctor." Mrs. Hwang peered out from her thick glasses and strained to see past Mace's shoulder. Switching to Cantonese, she asked, "Who's that? Is that a boyfriend? Did you bring home a boyfriend? I know the other one isn't your boyfriend, because he's seeing your blond brother, the one with the motorcycle. So who's this?"

Rob chortled under his breath, and Mace was trapped between answering the old Chinese woman dragging a pair of trash bags down the stairs or pretending he didn't understand her and hoping Rob didn't know Cantonese. The smug look on Rob's face did nothing to reassure Mace.

"I know the sound of a woman digging for gossip no matter what language she speaks." Rob's smirk grew until dimples appeared in his cheeks. He took a few strides over to Mrs. Hwang and held his hand up to her. "Hi, I'm Rob, Mace's friend. Let me help you with the trash."

"Let me get rid of the cigarette," Mace replied in Cantonese. The old woman had her chin up, but she let Rob take the bags from her. Mace wasn't fooled. Mrs. Hwang was gearing up for a fight, and he was going to have to go a few rounds with her before she surrendered her contraband... providing he won the argument. "You can't smoke. It's not good for—"

The sound of Mrs. Hwang coming down the stairs was as familiar to Mace as the clang of the station's bell for an alarm, but the heavy tread of boots coming up the slight incline of the driveway into the parking structure was unfamiliar, especially close to midnight. It was rare for any of the residents to use the driveway to enter the building, especially since the elevator was closer to the front door. A car pulled in behind the large man walking toward them and threw him into a silhouette.

"Rob, drop the bags and get Mrs. Hwang upstairs," Mace ordered firmly. He didn't need to see the man's face. He knew exactly who was walking across the painted concrete. He'd felt those fists clenched at the man's side, and his ribs ached on cold wintry nights where the man's boots had stomped on his torso. "Move *now*. Don't ask—"

"Now is that any way for a son to greet his daddy?" His father lengthened his stride, and the car came to a stop, angled across the narrow driveway, and blocked them in. Mace glanced quickly back as another man got out of the vehicle, but he twisted around when he heard Mrs. Hwang shakily ask him to explain what was going on in a string of stuttering Cantonese.

"Mrs. Hwang, you and Rob go back to your place." He tried to keep his voice steady, but a thread of strident begging wove through his words. "I'll be up in a bit."

"You just park your ass right there... Rob, is it? Tell you what, you keep the China lady from doing anything stupid and I won't blow your brains out." His father pulled a wicked-looking gun from his waistband and let his jacket drop back into place. He held it loosely at his side, but there was no doubt in Mace's mind that Rob and Mrs. Hwang would be shot the moment they turned toward the stairs. Moving into the light, his father's face peeled out of the shadows and revealed a network of bruises that ran down his cheek and over his jaw. "Boy, you and I need to have little talk."

"Leave them alone." Mace slid over and placed himself in front of the others. The gun was up now, raised as soon as Mace closed the distance between them. His father was a couple of yards away, but Mace could still smell the reek of cheap gin and stale cigarettes that rolled off of his father's clothes and skin. "You and your friend need to go. I don't want any trouble with you. And you don't want any trouble from me. Just walk away and your parole officer won't ever know you were here."

"See, that's the problem, Johnny. I was in jail. Do you know what they do to a man in jail? They make it impossible for him to earn any money, so when he gets out he's got to go begging like a dog, because the kind of job he could get hired for, a damned immigrant came across the border and took it from him." His father's hand shook slightly, but the muzzle of the gun was tilted up, aimed at Mace's chest. "And since you couldn't see to doing right by your old man the first time, I thought I would bring Bruce by, and we could teach you some manners until you changed your mind. So, what's it going to be? You going to see the light and cough up some cash for your daddy, or do I have to remind you how little a shit I give about people who aren't good enough to wipe my ass?"

THIRTEEN

THERE WAS nothing more ironic than standing in the shadows in front of a tattoo artist you were falling for and an elderly woman who taught you Chinese and facing down the man who'd forged your fear of darkness. It was also the moment when Mace realized the only thing more bitter than irony was regret. If they walked out of this, he was going to spend the rest of his life making sure he told everyone he cared for how much they meant to him, and he hoped he wouldn't die trying to prove it.

Because his father's face held no affection, no concern over Mace's well-being. He would as easily pull the trigger as he would kick a dog walking past. And Mace had seen his father kick many a dog.

"I don't have a lot of cash on me." Mace held his hand out slowly. "I can give you my wallet and my cards. Then you can walk away."

"Found out a few things about you, Johnny." His father hocked spit from the back of his throat, then spat it at Mace's feet. "Did some asking around and found out you turned queer on me. Bad enough you keep company with animals like them, you have to fuck one of them too?"

"I don't owe you anything—not an explanation, not an apology for how I live." Mace kept his voice as steady as he could, but the tremors were already beginning to roil up his spine. "All I've got is my wallet. Take it with you, and I promise, there's not going to be any trouble."

"Soon as we get into the car, he's going to call the cops. The wallet's not enough." The silhouette of the man standing behind Mace's father shifted unsteadily and moved his weight from foot to foot. "Betcha the old lady has cash up in her place. Her kind doesn't like banks, remember? Why don't we just take them upstairs—"

There was no way in hell Mace was going to allow his father and Bruce to get them into Mrs. Hwang's apartment. As soon as they were inside, Mace would be sealing them into their own death chamber, and no one would ever know who'd killed them. He'd also be damned if the men believed he would let them lead him to the slaughter so he could die behind a closed door.

He'd done enough dying behind closed doors.

"Tiger, don't." Mrs. Hwang grabbed his arm and tugged at his sleeve. He didn't dare look at her. Her broken, scared warble roughened the edges of her Cantonese, so he almost lost the rest of what she said, but his brain latched on to the ends of words he knew and pulled everything into place. "Let them take everything they want. I have no money upstairs."

"You're not giving them anything, Grandmother," he answered back in her own tongue. "Stay with Rob. Let me take care of this."

"Jesus, you even talk like one of them," his father sneered, his lip lifting in disgust. Again the gun wavered, dropped down a few inches, and then rose up again. The barrel was a deep black hole Mace was trying not to fall into, but with every sweep of his father's arm, it got more and more difficult. "Did nothing I taught you stick? Am I trying to put a lipstick on a pig here?"

"Why the fuck are we standing here talking about it?" Bruce lumbered out of the shadows. He was a big man with a sparse shock-white crew cut and a round, jowly face flecked with red splotches. His bulbous eyes gave his features an almost innocent, guileless impression, but his thin mouth twisted at the edges and added a layer of mean to his expression. He hovered a few feet away and glanced nervously over his shoulder. "Just fucking do what you've got to do, Danny John. We've got to… you know what? Fuck this shit."

A boom hit them hard, as did the flash of light from the gun Bruce fired. There was screaming, a high-pitched wail, and the nerves in Mace's shoulder caught on fire. He stumbled back, stunned by the hard shove of a bullet. Pain yanked at his guts, but fear kept him on his feet.

The impact punched him halfway around, and he held up his hand to stop Rob from coming to his aid. He needed them to run upstairs, wanted them to pull up the world behind them so he could fight off his demons in the dark they'd been birthed from. Mrs. Hwang struggled and fought Rob's grasp, trying to reach him. Her rollers were coming loose out of her dark hair. One fell to the ground, a splash of fuchsia plastic bristles scrabbling as it rolled across the oil-stained floor.

"Get upstairs," Mace yelled at Rob. "Get her upstairs before—"

Then another burst and roar stole away the world's murmur and left Mace in a numb silence. There was a distant ringing, but the rest of it—all the street noise, Mrs. Hwang's frightened shouts, and his father's toxic slurs—was *gone*, muted beneath a chatter of gunfire.

His father plunged him back into the quiet, but the humming nothingness in Mace's ears was forgotten, drowned under the torrential gush of blood that poured out of Mrs. Hwang's chest.

"No, no, no," Mace gasped as he lurched across the cement to get to Mrs. Hwang's side. Rob cradled the slender, brittle body of the old woman against his chest. Something dark dripped on her face, and Rob's look of horror nearly dropped Mace to his knees.

Rob was telling him something, screaming at him, but Mace couldn't hear him, not clearly, not through the screaming buzz in his ears and the *pound-pound* of his blood in his temples. It hurt to bend over her, not just along his side and shoulder, but in his heart. She was the woman he came home to after a long, hard day and the grandmother who made him dumplings and then lied about making too much for church.

The man who held her was just as precious. Rob made him feel… alive. For the first time in his life, Mace felt as though he owned himself, felt pride in the little things he'd accomplished, and knew deep in his heart that Rob was right—his brothers would never turn away from him. Rob made him feel the love he'd been given. Even in the short time they'd been together, he'd opened up dreams that Mace had mortared behind thick brick walls.

He wasn't going to let his father take that away from him—not again, *never* again.

The world snapped back into place, and the first thing Mace heard was the whooshing sound of Mrs. Hwang struggling to breathe, her panic-stricken face growing paler and paler with each heave. The sensation of being dipped into lava ran over his torso, and each flicker of heat was punctuated with a flash of pain so intense it made his eyes cross. In the middle of the chaos, he clenched his fists, or at least his left, because the right didn't seem to be responding, and he flailed and tried to strike the gun out of his father's hand.

He caught a glimpse of Rob dragging Mrs. Hwang to the side, leaving a streak of blood on the concrete, a river thick enough for him to fall into, deep enough to drown in, and Mace found himself fighting to breathe.

His father was shouting at him—a low hum of garbled buzzing—and just beyond him, the other man, Bruce, fought to get past his dad's arm. Their words were floating in and out, but Mace didn't care. The agonizing pain in his shoulder grew until he felt he could reach behind his back and pull out the spear someone had shoved into him. Things were beginning to not make sense anymore. The lights in the parking lot were getting brighter, but the edges around his eyes were thickening with a black he couldn't pierce.

"I'm not going to let you take them from me," Mace growled. "You've taken enough. I'm not going to let you have Rob and... *my grandmother.*"

"Dan! The fucking cops are coming!" Bruce shouted as he headed toward the idling car parked across the driveway. "Just fucking shoot him already. Grab the bitch's jewelry, and let's get out of here."

Mace's right hand was slippery with blood, but he reached for the gun in his father's hand. They were close enough for him to smell the booze on his father's breath, and Bruce's shouting became frenetic, ear-shattering shrieks urging Mace's father to get into the car.

"Let go!" His father's eyes were wild, and as they struggled for control of the weapon, Mace's blood splattered over the man's face and dappled his uneven beard. The recoil was immediate, followed by a look of disgust so wretched it curdled his father's expression and turned him monstrous. "Fuck!"

The slap of his father's hands on his own face was as loud as the gunshots moments before. He let go of his shriek and then turned to face Mace, his anger vividly reddening his skin. The gun was forgotten, released as soon as the spray shot across his father's mouth, and the weapon was heavy in Mace's grip and dragged his right arm down. He wanted to fling it away, but his shoulder wouldn't respond, and the numbness had moved down from his collarbone into his chest and seized his lungs.

"You fucking faggot! You son of a bitch!" His father screamed and scrubbed at his face with the hem of his T-shirt. "You got your fucking blood on me."

As heavy as the gun was and as hard as his arm trembled, Mace lifted the weapon and pointed it at his father. It would be so easy to squeeze the trigger and end his nightmares. He could live with the image of his father's skull being shattered apart by a bullet. His father probably wouldn't even realize he'd been killed. The man was in full panic, raking his face raw with the rough fabric. His ignorance and hatred would die with him. The mutilated scarification Mace bore on his shoulder itched as though it needed to be lanced and for the poison left inside of him to be released once and for all.

It would just be so damned easy to pull on the small piece of metal that rested against his index finger and erase the person who ruined his life.

"Mace, I've called the cops." Rob's voice punched through the haze settling over Mace. "Don't do it."

The two seconds it took Mace to fully absorb what Rob was saying to him was enough time for his father to realize he'd been drawn down upon. A small shuffle of his feet took him a few inches back and lengthened the distance between him and Mace. The blood was still there, speckles across his forehead and cheek, but it was the gun that held his attention.

"Get out of here. And you need to thank Rob for saving your life, because I sure as hell don't want to." Mace coughed, and the fire began once again and crept through his muscles. "You ever come near me or mine again, nothing Rob says will save you. And I mean *nothing*. Because if a piece of shit like you can do time, I'll be glad to mark off every single day they give me because I took you off of this earth. Understand, I will have no regrets, because I know my family waits for me. Hell, I'll bet you they'll even fucking bake a cake while I'm in there."

The sirens drowned out anything his father might've said to him, but Mace didn't think he had a reply. The only thing he saw was his father's back as he pelted toward the car, and the only thing he heard was the squeal of the tires and the thump as it jumped the sidewalk to the street.

Mace stumbled around. His legs refused to move correctly, and his arm was useless at his side. He bent over and tried to lay the gun gently down on the floor, but his fingers jerked and spasmed. It dropped. Clattered. Metal on concrete. A short mariachi burst of castanets and then Mace's knees hit the ground.

He didn't feel the impact. Not on his knees or his hands when he pitched forward, arms flailing out but useless to brace his fall, but he never hit the floor. Instead the darkness he'd been fighting since the moment his father walked out of the shadows finally consumed him.

MACE KNEW who was holding his hand before he even opened his eyes. He'd grown up with the touch of those hands, felt their calluses grow and their knuckles thicken with each punch thrown to defend one of the brothers during the occasional bar fight. He was the reason for more than a few lost thumbnails, and his shitty aim with a hammer became practically a legend in the house, but Bear continued to trust him, continued to hold nails steady in tight spots until they could save for a much-needed nail gun. They were hands that fed him, comforted him, and washed the stink of other men from Mace's skin during the times when he'd been unable to find his own worth except through sex.

Now he held on to Mace as though Mace would slip away if he let go. His grip was tight, nearly painfully so, but Mace was glad for the pressure.

It meant he was still alive.

"Gonna lose my fingers." It hurt to talk, and when Mace swallowed, his throat was dry and raw. Despite his garbled croak, Bear must have understood him, because he eased up. Wanting to say thanks, Mace grumbled something but couldn't get out more than a cough.

"Hold on. I've got ice chips for you," Bear promised. There was the sound of rattling in plastic, and Mace tried to blink. "Suck on these slowly. Okay?"

The light hurt as much as his shoulder did—a throbbing dull ache that edged toward a full-blown pain. Another blink and the bursts of white in his vision faded and left behind polka dots when he closed his eyes. His lashes stuck together, and Bear murmured for him to hold on. Then Mace felt the dab of a damp cloth across his face. Blinking became easier, and then a cold sting touched his lips.

"Open. Hold it on your tongue and let me know when you need some more." Bear emerged out of the white-and-beige haze. The room snapped into place behind his worried face—a mishmash of blue curtains, an open window looking straight out into another building, and the small phalanx of machines chirping a soft medley as they kept time with Mace's vitals. "How're you feeling? You've been out of it the last couple of times you woke up."

The hospital room was cramped but private. Its walls were painted in tones of warmed-up bread and tepid tea, and an open wooden door on the far wall from the bed gave Mace a peek of a mint-green bathroom that he vaguely recalled Ivo coming out of at some point. Flashes of lucidity were interspersed with burning agony and disorientation, many of them filled with his family's worried voices and a compassionate sea of nurses dressed in a rainbow of scrubs.

He didn't remember Rob in any of it, and Mace ached at his absence. It wasn't that he didn't love his family, it was just that he'd found something elusive, something organic and natural with Rob, and he wanted to have that touchstone.

Even when he didn't know how to tell Bear he was falling in love with someone he never should have given a second glance.

"Hey, open up. Take another one." Bear offered up another ice chip, a thicker piece than the one he'd slipped onto Mace's tongue a few moments before. "You seem more awake this time. Been a couple of days. Your eyes are clear this time. Good."

His brother was worn out around the edges, burned to a crisp, and knitted together by sheer will. After so many years of watching Bear working himself down to the bone, Mace recognized the signs of burnout on his face, in the slump of his shoulders, and in how he kneaded at his own fingers, sometimes turning the gold ring he wore on his pinky. The dull matte band was all that remained from his parents.

The others had to be somewhere nearby, probably held back by rules and administrators, but Gus would be pacing the halls outside, unwilling to be cowed by nurses, while Rey hovered nearby. He believed Ivo and Luke would sit quietly in a waiting room or even work the shop, anything to keep their minds and hands busy. They were the ones who would push the family forward and trust Bear to lead the way while Gus wandered off and came home when they needed him. Thankfully Rey was now there to tug him onto the right path.

Just like Rob was there to light the way for him, if only Mace would be willing to take that step.

"You doing okay, little brother?" Bear prodded gently and scraped the chair's legs across the floor with a hitch. It brought him closer to the bed, close enough for Mace to smell the spicy orange soap Bear liked. "Here. Another one. Get enough water in you and they'll yank that IV they've got you hooked up to."

"Throat hurts." Mace struggled to swallow, and then the cold water eased down and soothed away the rough gravel feel. "Shoulder too."

"They had a tube down your throat when you came out of surgery. Standard stuff." Another ice chip and Mace stared up into the weariness ground into Bear's face. He looked as though he'd aged ten years, and flecks of silver sparkled among the dark hair at his temples. "You fought it, and the doc thought you weren't in danger of getting fluid in your lungs, so it came out. You were lucky with the bullet. Went all the way through and then...." Bear swallowed hard, and his deep ocean-blue eyes turned misty. "Went out the other side but didn't have enough to puncture your clothes. Kind of bullet that's supposed to shatter into pieces. Doc said it's a miracle it stayed intact, but fuck it, kid, I'll take it."

"Fuck knows, I took it." The joke was feeble, but it pulled a slight smile from Bear, and Mace tried to grin back, but his lips stung when his skin cracked. "Shit, that hurts. Talking hurts. Fuck, *breathing* hurts."

"Breathing's good. At least you're doing it," his brother reminded him. "Hold on. I've got lip balm here."

He couldn't move much, or at least his muscles were reluctant to respond, but eventually Mace got himself comfortable and got his arms stretched out. His shoulder once again felt like someone had stuck a hot poker through it, but his fingers weren't numb, and his throat eventually was hydrated enough for him to speak without feeling like he was coughing up a caltrop with every word.

Mace didn't know where to start or who to ask for, but the flicker of something sad in Bear's eyes forced him to finally ask, "Mrs. Hwang... Grandmother... is she?"

"She's still in the ICU. Hasn't woken up yet, but she's strong. Everyone's... hoping." Bear's shoulders bunched up, and his plaid flannel shirt strained to hold its seams together. "And before you stress out about it, your captain's been here a few times, and your brothers in blue are shaking down the city looking for that asshole father of yours."

"Okay... okay. Good." He exhaled, glad for the aches that worked through his muscles. Fatigue flirted with him, a coy nudge that urged him to fall into the bed's soft warmth, but he shook it off and focused on his brother's handsome face. "He... shot her. Fucker just.... Jesus, Rob. Bear—"

"Yeah, Rob. He's... worried as fuck. Threw up a couple of times while they were working on you, but thing is, from what I've seen, you guys were always butting heads. But here he is, pacing the hall like the rest of us." Bear slid to the edge of the metal chair and rested his meaty, inked arms on the bed. "So when you're up to it, you and I are going to have a small talk about Rob. No, don't look at me like that. Don't. Because if there's anything I want for you, it's for you to have someone in your life… in your heart."

FOURTEEN

"YOU'RE GOING to have to go in deeper with that black," Ivo judged over Rob's shoulder. "You're leaving enough space for the skin to breathe, but you're lacking depth. Pack it in and stipple out into a tight blend on those curves."

If there was one thing Rob hated, it was someone throwing out directions while he worked. He loathed it nearly as much as he hated Ivo being right all the damned time. Because damned if the bastard wasn't right. There wasn't enough depth to the piece, and if he didn't correct the tones, none of the vivid oranges and golds he'd worked in would pop off the man's olive-hued skin.

"Fuck." It was a quick mutter, mostly to himself, and thankfully, the guy didn't hear him, because he was caught up in whatever was playing through his headphones. Rob sighed, wiped down the area, and assessed how much he could do now without shredding his client's skin.

His mind wasn't focused on his client, and if he wasn't careful, the whole damned tiger would end up looking like a paint-by-numbers kitten done by a color-blind preschooler with a unicorn fetish. He couldn't stop thinking about Mace. It was stupid to wonder if Mace was lonely, silly to worry about a man with enough brothers that he could form a basketball team, but Rob couldn't help it. His brain gnawed on the persistent idea that Mace's family knew jack shit about what made him happy or even how much Mace tortured himself over his asshole father and the legacy the man had beaten into him.

"I'll go back in," he promised, and then before Ivo could chime in, he added, "and I won't overwork it."

There was an unspoken moment between them, an electrified sizzle rising from the clash of Rob's temper and Ivo's experience. They might have been the same age, but Ivo was practically born with a tattoo gun in his hand, and he'd sucked in every trick doled out to him by the rounds of visiting inkers who'd come to ply their trade at Bear's pierside shop. Instinct rather than application now drove Ivo's work, and his years of working skin and watching others' mistakes gave him a knowledge base that Rob lusted after and would only achieve if he swallowed his pride and listened when Ivo offered up a suggestion.

Especially when the client was poised for the next pass of needles over his skin, his muscles tight from the already-two-hour stretch of inking.

The guy was good for another half an hour before he tapped out, and Rob was more than willing to let him go. After a thorough wipe-down with green soap and a careful application of clear skin covering, Rob tallied up the charges, cashed the guy out, and put his tip aside. As late as it was, the sidewalks outside of the shop were still packed with people, a mixture of tourists and locals taking advantage of the clear temperate night, and when the guy wheeled his bicycle out of the shop, he left the kick-down doorstop locked into place and the shop open to the street.

A salty damp was in the air, and waves of laughter, conversation, and street noise spilled in and broke through the odd heavy silence that had built up over the past few hours. Ivo'd come to work on the heels of Gus leaving barely ten minutes into Rob's shift. The brothers had a hot, spitting conversation made up of whispers and wild gestures, their body language tense and combative while they spoke in the hallway at the back of the shop.

Whatever was said, whatever they were arguing about, Ivo appeared to have won because, after a few minutes, Gus shoved his arms into his leather jacket, muttered a goodbye to Rob without making eye contact, and was out of sight before the bells hanging over the front door stopped chiming. Ivo then changed his heeled boots to a pair of Converses and the quiet began.

It cracked a couple of times during the shift, mostly with professional tidbits dropped here and there, but every attempt at conversation Rob threw out was met with a stony nothingness and a blank stare until the next time he needed a bit of a push in the right direction on a tattoo or a sketch. Then Ivo shoved... and hard. The jabs were sparse, quick, professional strikes Rob couldn't disagree with, because under it all, Ivo knew what he was talking about, even when he delivered the advice wrapped in razor blades and a sly tone.

Rob didn't have it in him to dodge the verbal jabs. Rolling with the punches seemed easier, especially when he couldn't get a damned thing out of any of the brothers now that Mace was out of the hospital.

And Rob couldn't go sneak in to check up on him when no one was looking.

He worked himself to death those first few days, covering shifts and rescheduling appointments for Bear, Gus, and Ivo. When he was done, he'd slip off to the hospital, hoping to catch Mace awake, but his timing sucked each time he could break free. As usual the brothers closed ranks and let very little out, but there were a few times when he'd notice Bear looking at him with a curious expression on his face. Rob was caught between worry over Mace and wondering if he'd still have a job once Bear came up for air. Something was definitely going on.

He just didn't know what it was.

"You know they let Mace go home, right? He's over at the house. Not his apartment." Ivo appeared at Rob's side and peered over his shoulder. Using the reception desk as an elbow rest, Ivo casually angled his body and cornered Rob. "Did anyone tell you that? Or have you already moved on, so you don't care?"

As usual, the youngest of the patchwork family Bear pulled together came out swinging, and the glitter in his eyes was intense and personal. Shock stilled Rob's tongue and left it dead in his mouth. Swallowing didn't help. No amount of spit could clear the gravel lodged in his throat. Ivo on a normal day was hard to read, cloaked in a complex push-this-button, pull-this-lever kind of personality where the rules were more complicated than a round of Calvinball, but even as little as Rob understood him, he was certain Ivo was fucking pissed off.

"Okay, if we're going to fight, at least let me close the front door and wait for me to finish entering this session. Guy paid cash, so I've got to log it," Rob shot back, and his fingers shook while he wrote down the amount of cash that he sealed into a session envelope and mentally calculated the store's cut in his head. "Step back and let me do this."

Before he walked through the shop's door, he'd put Mace to the back of his thoughts, far enough for his worry not to spill over, but the dam he'd built out of nerves and professionalism was slowly cracking. Small things surfaced during the oddest moments in the day—the blasts of the guns going off, the scent of blood in the air, and Mace's pleading cries for his neighbor to survive.

Rob also held on to the sound of his name on Mace's lips when the medical team loaded him into the ambulance and the final quick squeeze of Mace's fingers on his wrist before the EMTs pulled him free. His skin burned where Mace touched him last, and when Rob could sneak in a few minutes at Mace's bedside, he'd absently rubbed the spot until it was red as he watched Mace sleep.

He felt like a stalker, obsessed with a man who'd fought with him, fucked him, and then fed him, all the while promising Rob nothing more than a bit of his time—until everything changed and Rob found himself drowning in a pair of heartbreakingly sad blue eyes while Mace stripped off tiny pieces of the persona he'd hidden behind.

He wanted Mace's fingers on his wrist again, his lips touching Rob's mouth, and the sound of Mace laughing at something stupid he'd said. And he was beginning to resent the hell out of Ivo judging him when he knew jack shit about what Rob and Mace shared... even if Rob himself didn't know where it was going.

"Seriously, unless you want someone walking in on you giving me shit, go close the front." He nodded toward the open door. Focusing on the register screen was taking every bit of concentration he had, and Ivo's looming presence didn't help. Satisfied he'd entered the right totals, Rob punched in his acceptance for the shop to take taxes out of his share, slipped the envelope into the till slot, and closed out the transaction. Ivo stood to get out of his way, and Rob planted his feet and stared up at him. "You're just standing there. So, no on the door?"

Shoving Ivo was never a good idea, not when he had his temper up, but Rob was taking a page out of Ivo's book and pushing back... hard.

Ivo studied him with cunning, intelligent eyes. Up close, no amount of makeup could cover the strain around his mouth or the furrow along his brow. He'd gone dark with his eyeliner, smoking out the curves of black under his thick dark lashes. Ivo's features never crossed the line of feminine the way Rob's did in certain lights. It came close at times, his facial structure sometimes skewed pretty, but today, under the stress and whatever inner battles Ivo fought, he looked so much like Bear, possessed so much of Bear's aggressive masculine traits that Rob nearly pulled back. It was an instinctive response to the similarities between the artist and the older man Rob openly admired.

"You're going to say it's none of my business. And yeah, if we were like most families, you wouldn't be wrong. We don't dig into each other's love lives. Hell, I'd need a damned abacus and a punch card to keep track of Mace's, but here you are, lurking but not stepping up when Mace needs some support." Ivo shoved his hands in his pockets, and when he cocked his head, the shop's overhead lights gilded the unshaven breadth of his firm jaw. "You were there that night with Mace. And then you hung around the hospital, and at the time, I figured you were just a hookup, a one-night stand dragged into the wrong place at the wrong time. Luke and Gus think different, and Bear? Well, he's Bear, so he doesn't say jack shit about anything anyone tells him."

"Is this going anywhere? Because if it isn't, I've got to clean up my station," Rob cut in as he pushed his shoulders back and stepped in closer to Ivo. Temper flaring, he let loose. "You've had half the shift to poke at me, and when you finally get around to it, you can't even adult up and spit out what you want to say. What your brother and I have going on isn't any of your fucking business."

Rob knew his words were a mistake nearly as soon as they left his lips. For all of the makeup, heels, and plaid skirts Ivo liked to mix in with his leather jackets, jeans, and Doc Martens, there was nothing soft about him. There was more than a little bit of venom beneath Ivo's practiced charm, and the rough life he'd led threaded enough steel in him that Rob knew he'd break his teeth if he bit off more of Ivo than he could chew.

"You want *me* to adult up?" His easy grin was a lie, a social grace Ivo could slap on when he needed sleight of hand. "How about if you do the same? First thing Mace asked when I was let in to see him was if you were okay. And the next time. Then the time after that. He sneaks it in. Comes around to it, but he gets it in there. It's always about you, but I don't see you there. I don't hear you asking about him here, but I catch you leaning in when we talk. So what's the deal?"

"Like I said, I don't see how it's any of your fucking business." Truth was, he wanted to beg Ivo to tell him more than what he'd been able to scrape off of their conversations. He'd seen Luke once at the hospital, but he'd ducked around the corner, not wanting to be seen. Things with Mace were complicated, hung out to dry in a limbo splattered with blood and maybe regret.

"Mace is my business. He's my brother," Ivo spat.

"See, that's the problem right fucking there. You guys circle in, making a wall," Rob snarled back, leaving any niceties behind. Ivo wasn't going to give him any quarter, and if he didn't push back, Ivo would eat him alive. "I *tried* to get in there. You four wouldn't let me. Every time I went in, one of you told me to go home, you had it under control. I had to sneak in after visiting hours because I couldn't get past any of you. None of you let anyone who isn't family get in. Not at the hospital. Not here."

"If you'd told us—"

Rob snorted hard. "Yeah, right. If I dropped *anything* about me and Mace, you'd have torn me apart, maybe even packed my gear from my stall and dropped it off on my front porch. The shop's got rules and—"

"Ivo, back off," Mace's deep voice rumbled behind them and jerked Rob from his rant. "Love you, kid, but you're fighting a windmill here."

From where Rob stood, Ivo had no intention of backing off, windmills be damned. He turned to face his older brother, and if anything, the sight of a battered, gun-shot Mace made Ivo's hackles rise. His shoulders squared off, and if Rob were a betting man, Ivo was about to tear a piece of Mace off and feed it to the dogs.

Mace looked… damned good. A bit beaten up around the edges, but he was walking, breathing, and even with his arm in an ugly blue denim sling, he made Rob's mouth water. His hair was long enough to stick up from his scalp and fall over his forehead a bit. A tousle of amber, sienna, and dark brown strands nearly brushed one eyebrow. There were crow's-feet at the corners of his eyes, and they deepened when he moved. Pain lingered at the edges of his expression, and Rob caught the tiny hiss of tension when Mace padded slowly into the shop's main space. His shoulders were tense beneath his gray T-shirt, and his thigh muscles clenched to hold his balance with every step. But Mace's smile… it was like a ball of stars punching through Rob's aching heart—bright, warm, and only for him.

"Who the fuck let you out?" Ivo snarled at his brother as he walked over to meet Mace. "You're supposed to be resting. Fucking hell, dude! They make people who have their wisdom teeth pulled out rest for a couple of days. You got fucking shot!"

"I got it, kid." Mace caught Ivo's waist up in a one-armed hug, gave him a light squeeze, and then let go. "I'm okay. Just…. Rob and I need to talk, so—"

"Phones exist, man, and Ivo's right. You shouldn't be on your feet." The reception counter was a hard line against his back, but he didn't trust his legs to hold him up if he dared to walk. Every bit of fear he'd held on to dug claws into his chest and bled him out as the swarm of what-ifs and maybes fought to gain traction.

The back door opened again, and a disgruntled-looking Bear stomped in and shook something off of his boot. Earl shot past his legs and galloped down the hall. Ivo's sharp "Stop" brought the dog to a skidding halt, and his long legs went out from under him as he slid. Mace braced himself on one of the stall's short walls and gave the canine a wide berth.

"I know about phones," Mace finally replied. He scratched at Earl's floppy ear when the dog snuffled up to his side. "It's just sometimes it's good to see someone's face when you talk to them."

"Asshole was going to drive down here. Nearly broke his other arm before he'd let me bring him down," Bear grumbled at Ivo and stalked toward the reception area. He jerked his thumb toward the back of the shop and nodded at Rob. "I'll cover the rest of the shift for you. And why's the front door open? Am I paying to heat the sidewalk? Ivo, go close the door. Rob, go clean your station. Then you two can go have your damned talk. Just... don't go far. Use the art room, and I can't believe I've got to tell you this, but considering it's the two of you, no sex on the tables. Okay? Actually, no having sex at all. Last thing I want to do tonight is drag your ass down to the hospital, Mace. Bad enough I had to drive it here."

MACE COULDN'T get comfortable. Coming down to the shop had stretched the last of his energy, and when Earl's polite bump against his knee jerked him awake, he questioned his sanity for dragging himself down to the wharf. He just knew he couldn't go another day without seeing Rob— to touch him and make sure he was alive, well, and whole.

Bear hadn't agreed. His brother actually disagreed violently, but when he understood Mace wasn't going to budge, he gave in. Then he harped on him all the way over, especially after the shakes hit Mace and his teeth rattled when he rested his temple against the passenger-side window.

The dog was leaving a drool puddle on his thigh, and Mace shifted his butt and angled into one of the wide armchairs they'd dragged home from a thrift store a few years before. His shoulder felt like it was on fire, and it was probably past time for him to take another handful of pills, but he'd left them on the kitchen counter because he was more focused on hurrying Bear out of the door.

"Fuck, that was stupid, pupper," he informed Earl, who keened when Mace found a sweet spot on his jaw to scratch. "But I also don't want to be stoned out of my gourd when I talk to him."

"Well, you've got no choice on that," Rob said as he entered the former storage room. Holding up a Ziploc bag of pills and a water bottle, he edged past the dog. "Bear said to make sure you get these down, because you're an idiot. Rule one of getting out of the hospital is to take the medication the docs give you."

"Huh, and what do you know about that?" Mace held his hand up for Rob when he shook the pills out and caught them in his palm.

"Well, considering I was headed into medical school before I decided to throw it all away for the glamorous, extremely profitable world of tattooing, I'd say quite a lot." Rob tossed the empty bag onto the broad table the artists used to draw on and then worked at opening the water bottle. "Take them. You look like shit. If Ivo takes a peek in here and sees you passed out on the floor from the pain, he's going to take me apart bone by bone. And probably make me into a soup while he's at it."

Mace took the pills.

"Sit down," Mace mumbled through a mouthful of water. "You're making the dog nervous."

"Give me a fucking break. The only thing that bothers Earl is the ice cream truck going by and he doesn't get a vanilla cone out of it. *Swallow*." Rob glanced at the dog sprawled on the floor by Mace's feet. He snorted. "And then we can talk about what was so damned important you had to come down here when you're half dead."

"You are." Mace carefully took another swig and hoped the rush of water down his throat would dislodge the lump he'd carried there since he first woke up in the hospital and panicked, thinking Rob had been ripped from his life before… anything they could build between them. "I came down here to see you. Because you're that damned important. Or at least I think I want you to be."

FIFTEEN

"SO WHAT did you say to him after he swooped in and slayed the dragon for you?" Lilith asked from her perch on the double-wide armchair facing the fire station. "And are you *really* eating ice cream for breakfast?"

Rocky road wasn't his first choice, but since it was the only flavor left in the freezer, it was going to have to do. It was a drugstore brand he'd always wanted when he was a kid, but nothing they would ever stoop for. His family's preferences ran to shops with *creamery* in their name or exotic flavors handcrafted by French-trained dessert chefs. There was something satisfying about walking into a store that smelled of pharmaceuticals, charcoal briquettes, and household cleaners just to pick up a hand-packed pint of ice cream.

His favorite was butter brickle, but malted-milk-ball crunch was a close second. Rocky road and dark-cherry chocolate chip usually fought a tight battle for third, but he was pretty much good for anything without berries in it—although strawberry ice cream would also do in a pinch.

"See, that's the best part about being an adult," Rob said around a mouthful of marshmallows and nuts. "If I wanted to eat chocolate cake and a chicken quesadilla for breakfast, I can. No one's going to stop me. Some people—like the trash whore you are—will judge me, but I can gleefully eat anything I want and wash it down with a bottle of Mountain Dew if I want to. So, today breakfast is going to be rocky road ice cream and coffee. And as for last night, I don't know if he came to slay my dragons or admit to his demons. What I do know is we agreed to see each other, and then he turned white and looked like he was about to pass out."

"That's because he was shot. The man literally took a bullet for you." Lilith pushed her hair away from her eyes and got her rings tangled in the strands. Working them slowly out, she said, "And the family knows about you, then? How did that go over?"

"I think Bear knew, but Ivo thought I was just a fuck buddy, which to be fair, I kind of was." Rob dug back into the pint. "They probably have to talk about it because it's a pretty big rule. They don't want anyone coming back and saying shit like I was coerced into having a relationship with him. I've seen what happens when someone is sleeping with the owner. They start to get all sorts of special privileges, and when it goes south, things get really ugly. It makes sense for them to be protective of the shop. It's what pays their bills, and all of the brothers own it. They don't want anyone fucking it up."

"Well, now that I've seen him up close, I could totally be coerced into having a relationship with him," she purred. "Those arms and that chest? That fucking face? If his ass matches the rest of him, I wouldn't let him out of bed."

"See? That's why men don't like to date you. You don't respect them." He pointed at her with his chocolate-smeared spoon. "There's more to Mace than just a pretty face and a tight body. He's been through some heavy shit, and his dad is… he had a gun to come talk to his son. And he brought a friend with another gun. The one thing that I can't wrap my head around is that Mace wasn't surprised. Through all of the crazy shit and how scared I was, it was like Mace had been in that situation so many times he might've been ordering the cheeseburger and asking for no onions. He was *resigned* to it. Things didn't get hairy until his father's gun went off."

He couldn't swallow, not with the lump in his throat. It was too easy to remember how scared he'd been. The fear of that night lingered and haunted him. His arms still burned with the memory of the old Chinese woman's hot blood pouring down them from her wound. His back was bruised from the edge of the railing he'd fallen against, when her slight weight drove them back as he caught her up. Rob could still taste the bitterness in the back of his throat from the fear that ran through him as he curved his shoulder around the woman's trembling body. He knew he could do little to shield her from any more bullets, but something inside of him made him try anyway.

The ice cream tasted of ashes and regret. Logically Rob knew there was nothing he could have done to prevent what happened that night, but doubt clawed at him. Seeing Mace lying so still on the hospital bed gutted him. When he closed his eyes at night to go to sleep, the image of Mace's haggard, pale face surfaced. Seeing him today was a punch to the gut, but at the same time his heart sang.

"You've got it bad, don't you?" Lilith's question burrowed into the back of Rob's thoughts. "And not just because he stepped in front of a bullet for you. You had it bad before, didn't you?"

He joined her on the armchair, squeezing in next to her while silently offering up the pint of ice cream and his spoon for her to join him. It was a tight fit, but Rob needed her warmth against his chilled skin. Outside, the city was slowly waking and the fire station's rolling doors were partially up, giving them a peek of its iconic trucks. Because he'd watched them through the windows, Rob recognized a couple of the firefighters working at the front of the bays, and he caught himself looking for a familiar inked man, despite knowing he was elsewhere.

"I wasn't sure about it until I saw him last night. And he was so fucking stupid for coming down, because he's really hurt and he just got out of the hospital, but it did something inside of me. I couldn't breathe, and I just wanted to cry because I was all ready to fight with Ivo about him. Then there Mace was, walking through the back door as if he heard me needing him." He opened his mouth to accept a spoonful of the melting ice cream when Lilith offered it to him. Then he mused, "I was so angry at Ivo for saying I didn't care about Mace. I think some part of my mind was already calculating how much money I had in reserve and if you would carry me over until I found another shop, because I was going to lose my job after I punched his face in. And because he's so hardheaded, I would probably break my hand, and then I wouldn't be able to tattoo until that was healed so… that's where I was in my head when he walked through the door.

"He looked like shit, Lil, but I wanted to kiss him until he was blue in the face. I was so scared to touch him. It was like he was broken and weak but strong at the same time. I can't get over his father. And I can't even imagine the kind of crap that man did to him. It blows my mind he's even functional, because I can't see how anybody could be if they were raised by someone so disgusting." Rob shook his head when Lilith offered him another spoonful. "It's not even that his father is racist. It goes beyond that. He actively wants to hurt people—kill them, I think. That night, I thought we were going to die, because neither one of those guys saw us as people. It's like those kids who chase pigeons in the park, and their parents think it's cute, but nobody thinks about how terrorizing that is to the pigeon. He's the kind of man who actually would get sexual pleasure from hurting someone that way. And the sad thing is, I think Mace is afraid there's something inside of him that will one day turn him into his father."

"That's bullshit, because I've seen his friends and brothers. They're all kinds of colors," Lilith scoffed. "From what little I've seen of him, I think he's harder on himself than he is anyone else. He runs into burning buildings to save people for a living. And maybe I'm glorifying that, but he seems like the kind of guy who's more concerned about saving someone's skin than worrying about its color."

"He speaks Chinese." He chuckled. "Apparently it's pretty bad, but he speaks Chinese to that old woman, and people *like* him. His younger brothers think he's an asshole because he's always pushing them to do better, but isn't that what an older brother's supposed to do? My brothers just pushed me around. He really loves his. I can see it. And Gus gets grumpy about it, but sometimes it hurts to watch them, because it reminds me I don't have that kind of family."

"Well, if you follow your heart," Lilith murmured as she rested her head on his shoulder, "they'll become your family."

"I HATE family meetings," Ivo grumbled while he poured himself a cup of coffee. His brother's morning ensemble ran to a pair of black sweats and a tank top with a sparkly unicorn dancing across his chest. His hair was a tangle of muted colors, but Mace wasn't sure if the odd ombré effect was on purpose or a result of fading, and he sure as hell wasn't going to ask. Glancing over at Mace, Ivo held up the pot. "Do you want some? Since I'm here and you can't use that arm?"

"Yeah, thanks." Mace spent more than a few minutes trying to maneuver around Earl to get to the kitchen, and the scruffy mutt appeared bent on tripping him as Mace walked through the house. "If you could bring it into the family room, that would be great. The damned dog keeps getting in between my legs."

"That's because the damned dog knows you're hurt," Rey said with a laugh and closed the back door behind him. "Has he already gone outside, or should I go on potty duty before we start talking?"

"Luke already took him for a walk." Ivo scooped enough sugar into his coffee that Mace could almost taste it in the air. "Bear grabbed some doughnuts, but he said we can't have any until we sit down. I'll bring your cup in, Mace. *Earl*, come with."

The shaggy mixed breed mournfully glanced at Mace and then sighed dramatically and fell into step with Ivo as he headed to the family room. Rey laughed, crossed over to where Mace stood, and clasped his hand on Mace's uninjured arm.

"I'm glad you're okay, man." Rey's voice grew husky with emotion. "If anything happens to you, I won't have anyone to play tag with me through Chinatown."

Rey Montenegro and Mace's friendship began as adolescents, when Mace pulled Rey out of a fire set by Rey's drunken father, and they'd weathered more than a few storms. It'd been hard when Rey and Gus had a fling and Rey chose to break it off, which sent Gus into a spiral and, oddly enough, drove him into a one-night stand that resulted in his nephew, Chris. When Jules, Chris's mother, finally contacted Gus to tell him about their son, Gus came home and faced Rey.

Through it all Mace secretly ached for both his younger brother and his best friend. He hoped they'd patch things up and then celebrated as they fell in love. As much as Mace would miss having Rey as a roommate when the house he and Gus bought became livable, he loved having Rey as a future brother-in-law, and it wasn't as though he didn't live in Rey's back pocket when they shared shifts at the fire station.

Their games of tag were born from Mace's inability to sleep and a driving need to pound the doubt out of his body. Their runs were brutal and spanned blocks, but by the end of them, Mace's back stung from Rey's hand slapping him as he jogged past him, and his belly ached from the food they ate at the restaurant they chose as their endpoint.

"Well, the doctors say I'm out of commission for a few weeks, and then after that, I've got physical therapy. Captain says I can come back to the station and work a light shift once I get cleared. So don't get too comfortable," Mace warned and shot Rey a wicked smile. "I don't need my arm to run. And I sure as hell don't need it to beat you."

"I swear to God, if the two of you don't get your fucking asses in here, the only doughnuts that are going to be left for you are the cake ones with rainbow sprinkles," Ivo threatened loudly from the family room. "And your fucking coffee is getting cold!"

"I don't know why Bear buys those," Mace muttered. "Nobody likes them."

Rey shrugged and helped himself to a quick cup of black coffee. "*I* like them. Gus says he gets them for me, but I don't know if that's true."

"It has to be true. *None* of us like those. They're disgusting." Mace pushed off of the counter he was leaning on and winced at the ache in his side and shoulder. "Okay, let's head into the lion's den so I can get my head bitten off."

"I'll stand with you, my brother." Rey saluted him with his cup. "I'll just be a few feet back so the blood splatter doesn't get all over me. These jeans are new. I don't want to ruin them."

FAMILY MEETINGS were a tradition in the house, a practice born of living in communal houses and foster homes. It was normally a weekly gathering to air gripes or to vent about someone else. In the early days of their family, meetings were few and far between until all five of them moved in and Bear decided he'd broken up his last fistfight. None of them had good communication skills back then, and because they were raised in an environment where physical dominance outweighed logic and compromise, fights were bound to happen. But when Gus and Luke cornered Mace in the front hall, Bear finally put his foot down and demanded they come up with a better way of doing things.

They'd all been so different then, so angry at the world and desperate to find a place in it that they almost tore one another apart while they tried to carve out where they fit in the family they'd made. The meetings were a start, and the roles they found while talking things out proved to be prophetic in a lot of ways. With Bear anchoring them in place, Luke became the mediator while Mace found himself more comfortable keeping track of the things they'd decided on before and reminding them of past instances and what they did to solve those issues. Gus usually hovered around the corners, unwilling to give an opinion unless pushed or raging to be heard if it was something he was passionate about. The youngest, Ivo, glided along and disagreed every once in a while, but to the credit of the way they raised him, he usually reasoned his way through any problems. He was particularly stubborn during his teenage years, but he evened out when he got older.

Throwing Rey into the mix was new, but he brought the same steadying influence as Bear did, so his voice was very welcome in the volatile stew of their family dynamics.

And luckily for Rey, the cake doughnuts with rainbow sprinkles were waiting for him in the box, as well as a yeast cinnamon twist that Luke had put aside for Mace.

It took a bit of shuffling on the sectional to find a place for Rey. Habit meant each of the brothers had a little bit of space around them on the couch, with the exception of Ivo, who liked to drape himself over whoever he felt like bothering that day. With Rey settled against Gus, Mace made himself comfortable in the corner and nudged Earl to the side before the dog jumped up onto his lap.

"I'm confused." Gus spoke up first. "What are we having a meeting about? Mace sleeping with Rob?"

"I'm not *sleeping* with him." Mace grimaced when Bear shot him a withering look. "Okay, I had sex with him—"

"In the shop," Bear interjected. The gasps from the other brothers would've been funny if Mace hadn't been in the middle of the problem. "But that's not why I thought we should have a family meeting."

"I think that's exactly why we should have a family meeting," Ivo argued. "Sure, Gus did it too—although not in the shop—and while Mace can't get Rob pregnant, he works for us. What's the point of agreeing not to sleep with employees if everybody keeps doing it? We've all been to those kinds of shops. We've all worked where there's so much drama between who's fucking whom that it damages the shop's reputation and nobody can get any ink done."

"It's not like that with Rob," Mace replied. "I promise you, it's not."

"Maybe you should tell us what it *is* like so we can understand." Luke caught up Ivo's hand and squeezed it when Ivo looked away. "Does he mean something to you? That's something all of us are asking because he was there that night with you. While we have to protect the shop, we also need to protect you, and part of doing that is understanding where you are right now and who's becoming important to you."

Mace could always count on Luke to peel back the layers of emotion and get to the rawness inside. Never before had he felt so much on the edge of a cliff, especially with all of his brothers and his best friend looking at him with varying degrees of sympathy, concern, and mild anger. He couldn't carry around secrets anymore. They'd become too heavy, and with the damage his father had already done to his life, he needed to know where his family stood.

He needed to know if they would love him, even if they knew the filth he was stained with.

"I care about Rob. I've been fighting my *thing* for him for a long time, and then one day we just gave in to it," he confessed with a shrug.

"I thought if I could somehow satisfy that itch, it would go away and we could go back to aggressively ignoring each other, but it didn't go away. Then we spent a little time together, and I thought maybe I could have something with him. Because, except for you guys, I never imagined anyone would ever love me.

"With Rob, I find myself talking about the shit I've always wanted to ignore, the crap that my dad did to me and everything that I did for him." Mace rubbed at his face, his unshaven jaw rough against the palm of his hand. "I've done some horrible things, things I'm not proud of. And Rob's been pushing me to talk to you guys, to share with you, because he's like Luke—lots of talking about how you feel and what will make you grow. I've been scared to talk to you guys because, if you know everything about me from back then, I worry that you won't love me anymore. And the one thing I cannot lose in my life is you guys. I just can't."

"You're not going to lose us, Mason," Bear reassured him. He reached across the couch to place his hand on Mace's thigh. "There's nothing that you can say that's going to change that."

"That's what Rob thinks. He also said all of the crap inside of me would be easier to deal with if I shared it with you guys, trusted it with you guys, because it's killing me inside to hold on to it." Mace looked up at his brothers, suddenly aware of the tears in his eyes. Swallowing hard, he said, "I need to tell you what kind of monster my father is. And what kind of monster he tried to make me into."

Sixteen

"This is really fucking hard," Mace confessed slowly. The rug was fascinating, the patterns in the nap a variegated blend of light and dark colors he'd never really noticed before. His hands were heavy and cradled an invisible weight as he laced his fingers together and crouched forward to stare at his feet.

Talking to his brothers about his childhood and the man who'd taken him from a life he barely remembered seemed easy enough in theory, but once he opened his mouth, the words he needed fled, driven from his mind like pigeons taking flight during a hawk strike. It was easier not to look at their faces, to avoid the disappointment and disgust he feared he'd find in their expressions once he told them who he really was—who he'd come from—and the man he always feared he truly was beneath the thin veneer of humanity he'd fought so hard to slather over himself.

Mace just didn't know if any of it stuck.

"Anything you say, you know it won't change how we feel about you, right?" Luke moved over and sat closer. Mace's thoughts flashed to another Hispanic man, his terrified face bloodied from a vicious beating, and all he could think about from that moment on was Luke curled up in an alleyway and the feel of a baseball bat clenched in his hands. "All of us here have dark places and secrets. No one can judge."

"I can sure as hell judge," Mace snorted.

Bear edged in and sat on the ottoman, so close his knees nearly touched Mace's leg. "You tell us what you think you need to. And Luke is right—every single one of us has had shit to eat, served up by people who should have taken care of us. Whatever happened, whatever you're holding on to, we're here to listen. That's all."

"Speak for yourselves," Ivo piped up and nudged Mace's thigh with his bare foot. "I was raised by you guys. I'm golden."

"Can't be as bad as our mother," Gus interjected from across the sectional, his head resting on Rey's shoulder. "And really, we've all seen a lot of ugly. Pretty sure we can take it."

The sight of his brother and his best friend sitting intertwined and attentive twisted something in Mace's heart. He wanted what they had. He'd never given a thought to sharing his life with someone, but seeing their relationship—their solid, chaotic relationship—made Mace realize he was missing out on so much of life by trying to hold on to his heart. Breaking through the wall he'd put up between him and his brothers was only the first step to reclaiming himself. After that, there was a certain golden-eyed tattoo artist he wanted to get to know much better.

Earl's head on his thigh did him in, but the dog's mad scramble to get into Mace's lap became a battle of wills and caused him a few shots of pain. The shouting was loud, but Earl was determined, and eventually everyone settled down when the shaggy mutt had gained his purchase, wedged between Mace and Ivo.

If his hands were a distraction, then the dog was a balm, and Mace soon lost himself in the texture of Earl's fur on his fingers and the coarse hair that tickled his hand as he worked it through Earl's rough coat.

"It all started when my mom left him, or maybe it started after she gave birth to me. I don't know. I don't really remember him before he took me. I knew who he was, but he wasn't a part of my everyday life until… he became my entire life." Mace took a breath, but it did nothing to ease the tightness in his chest. "He tried to change everything about me—my name, my thoughts, anything that my mother had given me up to that point.

"But mostly he tried to make me—turn me into—someone exactly like him." He forced the words from his mouth. "He has ideas about race that I don't agree with. Or at least I don't now, but back then, everything he pounded into my head was hateful and destructive. Anyone who wasn't our skin color—not of European descent—was nothing more than a talking animal, someone—*something*—to be used and subjugated."

Luke's hand on his knee almost undid Mace, and he had to look away. Earl shifted against him, whined slightly when Mace's fingers stilled, and then heaved a sigh of contentment as Ivo took up where Mace left off and lightly scratched the dog's back. With his head down and his focus on the tufts of loose hair coming out of Earl's coat, Mace continued.

"When he first took me, I fought him. There were nights when he would throw me into the bathtub—into ice water—and then beat me until it ran pink. He would starve me and lock me in a closet and leave the apartment or the house we were at. Sometimes it was just for a few hours, but there were times when it would stretch on for days." The memory of biting his lip to satisfy his thirst rose up and blended with the bile of his stomach as he fought to maintain control.

"The hardest thing to deal with was the silence. I couldn't hear anything. He would duct tape the door and cover it with bubble wrap so no light would come in and no sound would reach me. Sometimes I could hear the bang of a pipe when someone turned on the water or the rattle of an air vent, but usually there was nothing there. It got so I hated the sound of my own heartbeat in my ears, and my throat would hurt because I couldn't talk anymore. I used to talk to myself just so I wasn't alone.

"I would tell stories. It made the darkness seem not so scary anymore." Mace shifted to take the pressure off of his shoulder. "And it's going to sound stupid, but if I closed my eyes when I was telling them, it was like I was making it dark and I had some sort of control over it. I could usually do that for a few hours, but if it got longer than that, my voice would give out."

"Well that explains why your voice is so deep and raspy," their youngest brother teased.

"Ivo, not now," Bear scolded in a sharp rumble.

"It's okay," Mace said, looking up. "It helps to laugh at something sometimes. Now, it's easier to think about it because it's like all of that happened to someone else, to a little boy named Johnny whose father drank too much and did drugs and had his friends come over to talk about doing horrible things to other people, who did horrible things to me.

"It's hard to remember being that little kid because, if I shove it away, I can pretend it wasn't me, that I wasn't the one who chewed my fingernails because I was hungry or drank my own piss because I didn't have any water. I hear about kids that Luke sees, and all I can think is, at least that wasn't me. I had it better." Rubbing at his face, Mace got a piece of dog hair in his eye, and he flinched when Luke pushed his hand away to help him.

"Hold still. Let me get that," Luke whispered, his fingers gentle on Mace's cheek. A whisper of an accent thickened his words, and a heat rolled beneath them. Mace pulled back a little and tried to meet Luke's gaze. Luke smiled at him and then said, "You should never think that you deserve anything less than the best. No matter what your father tried to turn you into, he didn't succeed."

Mace shook his head, and from across the room, both Gus and Rey objected before he spoke, their murmurs a soft admonishment against anything he was going to say.

"I helped him. There were a few times when he would take me with him, and they would go hunting Mexicans or blacks, anyone who didn't look like them. It didn't matter." Mace caught himself before he could be sick and swallowed hard. Breathing through his cold sweats, he continued, "Usually men, but there were a couple of times they'd come back and say they found themselves a good time, and what does it matter, because it's not like they were real people.

"That's who I was when the fireman found me that day. I didn't want to go with him because he was darker than I was, because he was a different race than me. I didn't believe him when he said he would save me because… I guess I knew deep down inside what we were doing was wrong." He heard Bear murmur something—a soothing sound meant to console—but Mace pushed on, needing to say the rest of what he'd built up in his head before he lost all his nerve. "I didn't deserve to be saved. And I sure as hell didn't deserve to be rescued by a man my father and I would beat up if we caught him alone late at night. That's the kind of person they found."

"Mace, you are *not* that person." Luke grabbed at Mace's hand and pulled it away from the dog. He ducked his head and forced Mace to make eye contact, but it was too much. He had to look away from Luke's beautiful, emotional face. "When I got here, you were the first one to make me feel like I had my feet underneath me. Bear was working to make us safe and give us a home, but you were the one we fought with because you'd get us out of bed to go to school or make sure we got to whatever part-time job we were working at that month. For fuck's sake, you made sure we got dressed up to go to Ivo's school for that stupid art show where they put black bars over the nudes he did. *That's* my brother."

"If I had met you just a few years before, I would've pounded your face in," Mace confessed through a veil of tears and the thick gravel in his throat. "Don't you understand that? I would've been one of those guys you work to get your kids away from. I *enjoyed* it. I used to look forward to the closet door opening up so I could be let outside, and the price I paid for every single one of those nights was someone else's blood. The first time, I bashed some guy who looked a lot like you. We nearly beat him to death. Hell, for all I know, he died. I was a kid. Sure, I can use that as an excuse, but that doesn't wash the blood off of my hands. It doesn't make it okay that I got excited to go with my father and his friends on those nights."

"You know what pisses me off the most?" Gus called out from across the room. Untangling himself from Rey's embrace, Gus stood up and worked his way around the ottoman toward the open space in front of the television. "All of the fucking times I give you shit about needing to leave the light on or having the stereo playing, like you were a little kid who was scared to go to bed at night, and all you had to do was tell us about this crap. All this time I went around thinking you were an asshole because, no matter how much I needed quiet, you made sure there was all this noise."

"Don't make this about you, babe." Rey moved to get up, but Bear's hand was on his shoulder before he could do more than lean forward.

"It's not about me. It's about this fucking asshole pushing us every single goddamned day to be better—just like his father pushed him to be a monster—and we would curse him out. Nearly every night the three of us would bitch the fuck about how much Mace pissed us off that day, and never once did he think maybe we needed to understand where the hell he was coming from." Gus turned and faced Mace with a snarl. "I fucking hate you as much as I love you, because nothing I did was ever good enough. And what you're telling me right now is that you were that much of a fucking asshole, not because I wasn't good enough, but because you thought *you* weren't. And that's a big fucking bullshit, because the first thing we all swore to each other was, no matter what the fuck happened to us, we would stick together. Right?"

"How did that go? Forgive us our trespasses as we forgive those who trespass against us?" Ivo's words dug beneath Mace's skin. Pushing his riot of pastel hair away from his face, Ivo smirked. "Wasn't that the point of this family? I mean, I came to this really late in the game, and anything I did or that was done to me—with the exception of Puck, because yeah, I knew he tried to kill me—but everything else is pretty low-key. All of my drama and shit is nothing compared to you guys, but the deal was no matter what happened, we held on."

"And that's what we're going to do right now, hold on to him." Bear nudged Earl off of the couch. The dog grumbled but shuffled off, and then Bear shifted closer until his knees nearly touched the couch and forced Mace's legs to either side. Bear's hands were enormous. When he reached for Mace's face, Mace almost recoiled from the heat and strength in Bear's touch. "I would hug you, but you've been shot, and right now I think you're just wrung out. You're carrying a lot of stuff you don't have to carry alone, little brother. I knew about the guys you had sex with because you thought it kept you safe. Not the only one who did that. A lot of the kids who were in fucked-up places did what they could to survive.

"And that's what you were doing. You were surviving. Every time he opened that closet door, you were living another day. I'm angry you had to make the choice between your suffering and someone else's. That's not anything a kid should ever have to choose. It's nothing anyone should ever have to endure, but you did." Bear glanced back and tracked Gus's pacing. Then he shifted over to Ivo, who got a small smile. "I left you here to raise these three. Sure, I was around, but a lot of it fell to you because I was working so many hours. And you didn't let the family down. None of us would be where we are if it weren't for the sacrifices you made. You could've walked away."

"Hell, people were probably betting on it, and no one would've blamed you." Luke chortled. "We were such a damned mess."

"Not me." Ivo preened. "I am a *fucking* delight."

"You just keep thinking that, bucko," Gus snorted. "I'm surprised Rey didn't kill you, and he's the most easygoing guy we know."

"Don't drag me into this." Rey shook his head, but a small grin crept over his face. "You pulled me out of a fire, Mace. Remember? I owe you my life. You gave me a passion and a career and eventually a husband who came with a kid so I don't have to work so hard to get him pregnant."

"We would all appreciate if you guys didn't work so hard on that," Ivo shot back.

"The point of this is, you have to let us carry some of the weight." Bear took back the conversation and eased the focus back onto Mace. "The sick things he made you do were not your fault. He waged a campaign of emotional terrorism on you, and you were just a kid. I look at everything you fought to become, and I'm proud to call you brother."

"We all are." Luke's words were soft and nearly a whisper. His gaze at Gus, however, was quite sharp. "All of us, right?"

With Bear's hands still cupping his face, Mace couldn't look away, so he caught every inch of remorse and apologetic embarrassment on Gus's face. Gus nodded and mumbled, "I was just pissed off he didn't trust us with everything. I mean, everyone knows about what my mother did to me and Puck, and all this time we've been not talking about what Puck did to Ivo to protect him, but apparently that's gone to shit because he knows. Luke's life was a shitstorm, but he's the best of us. And everything shitty that's happened to Bear was pretty much inheriting all of us. So why did you think we'd just throw you away? That's gotta be the stupidest fucking thing that's ever gone through your head, dude."

"Inheriting all of you—as you put it—were the best moments of my life," Bear corrected him. He dropped his hands to Mace's thighs and squeezed gently. "Nothing is going to break us apart. We're family. You're my brother. All of you are. And I think I can speak for all of us when I say we would die for each other, and we would rather die than turn one of us away. And that includes Rey."

"Not me." Gus shook his head when everyone turned to look at him. "About the Rey part. I don't think about him as a brother. Just so we're clear on that. All of you—especially *you*, Mace the asshole—can love him like a brother all you want. Me? I've got other things on the agenda."

"And once again Gus takes it back to himself," Ivo sighed.

Luke clasped both his hands around Mace's and squeezed as he rested his forehead on Mace's temple. The air around them was growing warm from their body heat, and it was stifling, but at the same time, the tightness Mace held in his chest released and opened a space for his heart to begin beating again.

"Thanks" was all Mace could choke out. The dog whined at his feet and crept into the tight space between their legs, the sectional, and the enormous ottoman. "Yeah, you too, Earl."

"I love you a lot. We all do," Luke whispered. "And just so you know, blood washes off your hands pretty easily if you use water and soap. It worked for me, so I know it'll work for you."

THE BED wasn't uncomfortable, but Mace felt every fluffy pillow-top mound on the mattress beneath the squillion-thread-count fitted sheets

Luke liked to sleep on. He'd tried to make it up to his own bedroom, but climbing the uneven stairs with only one arm was difficult, especially when the medication made him a bit drowsy. After the second bump of his shoulder on the stairwell, Mace's sleeping accommodations moved to the former front parlor that Luke had taken over for his bedroom years before.

It was odd how the room smelled like Luke despite him not being there all the time—a slight hint of citrus and Ivory soap. Unlike Gus and Ivo, Luke preferred things to be neat. His furniture was nearly spartan, and the four short bookshelves he'd lined up under the street-facing windows boasted a mixture of fiction, nonfiction, and textbooks nearly as wide as Mace's head. The walls were a silvery sage in the sparse glow from the lamp on the nightstand, and despite the softness of the bed, Mace drowsed, lulled by the sound of the light rain outside.

When his phone rang, Mace jerked awake and badly twisted his shoulder when he tried to sit up. The covers wouldn't seem to give him up, and "Polk Salad Annie" growled through the room at a volume loud enough to wake the dead. He gave it about three seconds before one of the guys beat at the floor above him.

"No, that's right. Bear's room's above me," Mace muttered when he worked out the layout in his head. He grabbed the phone. "He'd come down and yell at me. Hello?"

"Hey. You still mostly awake?" Rob's sultry voice reached out and stroked at the simmering want Mace had for him. "I know it's late, but I wanted to make sure you were okay. I got your message earlier, but the shop today was really busy, and the guys were a little bit weird. I figured I'd call you when I got home."

"Weird how?" Mace sat up, but agony bloomed in his shoulder and then worked down to seize his spine. Grunting, he forced himself to get at least partially upright and leaned against the slightly cold wooden headboard, grateful for its chilly surface. "Anybody say anything to you? Did they give you a hard time? Because if they did—"

"No, it wasn't like that. It was more like everybody had gone a few rounds and then came into work. It was weird because Ivo was *nice*. Most of the time he's chewing on my ass about one thing or another, a hell of a lot worse than Bear, who should be giving me shit because he's, like, the head guy. Well, that was stupid. You know he's that guy." Rob chuckled. "I was kind of surprised to see Gus here for the whole day. Like I said, it was just weird. How are you doing?"

"I'm doing okay." Mace almost shrugged, but he caught himself. "Tired. And I keep doing really dumb things like reaching for things with the wrong hand or calling Earl up to the couch. And before you ask, I talked to them today. Or at least a little bit of it. Enough so that they understood how I feel inside."

"And what'd they say?"

"That I was a fucking idiot to think they would walk away from me." The emotions Mace held in all day broke and pierced through the thin layer of control he had left. A sob ripped through him, and its serrated edges tore him apart.

Fear was too small a word for what he'd held inside of him for so long. Without his family—without his *brothers*—he'd be too devastated to go on. They were everything holding him together, weathered and beaten leather straps fastened tightly around the pieces of himself he'd picked up and tried to make a man out of. They'd given him purpose and salvation, and he'd been so frightened to lose them that he hadn't trusted them to help him with what he needed the most—to be free of the man who'd broken him and then remade him in his own image.

"Do they still love you?" Rob's laughter mocked him. "Because I spent the day with them, and they seem fine to me. Jules even came by with the kid, and they all talked about having a barbecue when you felt better. Or are you calling me from a cardboard box behind the grocery store because they've kicked you out?"

"I would tell you to fuck off, but that would probably end my chances of a date." He shook his head and ground his teeth slightly at Rob's derisive snort. "They still love me. And yeah, you were right. Is that what you called to hear?"

"No. I called to hear your voice." The line was silent for a few moments, and then Rob said, "I visited you in the hospital, but you were never awake when I was there, so I guess I never heard you say you were okay. And it's silly because you almost killed yourself coming to see me—"

"I did not almost kill myself," he objected. "Despite what my brothers think."

"I saw you. You were one step away from a frizzy-haired doctor strapping you to an operating table and lifting you up so lightning could hit you. Throw in some werewolves and neighing horses and you would've been all set to go." Rob sighed. "What is it about you that you think you need to be invincible? That symbol your dad carved into your back wasn't an *S*, but that doesn't mean you have to try to make it one. It's okay to fuck up, and it's okay to say you need help, dude. We all need help sometimes."

"That's the hardest thing for me to say. Hardest thing for me to ask for. Right before telling people what I need or want." Mace echoed Rob's exhale. "I'll try to do better. I promise."

"Good. You do that." Rob's whisper grew husky. "Because there's nothing hotter than a guy who knows what he wants—and can tell me about it—when we're in bed."

SEVENTEEN

"IF YOU guys need anything, please let me know." Mace's Cantonese stumbled, forcing him to patch in English words when he reached the end of his knowledge. On the other end of the phone, Mrs. Hwang didn't seem to mind. Her cheery voice was a welcome balm to Mace's troubled mind. "Mrs. Hwang—"

"No, no, no. Do not call me that." The silence on the phone was loud enough to hush Mace before he went any further, but then Mrs. Hwang remarked in a gentle, scolding voice, "You called me grandmother—*intimate form*—in the garage. After those men shot us. It helped me get through the pain, knowing how you felt. So I would not mind if you called me that. Grandma Yu, okay?"

Mace dug his fingers into Earl's ruff and scratched his nails through the mutt's coarse fur. The dog's weight against his thigh was welcome, although he could have done without Earl digging his back paws into his hip. The sectional was a comfortable retreat for Mace, someplace he could listen to the house and sip his coffee while he talked to a woman who could have broken his heart if she wanted to.

He hadn't expected her to heal, so the words he found spilling out of his brain were disjointed and probably the worst Cantonese he'd ever spoken, but Mace was going to try anyway.

"I'd be honored to call you grandmother," he choked out. "Just get better so you can come home and cook for me. Right now I am at my brothers' house and the food is horrible. Nobody knows how to make *xiao long bao*, and don't get me started on their chow fun. Besides, I still have to put those shelves up for you, and I need you there so I don't hang them too high, because I am tall and you are short."

She hurled gentle abuse back at him, and after a few promises to get better wrapped around an admonishment for him to do the same, his grandmother hung up and left Mace holding a warm phone in his hand. The dog, sensing he had Mace's full attention, rolled over for a belly rub, and his back paw connected solidly with Mace's chin.

"Dammit, mutt," Mace grumbled, giving in to the dog's demands. "And what did you roll in? Did you get into the herbs? Because you kind of smell like Italian food. Bear is going to skin you alive if he goes outside and finds his rosemary is flat again."

"That's a lie if ever I heard one," a very familiar and welcome voice called out from behind him.

Earl scrambled to get off of the couch, startled by an intruder he hadn't heard coming in, but in true Earl fashion, he was more interested in reading the new person than defending Mace against attack. Although, he realized, Rob was a part of Earl's day-to-day life, and he probably saw Rob more than he ever saw Mace.

Carrying in a couple of plastic takeout bags from a taco shop down the street, he was dressed for work in a pair of old jeans, a T-shirt from a band whose members got inked at the shop, and a pair of scuffed black boots in need of a shine. His ink-black hair was a riot of spikes, the ends an intense sapphire blue with a hint of violet. A broad white smile creased Rob's tanned face, and his plumped cheeks were marked with dimples.

Rob's joy at seeing him grabbed Mace's heart and squeezed hard.

"Settle down, dog. You didn't even notice me knocking at the front door," Rob scolded when Earl flung himself at him. Lifting the bags up out of dog nose reach, Rob nudged a very interested Earl out of the way with his knee. With a soft woof, Earl declared his disapproval at the food's distance and snuffled at Mace's foot. "I hope you're hungry, because I grabbed some food for us. Since I didn't know what you liked, I have a carne asada burrito, a carnitas burrito, a pollo asado quesadilla, and a couple of containers of elote. There was a fish burrito, but I had to pay a toll at the door to Ivo, and since I'm working with him and Bear in a couple of hours, I thought it best to give him what he wanted."

"Don't take this wrong, but if ever you have a fish burrito, please feel free to give it to him." Mace straightened up but winced when he jostled his shoulder. "Hope he eats it on the way over, because Bear will want half."

"That's his problem. I was also told to make sure you took your painkillers." Rob set the bag down on the couch next to Mace. "So consider yourself reminded."

Watching Rob unpack food onto the ottoman was probably the most domestic experience Mace had ever had. His encounters with men were nearly always physical in nature—a quick hot bout of sex someplace Mace could walk away from—and he purposely kept his relationships shallow. There were men who intimately knew his body, but Mace didn't even know their last names. Then Rob happened. He couldn't imagine sharing anything as personal as his dislike for fish burritos with any of the men he'd been with before. It seemed like too intimate a detail, too much of a peek into his personal life, and a moment of disassociated sadness washed over him.

"What's up?" Rob quirked an eyebrow at him, a curious gleam in his golden eyes. "You've got a weird look on your face. Haven't you ever had a Mexican food picnic in your family room before? All the rage where I come from. Right up there with tea parties and 'painting porcelain rabbit statue' raves."

"Sounds more like Wonderland than San Francisco there," he teased as he took the handful of napkins Rob thrust at him.

"Babe, this is SF. It's one step away from Wonderland. Only thing we're missing is a mock turtle." Rob began to stack hot sauces on the ottoman and arranged the plastic tubs by color. "Ivo told me I'm the first person you've had over here. Well, as he put it, first one Mace fucked and the only one he's let come back for seconds."

"Sometimes I think we didn't beat Ivo enough as a child, not that we beat him at all. There's no filter there. He doesn't think before he speaks."

"He's very trusting. Maybe it's because he's secure, like he knows he can do anything outrageous and you guys trust him not to go too far." Rob snorted under his breath and added, "Of course a lot of people only see the skirt and high heels and not the guy who can fuck someone up if they push him. Learned *that* the first week I was there. But really, first guy you brought home? Who showed up with Mexican food and pushed his way past the gatekeeper?"

"Yep, first one. I don't normally mingle pleasure with personal. Hookups? All the time. Relationships? No fucking clue about what to do," he admitted in a soft voice. "So this is all kind of new to me. Am I supposed to kiss you hello? Offer you a drink? Which makes sense, because that's what I would do to a friend, but this—you and I?—is a little bit more than friends."

"Well, I've got a couple of bottles of water here, so we don't need any drinks. Mostly I guess I hug people hello, but a kiss?" He smirked. Rob put one of his hands on the other side of Mace's hips and precariously supported himself on his palm. "Not a bad idea."

Rob's lips were soft on his mouth. There was a bit of an ache along Mace's collarbone, especially when Rob's weight dipped the couch cushion down, and Mace couldn't hold back a hiss of pain. He wanted to enjoy a slow, leisurely taste of Rob's mouth and suckle on the plump of his lower lip, but the angle was all wrong, and his injury wasn't going to let him wrap his arms around Rob's waist and hold the man he longed to have straddle his lap. His cock flared into a hardened state. He knew how Rob's hands would feel on his chest, how his nipples would respond to Rob's fingers pinching at them, but Mace was going to have to be satisfied with a simple kiss.

Because he was in no condition for anything more.

Kisses were never gentle. In a lot of ways, they often mimicked the quick, hard sex Mace had with his partners. There was always a lot of give-and-take—mostly take—a profane amount of aggression, and a demand for more as each second went by.

This kiss was so very *fucking* different.

He could actually taste Rob in this kiss. There was an underlying sweetness, like a handful of pure water from a snow-fed stream. There were notes of brightness and a hint of blue, the ghost of mint toothpaste and something indescribably masculine. His tongue played with Mace's, a gentle velvet tickle that rubbed first on Mace's lower lip, overstimulated his nerves until they were nearly numb, and then slid into Mace's mouth to stroke at the back of his teeth.

A heat built up between them—a sticky tapestry of tightening electrified threads. Mace drank deeply and cupped the back of Rob's head with his good hand, his fingers tangled in Rob's product-heavy coarse hair. He angled his mouth, seeking for a way to get more of what Rob was giving him, but then something in Mace shifted and the kiss slowed and became a languid dance of barely touching tongues and pressed lips.

The angle of Rob's body leaning across of him was awkward, and the cushions shifted as they moved to get closer. Mace wanted nothing more than to plunge himself into Rob's warm, willing body. He lusted for the press of Rob's cockhead at the back of his throat and longed for the salty release he knew he could draw out of him. Yet their kiss was a delectable, fragile dance of tissue-thin control and a deeper emotion that Mace couldn't quite name.

It all came crashing down around them in a clatter of Earl's excited barks and Bear's surprised "Shit, I'm sorry" booming through the family room. Rob's tentative balance broke, and he toppled forward and slammed into Mace's injured shoulder.

And while Mace would've liked to let out a manly grunt, he probably sounded more like the scream his mother made once when a rat ran across her foot.

What followed was a few minutes of panicked examinations and apologies, first from a horrified, contrite Rob, who scrambled off of Mace's twisted body and then accidentally made matters worse by grabbing Mace's sling, and then from a few pokes by a not-so-gentle Bear, who had to fight for space on the couch against a very concerned Earl.

"All of you, *get off,*" Mace ordered as he lightly shoved at the dog, who attempted to climb onto his lap the moment Mace yelped. "Earl, *down.* Bear, help me get the dog off of me. Rob, you're fine. Just stay over there for right now."

There were definitely stars, and his shoulder felt like it would burst into flames any moment, but it soon settled down to a hot throb once everyone gave him some space. Breathing heavily, Mace reached up to adjust his sling and stopped Bear from helping him with a hard glare.

"You probably need some painkillers. Did you already take some, or should I get them from the kitchen for you?" Bear's massive body cast a long shadow over the couch. The apologetic look on Bear's face would've been comical if he hadn't seen it through a wash of tears. At Mace's grunted *please,* Bear clicked his tongue at the dog. "I'll grab them for you, and I'll take Earl down with me to the shop. I swung by to see if you needed anything but—yeah, let me grab your medicine and I'll just go."

"I actually should get going too," Rob said as he glanced at the clock on the wall. "Traffic's always a bitch, and today's probably going to be kind of awkward, considering my boss just caught me kissing his younger brother."

"You can probably bribe him with the carnitas burrito," Mace said through a hitch of pain. Then he laughed at Bear's snort. "He already had to pay Ivo off just to get let into the house." The burning began anew. "Okay, yeah. Pills would be good. And maybe a bottle of whiskey."

"No alcohol," Bear called back as he headed toward the kitchen.

"You okay?" Rob eased himself onto the ottoman, careful to steer clear of Mace. "Shit, I didn't even—"

"No regrets. Okay?" Mace tried to lean forward, but another stroke of pain poured down his arm. "I'd ask for a kiss to make it better, but I think all that's going to do is make me hard again."

"Dude, your brother's going to come right back. I don't want him catching us doing anything else."

"I think Bear knows I'm not a virgin. Pretty certain he knows you're not one either." Mace chuckled. "House rules are no sex in common areas. I'm pretty sure Rey and Gus have christened the kitchen counters and maybe the stairs. You and I just kissed."

"Yeah, almost broke you while doing it." Rob ducked his head back when Bear returned with a handful of pills and a glass of pink juice. "I'd stay and keep you company, but I've got a customer coming down in a little bit for a second session, and well, Bear's here, so it's not like I can call out sick. How about this? I can give you a call when I'm on break for lunch. It'll be around four o'clock. Maybe by then your arm will feel better and you'll have forgiven me for punching you in the shoulder."

"I've got something better to suggest," Bear interrupted. "How about if you ride down with me for the shift? And when it's done, I'll bring you back up here and you can have dinner with us."

"That sounds like an excellent idea." Mace grinned up at Bear. The throbbing in his shoulder was diminishing, but he chased after it with the painkillers Bear brought over for him. He hated the bitter taste on his tongue nearly as much as he did the numbing crash he would have in about ten minutes. "I'm going to be useless to the world in a little bit, but if you can swing dinner, I promise I'll try to remain conscious through it."

Rob's face creased with another soul-brightening smile, and Mace heartily wished his brother to go either to hell or possibly another city—someplace far enough away to give Mace time to kiss Rob senseless once again.

"It's a date." Rob dug through the plastic bag and came up with a wrapped burrito. "So, we're back to our original question of what burrito do you want? Carne asada, carnitas, or the pollo asado quesadilla? And don't ask me what I want. I'm going to get whatever is left over, because Bear's my boss and I owe him for not killing me when I nearly tore off your arm. Well, and for the dinner invite, because so far, other than your kiss, that's the best thing that's happened to me today."

ARGUMENTS WERE commonplace in Mace's family. Some people had pancakes on Sunday. Other families had movie nights together. Mace's band of brothers pretty much guaranteed a disagreement about something minor would flare up at least once a week. Normally cooler heads prevailed and the loser in the argument skulked off to sulk for a few hours and then came back and pretended like nothing happened.

This time was different, or at least for Mace it was. This time he wasn't going to give in, even if he was the only one on that side of the battle.

Because he was going to be damned if he didn't move back into his own apartment soon.

"Look, let's discuss this rationally," Luke said as he leaned over the back of the couch. "If you're going to have a family meeting, we have to agree—*again*—to hear each other out."

He'd been in the sun lately, probably working the raised gardens at the center he started for their young clients to care for and take home fresh vegetables. His cheekbones were slightly pinked, but the rest of his face had already deepened to a rich gold, adding a luster to his dark eyes. He was using his counseling voice, a smooth baritone meant to ease a troubled person into talking. At the moment the only thing Luke accomplished was to piss Mace off.

"This *isn't* a family meeting." Mace's objection appeared to fall on deaf ears, especially when the others murmured to agree with Luke. Pacing near one end of the sectional, he cleared his throat, but none of the brothers paid any attention to him.

"It's been a bit more than two weeks, right? The doctors say he's shown progress, but I'd rather wait until he's at least mostly done with physical therapy before we make any decisions about moving back in," Bear pronounced as he crossed his meaty arms over his chest. Behind him, a soccer game silently played on the big-screen television mounted to the wall, cutting to a cat food commercial featuring a singing tabby. "Suppose something happens and one of us isn't around?"

"I am literally standing right in front of you, so stop talking about me as if I'm in a coma in the other room." Mace lightly shoved at Bear to get his attention and schooled his face not to wince when he realized he'd used his injured arm to push at what was basically a mountain of muscle anchored to the family room floor. "It's been weeks since I was shot, and even the doctors say I'm healing great. With any luck I'll be back on the line before you know it and hopefully be able to play on the station's softball team next quarter."

"I think the question to ask is has he been cleared for sex? Because you know damn well he's not going to do it with Rob *here*. Not with all of us around," Gus piped up from his corner of the couch. "It's hard enough for me and Rey, and I'm not even on the floor with the rest of the bedrooms."

"Trust me, we know when the two of you are going at it," Ivo drawled from his spot on the sectional's arm and then rolled his eyes when Gus flipped him off. "We can all hear you. The neighbors' fucking deaf cat can hear you. It's like Rey is fucking an air-raid siren."

"You can't hear us. The walls are too thick," Gus protested, but his argument sounded weaker as he went along. He glanced at Bear and asked, "You can't, right?"

Bear unfolded his arms and then wiggled his hand back and forth. "Depends."

"Depends?" Ivo sneered. "The only way you can't hear them is if you're in *Oakland*."

"Can we stop talking about Gus and focus on why we're all here?" Luke sighed. "We're trying to decide if Mace should move back to Chinatown right now or wait a little bit."

"Okay, let me repeat this again," Mace groaned as he rubbed at the tension headache forming between his eyebrows. "You all do not have a say in this. I'm moving back home. I love being here, and I love you guys, but in order for me to continue loving you guys, I need to get the fuck out before I kill you. Rob has nothing to do with it, although Ivo is right, Gus. Yes, we can hear you. The walls are thick, but you are probably the loudest one of us. But since Bear hasn't had a date since forever, he's kind of out of the running.

"I want to sleep in my own bed, listening to my own neighborhood. I want to be able to write in my own space, maybe finish that damned book, and Mrs. Hwang—Grandma Yu—is coming back home in a week, so I want to be there to help her get settled." Mace quieted with a stern look. "Why can't you guys get it through your heads?"

"Maybe because they haven't found your father?" Ivo's steady gaze caught Mace unaware. "As long as that asshole is out there, he could take you away from us, and I'm sorry if it's screwing up your love life, because I know you've been spending a lot of time with Rob, but I couldn't really give a shit. I'd rather you be sexually frustrated and alive than have gotten your rocks off right before we have to bury you."

It was always their youngest who yanked off any bandage covering a particularly tender scab. Maybe it was Ivo's confidence or brash personality, but he could always be depended upon to walk right in where angels feared to tread. The past few weeks of living in the Ashbury Heights house were wearing down Mace's nerves. His frustration at having to steal bits of privacy to spend with Rob was growing, along with his impatience with his doctors to medically clear him. The aches only came when he moved wrong and after a long round of PT. His anger at being unable to go on runs with Rey and having to stop after a few kisses with Rob only made matters worse.

"He already tried to take my life once," Mace said quietly. "Actually a few times, but can't you guys see that I can't let him win? I need things to go back to normal, or at least move past getting shot. Yes, I would love to have sex with Rob. But I'd also love to play tag with Rey or go boxing with Bear."

"Yeah, I'm not so sure you weren't shot in the head if that's something you miss," Luke commented. "Who in their right mind gets into a boxing ring with Bear?"

"Distraction technique," Gus pointed out. "Ivo's right. And you know how much it hurts me to say that, but we feel safer with you here."

"Yeah, I know, but you've got to understand something, Gus." Mace slung an arm around Ivo's shoulders and leaned on him. "I'm not going to go back to living behind closed doors because of my father, so tomorrow night I'll be having Rob over for dinner in my own apartment, and *none* of you are invited."

"I know you like Rob, Mace, but you've got to ask yourself something," Bear rumbled. "Is it worth the risk being someplace your father's hurt you before? Is *he*?"

"I don't know if he is, but I am." He exhaled and then gave his brother a soft smile. "I've got to start living for me, Bear. Because if I don't, then nothing I do matters, even falling in love with Rob."

Eighteen

"Do you have any candles?" Ivo shouted from the back of the apartment. "I can't find any candles."

"What the fuck do I need candles for?" Mace crouched and flung open the kitchen cabinet he used to store odds and ends. It was useless for storing anything he'd use on a day-to-day basis, just a corner slot with a deep recess that ran along the wall, so he'd stacked it with half-full plastic tubs. He'd marked each tub with a few words in black marker on masking tape, but none of them said *candles*. Muttering, he pulled each one out and laid them on the floor by his feet. "I've got three labeled *kitchen stuff*. That tells me fucking nothing. What the hell does kitchen stuff mean? What was I thinking? And why the hell is he in the bedroom looking for damned candles?"

"Because, asshole, Rey's got more romance in his cutoff toenails than you do in your whole body." Ivo padded in, holding up a pair of candlesticks with half-burned white taper candles. "Why the hell are you cleaning your kitchen *now*? Rob's going to be here in a bit. You're not even dressed."

"I told him casual." Mace glanced down at his perfectly good pair of 501s and his SFFD T-shirt. "Don't give me that look. I even shaved."

"Why did you invite me here to help you if you're not going to let me help you?" Ivo rested his hip against the kitchen counter.

"Because you're good at all of this kind of shit. You read romance novels, for fuck's sake." Mace began to stack the bins back into the cupboard, only to discover they didn't fit anymore. "How the hell did all of this get in there?"

"I'll put all of that away. Just go change your clothes into something dressier. Maybe put some cologne on." Ivo put the candlesticks down and stepped aside. "What are you waiting for? Go change your clothes."

It pained him to admit it, but Mace swallowed his pride and muttered, "I kind of need help getting up. I can't push up with my shoulder yet. Just give me your hand."

"Jesus, you're a mess." Ivo was smaller but had a core strength Mace could only admire, especially when he didn't seem to struggle at all when he helped Mace get up off the floor. "If you end up in the hospital because you and Rob do some funky-ass shit tonight, don't come crawling to me. You call Bear and eat every bit of crow that he's going to serve you. And then we're all going to kick Rob's ass, because he should know better."

"Unlike you, I can go for months without sex." Mace rubbed at his sore shoulder. "Did you guys ever think I might want to have a little privacy? Not everything is about sex."

"Then all I have to say to you is you have some pretty shitty sex," Ivo snapped back. "And don't go all Amish on me. I've been with you at the clubs. You hook up all the time."

"Not since... actually, a few months after Rob started."

His admission made Ivo's eyes go wide and made him laugh. "See, you've had a hard-on for him since he started? And all this time I thought he just pissed you off."

"He did. The shit he did would get under my skin, and he would irritate the fuck out of me." Mace regretted his shrug as soon as he did it and rolled his arm back to release the twinge. "And that's all you're going to get out of me, baby brother."

"Actually, what I'd like you to get out of are those fucking jeans. If they had any more holes in them, I could use them to strain spaghetti." Ivo bent down and began arranging the bins into the cupboard. "Just come back out here looking like you'd be good enough to eat off of. And while you're at it, brush your damn hair. You're looking a little shaggy."

WHEN MACE returned, he wouldn't go so far as to say Ivo's sigh was heavy, but had they been on a pirate ship, it would've pushed them past Tortuga and straight into the Gulf of Mexico. There wasn't much in his closet, so Mace finally settled on a pair of black jeans and a button-down Marshall's Amp bowling shirt he'd won in a raffle a few years back. Holding up the only two bottles of cologne he owned, Mace waited for Ivo to respond.

"Fine, you can keep the jeans, but I'm going to find you something to wear in Rey's closet. Right now you look like you're about to go do battle with Danny and the rest of the T-birds," Ivo grumbled and brushed past Mace. "And after you change *again*, use the Cool Cotton cologne. But just spritz it and walk through the mist. Don't actually spray it on you."

"I know how to put on cologne," he objected, mentally storing away the knowledge. "Food should be here shortly. Let me put the oven on warm so it'll keep until he gets here."

The apartment's speakers burbled and thundered with Mace's favorite thunderstorm track. They'd spent more than two hours scrubbing the place down until Ivo threatened Mace with bodily harm and the toothbrush he'd been given to get at the grout in the spare bathroom.

Standing in the kitchen, Mace frowned at how worn out his couches were, but they were hand-me-downs from the main house when they all chipped in to buy the enormous sectional. He toyed with leaving the windows open, torn between the oddness of the storm playing over the speakers and the sometimes-raucous chatter of the bars down below.

The table he normally used to write at was cleared off and laid out with two place settings, complete with wine and water glasses Ivo had polished to a sparkle. He'd found the only two sets of complete utensils Mace had and let himself be convinced it was okay to mix and match the plates. There'd been a short, hot debate about Mace popping down to Grandma Yu's to borrow pieces of her everyday china—Mace for, Ivo against—before they finally decided neither one of them wanted to risk breaking anything that didn't belong to them.

Mace glanced down at his toes and suddenly panicked at the sight of his bare feet. Concerned, he called out to Ivo, "Should I put on shoes? Is that too weird? I don't ever wear shoes in the house. Maybe I should put on some socks. Or is that too weird?"

"You're wearing a faded bowling shirt you got from an old stoner who was giving away shit out of his storage unit as prizes at his coffee shop," Ivo reminded him as he walked back into the living room. "And now you worry about your feet? Fuck that. He's not going to care. Put shoes on. Don't put shoes on. What I want you to do is change your fucking shirt. Try this blue one. And if that doesn't work, we've got the green for backup."

"That's green? Looks kind of grayish." Mace caught the long-sleeved henley Ivo tossed at his head.

"And that's why you're not a tattoo artist." Ivo made a slight grimace. "Okay, not just because you can't see colors but because you can't draw for shit. And I'm pretty sure the sight of blood makes you queasy."

"Just *my* blood. I see bloody people all of the time. It's kind of my job." He stripped off his shirt, tossed it onto the couch, and then worked the henley over his head. "It's too tight."

"Unbutton the collar, you fricking idiot," Ivo scolded. "Seriously. How have you survived as long as you have?"

"Because my goal in life is to dance on your grave," Mace muttered. The henley was soft, a deep ocean blue, and it fit snugly across his chest and upper arms. Pushing the sleeves up made it feel more comfortable, and as he was about to tuck it into his jeans, Ivo hissed at him.

"Do not tuck that shirt in. I swear to God, you are like a suburban dad in training. Do you need me to get you a fanny pack?" Ivo sneered. "Maybe you do need those socks. I can run down to the corner and maybe get you some sandals to wear with them. Have you always been this uncool? How the hell have you ever gotten laid?"

"I do just fine. Fuck you." He lifted his arms up and twisted to check the fit of the shirt. "You don't think this is too tight?"

"Even as shot to shit as you are, your body is the best thing you have going for you, because right now, your brain has left the building." Ivo tugged down the hem and stepped back to get a better look. "Quit fussing with it. You look good. It's a nice color for you, matches your eyes. And God, you have hairy toes. If you weren't so tall, I would say you were Gandalf's second choice for the trip to the volcano."

"Fuck. I told you I needed to put on shoes. I just don't wear them in the house because of the floors." The doorbell rang just as Mace was about to head to his bedroom. "Shit. That's probably the food. Let me sign for it, and if you could throw it in the oven so it doesn't get cold, I'll go put on some sneakers."

"Who cares what you have on your feet?" Ivo threw his hands up. "Is this like your first date *ever*?"

"Yeah, it is. I don't date." He opened the door, still half facing his brother. "I didn't even go to my prom. Up until right now, my idea of a date was knowing the guy's last name."

"It's Claussen," Rob said, holding up a repurposed cardboard box filled with Chinese food. "And if it makes you feel any better, I didn't go to my prom either. But that's mostly because the guy I was dating at the time was voted prom king, and he didn't want his cheerleader girlfriend to know I existed. Hey, Ivo. So, it's a threesome tonight?"

"Nope, I just had to get him dressed and upright." Ivo grabbed his leather jacket off of the couch. "The bowling shirt over there is a reject. You can thank me later. Make sure he doesn't drink anything alcoholic. And Mace, your next round of meds is in an hour and a half or once you start puking from pain."

"Thank you for helping," Mace ground out. "And the pain isn't that bad. I'm not puking."

"You will be if the two of you do anything more than eat and talk," Ivo warned as he slid past Rob and Rob edged out of the doorway and into the apartment. "Try not to kill him, Claussen. Pretend you're religious and saving yourself for marriage."

"Hey, umm… *hi*." It took Mace a second to break his brain off its quest for shoes and focus on the smirking man holding their dinner. "Come on in. Here, let me take that. I can't believe he let you sign for it. Usually he's an asshole about it when Ivo's around."

"I think that has more to do with Ivo than him," Rob said, but he angled the box away from Mace. "You've still got to pay for this."

"They have my card on file. It's already been charged." Mace frowned. "You didn't give him any money, did you? I should probably call them—"

"It's a good thing you're pretty." He chuckled, toeing off his Vans. "Let me go put this in the kitchen and you can pay me with a kiss."

The throb in Mace's shoulder was quickly forgotten, burned away by the sight of Rob's ass in a pair of blue jeans so tight they should have been illegal. His thin burnt-orange cotton T-shirt was the kind of casually distressed garment Mace knew probably cost at least two tanks of gas, if not more. He'd done something different with his hair, a less stylized version of the aggressive spikes he wore at the shop, and the tips appeared more purple than cobalt.

His full, lush mouth tasted the same, and Mace found himself cupping Rob's face, holding him still so he could savor every last moment of their kiss.

They pulled apart, gasping for breath, but remained close enough for their foreheads to touch. A hint of orange lingered in Mace's mouth, and Rob's breath ghosted a citrus scent in the warmed air between them. Mace allowed his hands to roam slowly down Rob's stocky chest, over his sides, and then farther downward to Rob's ass. Rob's hands made their own journey, stroking the length of Mace's spine, pinching his butt. Then he laughed at Mace's mock outrage.

"You grabbed my ass first," he teased and bit at Mace's lower lip. "Now don't take this wrong, because you're making me want to do bad things to you—which I shouldn't—but I am really fucking hungry, and whatever you ordered smells damned good."

"It's been a few weeks," Mace grumbled, not ready to let go of the delectable man in his arms. "Shouldn't I be healed up enough?"

"Dude, when I had my wisdom teeth taken out, it took me two weeks before I could eat anything firmer than orange Jell-O and soft tofu." Rob slowly extracted himself but stole a quick kiss before he pulled away. "You were *shot*. I'm surprised your brothers even let you move out of the house."

"Yeah, *that* was an argument." He was going to have to be satisfied with the kiss and maybe a few more, but just having Rob in his apartment seemed to stir up things inside him that Mace couldn't readily identify. "Well, why don't we dish out some plates and we can eat."

"Table looks nice. Kind of formal for you and me, but nice." Rob glanced about the apartment. "But what's with the army of candles on the kitchen counter?"

THE TABLE was left untouched. Its glittering utensils and mismatched dinnerware framed a centerpiece of white baby mums and lavender sprigs, and a quartet of candles eventually made it to keep the flowers company, but as pretty as everything was, the chairs looked too uncomfortable for Mace to sit on for any length of time. Or at least that's what Rob thought when he suggested they eat their dinner on the beaten-up couches in the living room.

Mace's broad coffee table became their buffet, and a couple of wide, low noodle bowls seemed a lot easier to handle there than Mace's stoneware plates. It also allowed Rob to sit next to Mace. They pulled their legs up onto the cushions, and their bare feet touched as they ate.

Rob recognized most of the food nearly brimming over the red-pagoda-emblazoned white takeout boxes, but there were a couple of surprises. The crispy boneless pressed duck with its tangy hoisin sauce was a luxurious delight on his tongue, slightly fatty but thick with a smoky tea flavor. Its skin nearly melted in his mouth, and the freshly made hot bao accompanying it gave a slightly sweet yeasty counterpoint to its richness. The noodles in the beef and chicken chow fun were definitely handmade, cooked just enough to grab at the savory sauce but retain enough heft to fold around the meats instead of falling apart when bitten. A container of flash-fried eggplant in black bean sauce had enough garlic in it to ward off an entire bus of vampires, but it was the crackling pork and fiddleheads Rob couldn't seem to get enough of.

They ate in silence for about ten minutes, and then Mace asked Rob how his day went. A brief discussion of art and how Mace's lack of color sense guaranteed he would never work the shop in any capacity other than taking money and making appointments led to Rob discovering what he figured was Mace's biggest secret.

"You write?" Rob tried to keep the surprise out of his voice, but it flooded through. "Okay, I sound really shitty here, but I never would have thought you wrote. That's kind of awesome. What do you write? Can I read it?"

"It's not shitty. I don't look like somebody who writes. I guess? I never thought about putting anything down until Ivo suggested it." Mace picked at the food on his plate and gave Rob a quick, bashful glance. "And no, you don't want to read it. It's *crap*."

"Okay, so let me ask you something." He dug a sliver of duck out from under a pile of noodles. "If Gus or Ivo said that about their stuff back when they started drawing, would you let them, or would you jump on their asses?"

The flare of heat in Mace's blue eyes was enough for Rob to know he'd hit his mark, and he sat back and chewed his duck morsel as smugly as he could.

"I… I would tell you fuck off, but that's not something I want you to do." Mace stretched to stab a *gau gee* from one of the containers, the fork wobbling slightly in his hand. His wince was nearly imperceptible, but Rob felt Mace's legs tense up when he sat back.

"You know, if you want something, I can get it for you." Rob gestured at the containers with his chopsticks. "You're hurt. I don't know why we have to keep telling you that. You would think the pain would remind you, but you keep overdoing things. And I know a lot of it's because you don't want to ask for help, but sometimes you've got to ask for help."

"It's kind of hard. When you're in foster homes, you spend most of your time trying not to be seen," Mace murmured and broke the fried dumpling in half against the flat of the bowl with his fork. "I know there are a lot of kids who—especially now—find a place with the families they're put with, but it's not really your place, not really your family."

"I still don't understand why your mom didn't take you back," he said as he set his bowl down on the table. "And I don't mean to slag her, but you're her kid. I mean, even as passive as my mother is, she would still fight for me if I'd been taken. I guess I don't understand how she could just walk away. You're a bit complicated, but you're a really solid guy. And I know I'm seeing you now and not then, but shit, I guess I just don't understand."

"I don't either. Can you put this down for me?" Mace let Rob take his bowl away, and he edged it into a spot between the containers. "Thanks."

Rob moved closer, sat sideways between Mace's parted legs, and slung his thigh over Mace's shin. He was careful not to put any weight against Mace's sling, and it was hard not to fold Mace into a tight embrace to chase out the pain and sorrow flickering over his face. He traced Mace's beautiful mouth with his fingertips and let his thumb slide over Mason's strong chin.

"I haven't heard from her in a long time, really. I think in her mind she'd already accepted that he'd killed me or changed me so much that she wouldn't recognize me, wouldn't—*couldn't*—love me," Mace whispered, his breath ghosting over Rob's palm. "She has a new family and kids who aren't touched by my father's craziness. You were there. You saw him. If she'd taken me back, she would've been stuck with him for as long as she lived. I'm the only thing that connects him to her, so I don't know if I can blame her for cutting me out of her life. He's violent and unpredictable. Who would want that around their family? Especially since I turned out exactly like him."

"I don't know if you've noticed this, but I'm a bit darker than you are." Rob tugged at Mace's lower lip and forced his mouth into a smile. "I'm a mutt, and you seem to be perfectly fine being with me. You call an older Chinese woman grandmother, and your best friend is Latino. You have a brother who likes to dress in skirts and high heels. And if I have to remind you about this, then I'm in for an uphill battle in this relationship, but your entire fucking family is made up of gay men. So, you're going to have to explain to me exactly how you turned out like him. Because I don't see it.

"What I think is your mother is selfish and a coward." He expected Mace to narrow his eyes since he'd just insulted his mother, but Rob hated the resignation in Mace's voice. "You needed her. You needed your mother to make your life normal and okay again, and instead she tossed you into a social service system that doesn't always have a kid's best interests in mind. The best thing to come out of that situation was you found Bear and discovered a bunch of guys you could call your brothers, which led you to me."

"So what you're saying is my life was the way it was just so I would be led to you?" Mace leaned his head back and eyed Rob skeptically. "It was a pretty shitty childhood. You better be really worth it."

"I am." Rob brushed his mouth over Mace's. "And I'm going to enjoy showing you that you're worth it too."

NINETEEN

"AT LEAST there was no earth-shattering kaboom," Ivo consoled himself while Mace began wiping off the cabinets. "I mean, the lid held."

"Yeah, good thing. It's awesome how the steam release chittered around like a lawn sprinkler. Now we've got tuna-casserole juice all over the kitchen." Mace glanced down at the sudden weight against his shin. "And the dog is licking the oven door. *Earl*! *Get out*!"

"It looks like soup. I probably put in too much liquid." As far as Mace could see, Ivo was not making any movement toward grabbing a paper towel or sponge to help. Instead he was peering down into the tall steel insert of the combination slow/pressure cooker. "Should I dump it and start over? Or try to fix it?"

"You should pick up a sponge and wipe down the damned counter." He could ignore the tiny ache in his shoulder, but he had to stop the dog's slinking back into the kitchen. He would have to use the big guns, a rare command meant to warn Earl that he was one step away from being in the laundry room behind a baby gate while they finished cleaning up. "Earl, *beanbag*!"

At least Earl recognized Mace's authority and stopped in his tracks before his feet touched the fish-peas-pasta water splattered over the floor. Earl met Mace's gaze and then schlepped off to plop on the leopard-print beanbag he'd been ordered to.

The multifunction cooker should've only held eight quarts of anything, but judging from the milky lakes on the counters and the rivulets pouring down the front of the cabinets, Ivo seemed to have folded space and crammed a kiddies' wading pool into the pot.

"How many of us are here tonight? And before you start yelling at me, *look*." Ivo waved a slightly damp sponge under Mace's nose. "At least I took off my boots. I got some that match the dog's beanbag. Pretty hefty, and they've got a great heel, but I would've fallen on my ass with all this water."

"Just. Clean. The counter," Mace ground out. Then he shook his head when Ivo flipped him off. "The shit you wear."

Ivo shrugged, wiped down the backsplash, and then moved on to the rice cooker. "I like to wear different stuff. You know what else I like? Takeout. Or delivery. Either one."

"I'm not getting down on you for what you wear. Just scared you're going to break your neck on those heels." The pot was still warm, and a quick peek confirmed Ivo's diagnosis—their dinner was pretty much soup. "It's just you, me, Bear, and Rob was coming over. Maybe pizza."

"Chinese?" Ivo wrinkled his nose. "Had pizza for lunch. Or here's an idea, why don't you guys go out? Like someplace fancy? Where you have to shower and maybe wear pants."

"Okay, that's rich coming from you. How many times did I have to make you go turn around and put on leggings or something under the skirts you wanted to wear to school?" Mace reminded him.

"So they were a little short. I was experimenting." He shrugged off Mace's words as easily as he had when he was a teenager. "Why are you picking on what I used to wear? It's been weeks since you were shot. Isn't it about time you and Rob did something other than play video games and watch old movies?"

"Because you don't learn. Now it's the heels. Back then, it was the skirts and booty shorts. You were going to freeze your nuts off. It was the middle of winter. Short was the least of—" The doorbell rang, and Earl burst out of his exile. His booming bark rattled the walls. Tossing his sponge into the sink, Mace ordered, "Keep cleaning. I'll go see who that is."

And once again the dog proved to be more mindful than his little brother, because Ivo followed him down the front hall and straight to the door.

"Do you listen to anything I say?" Mace muttered at his brother. "Because I swear to God, I say turn left and you turn right."

"The doctor just cleared you to wash your own ass with that arm. If there's somebody at the door and you need help, what are you going to do?" Ivo grabbed Earl's collar, and the muscles in his forearm bulged as he held the strong dog back. "You going to ask him? He'll lick somebody to death before he ever bites them."

"Just keep Earl inside." Mace opened the door as the bell went off again. "And back up a bit."

"Jesus, we have an eyehole thingy. At least check to see who's there first. It could be…." His brother's admonishment stuttered and then trailed off. Mace glanced back, but Ivo's attention was pinned to the man standing on their stoop.

He was a cop. Mace had been around just as many cops as firemen. They had a blue-red sibling rivalry bolstered by one-upmanship and boasting. He worked with a floater who was the only fireman in a family of cops, and the stories that guy could tell over a beer were legendary, especially when his siblings showed up at the pub and turned the tables on him. Cops had a set stance to them—an anchor of authority when they stood and spoke—and this one was no different. He commanded attention, squared off on the cement slab at the top of the short stack of stairs that led to the sidewalk. His flinty gaze fixed on Mace for a brief moment and then settled on Ivo.

Ivo, who'd gone stiff and cautious next to him.

The plainclothes cop flashed a gold star and held his billfold up for Mace to study, but his light green eyes never left Ivo's face. He was dressed for San Francisco's fluctuating weather, in a long leather coat over a gray cable-knit sweater and a pair of black jeans. His cowboy boots were worn in—a dark sienna nearly the color of his slightly unkempt hair. Its silver-shot strands brushed back from his aggressively masculine face, and the ends flowed over the collar of his jacket.

At some point his nose had been victim to a couple of right hooks, but his long dark lashes and full lower lip softened his harsh features. His face looked lived-in and openly wore his years with a hint of crow's-feet at his eyes and a two-inch-long scar running under his chin. About Mace's height, he was lankier, mostly leg with a hint of a bow to his knees, but his hard, assessing stare would be enough to give anyone pause.

"I'm Detective Ruan Nicholls. Are you Mason Crawford?" His voice was deep—a hint of Midwest and "rolling, dark waters chased with a shot of bourbon" deep. Giving Ivo one last glance, he turned his attention to Mace and tucked his billfold away. "Is that you?"

"Yeah." A panic hit Mace. He reached for his phone and was alarmed at the emptiness in his pocket. There were very few reasons for a cop to show up in the middle of the afternoon, and most of them would involve his brothers. Tamping down the fear rising in him, Mace blindly reached back and clasped Ivo's forearm in case the cop was bringing trouble to their door. "What's wrong? What happened?"

"I don't know if you want to have this conversation in front of your boyfriend," Nicholls said gruffly. "When I called your station to see if you were on shift, I spoke to a guy named Montenegro who told me you're up here, but he didn't tell me you had company. I don't want to take up too much of your time, but if you want this done in private—"

"My boyfriend?" Mace was confused until he caught Nicholls looking at Ivo standing behind him. "No, that's my brother, Ivo. Do you want to come inside? Is everything okay? My other brothers are down at the shop. Well, two of them are, but Luke… shit, did something happen to Luke?"

Ivo tugged free of Mace's wrist. "Let go. I'll get the car keys."

Mace moved aside to usher the detective in, but Nicholls only stepped over the threshold and stood in front of the open door. Earl slunk off, his head and shoulders down as he bumped the back of Ivo's legs. There was no traffic on the street, but Mace couldn't remember where he'd put his keys or even if he trusted himself to drive.

"Anything you need to say, you can say in front of Ivo too," Mace got out.

"Your brothers are fine. This is about your father. Your case was transferred to me a couple of hours ago. I work homicide." Nicholls's stern face turned into a mask of professional sympathy. "I know your situation is complicated, and I wanted to reach out to you in person, a personal courtesy to someone who works the line. There's no easy way to say this, but your father was brought in with multiple gunshot wounds last night by EMTs working Chinatown. He never regained consciousness, and by the time they ID'd him, he'd passed away. I know it's difficult, and you're probably experiencing a lot of emotions right now, but I wanted to tell you that face-to-face. It's the least the SFPD can do for you… the least I can do for you. I want you to know that I'm going to continue to work the case, and we're looking for the other man who assaulted you. Normally now I would say that I'm sorry for your loss—"

"No, it's okay," Mace shakily cut in. It was strange to find an emptiness opening up in his chest, and he nearly staggered with the rush of bitterness that filled it. He didn't know what to ask or what to say, and the cop seemed to be waiting for something when all Mace could think about was how happy he was that none of his brothers were hurt or, worse, lying in a morgue waiting for him to identify them. The finality of that thought jerked Mace back to his father. "Do you need me to come down and ID him or something? I don't think there's anybody else. I don't know."

"No. We have his fingerprints and dental records from his incarceration records, so you don't have to go down there if you don't want to," Nicholls said. "Someone might be contacting you about receiving his remains. Like I said, your situation is complicated, but we don't want to assume you wouldn't want responsibility. You don't have to make that decision now. It'll be a few weeks to process the body, and since it's still an open investigation, we'll want to gather as much evidence as possible. Someone murdered him, and it's a good bet it's the man who shot you. I want to make sure that guy is off the street.

"If you need anything or if you have any questions, here's my card." The detective held out an all-too-familiar SFPD business card embossed with the police department's shield and his contact information. "I doubt his partner in crime is going to stick around, but if you do see him, call me right away. I have your phone number from the report, so I'll let you know how the case is going in a couple of days. Until then, don't be afraid to call, and with any luck, the next time you hear from me, it'll be because I caught him."

THE CITY lights bleached out the night sky above their not-so-ramshackle house on the hill and whipped swirls of gold into the deep blue canopy. A hint of rosemary and lemon was in the air, evidence that their gardening attempts were at least semi-successful, the bed of herbs thickening and the citrus trees they planted at the foot of the slope in the yard bearing fruit despite Earl's assistance in watering them. The deck's wood railing was rough beneath Mace's forearms, an indication that the sealant probably hadn't taken. Behind him the house groaned and sighed as the cold evening air crept into its sun-warmed bones.

Inside, the excited shouts of his young nephew playing with an equally thrilled Earl broke the weighty silence he'd walked into a few minutes before. They'd talked around the news of his father's death and instead had a hard spangly clatter of conversation revolving around nothing heavier than a client who'd wanted a Tasmanian Devil inked on the back of his skull. The punch line of Bear's story came with a cockeyed Tweety Bird tattoo revealed once they shaved the guy's head— apparently the forgotten souvenir of a misspent summer in Las Vegas.

Mace laughed when he was supposed to, checked the door periodically when he heard a car drive past, and finally excused himself from the family room to get some fresh air.

He didn't turn when he heard the screen door slam shut against the frame, thinking it was one of his brothers. But then a pair of slightly chilled hands slid up under his shirt. Rob's cheek pressed against his back felt like heaven, and he sighed contentedly when Rob slid his arms around his waist.

"I'm sorry," Rob mumbled into Mace's shirt. "And before you say anything, you should know that I'm sorry you didn't get a chance to have a real dad. I mean, not like mine is a treat but… I'm just sorry. Okay?"

He leaned back into Rob until their bodies were pressed against one another and then let go another sigh. "You know what the hardest thing is?"

"No," Rob replied, his words a soft brush of air on Mace's neck. "What is it?"

"I don't really know how to feel or what to think," Mace admitted with a short laugh. "One minute I'm arguing with Ivo because he's blown the kitchen up trying to cook tuna casserole with that pressure-pot thing Bear bought, and in the next minute, a man with a gold star comes by to say someone has killed my biggest nightmare, slayed my metaphorical dragon, and the man I might have to thank for that is the one who tried to kill me. And in the middle of all of that, I *miss* my mother."

Rob turned him around with an insistent tug of hands on his waist, but Mace didn't resist. Slouched slightly against the railing, he was nearly Rob's height, and he parted his legs so Rob could nestle between them. The chilly air began to nibble at the still-healing muscles and tendons in his shoulder, but Mace didn't want to go inside. Mace couldn't stand another moment of brittle noise, churned up only to break the uncomfortable quiet as his brothers scrambled to think of what to say.

They held each other for maybe a minute or two, and then Rob heaved a shuddering sigh.

"Did you call her? I mean, does she know?" Rob asked. His eyes were cognac and stars, a romantic sunset hue in the oddly flattering lantern lights they'd installed on the anchor posts of the railing, and Mace could think of a million things he would rather have been doing that evening with Rob instead of sorting through the ramifications of his father's murder. "Did the cops tell you they called her?"

"I left a message on the number I have, but it's a work phone, so I don't know if she's even going to get it until tomorrow." The distance his mother put between them stretched out to an impossible chasm, and Mace stared down into that dark abyss and wondered if his mother was as dead to him as his father was. "I'm always the one reaching out to her. We talk for a few minutes, and then she finds herself late for a meeting or has to run an errand. I think I have to accept that I have no place in her life, and I think that hurts more than anything. Thing is, she walked away from me years ago, and I'm still chasing after her. Maybe it's time I let her go too."

"Wait and see what she says. Not because you need her but because she's missing out on someone who's worked really hard and accomplished so fucking much. If she doesn't see it, then that's her problem." Rob brushed his nose against his, a spot of warm on Mace's cold skin. "And as clichéd as this sounds, you do have all of those assholes in there—not the kid, he's cool but… maybe the dog counts—and me. Unlike the first time she walked away from you, you're not alone. You have every single one of us."

Rob's mouth on the edge of his lips seared a line of heat that poured down Mace's torso. He wanted to crawl into the comfort of Rob's body, bask in the warmth of his golden skin and bright white smile. He loved the feel of Rob's nails raking up his sides, and when Rob tugged at the hem of Mace's shirt, he didn't mind the cold bite along his ribs, because Rob's fingers soon chased it away.

They were hidden in the partial shadows, cloaked in an unfamiliar privacy. At any moment Mace expected one of his brothers to come through the back door, a rolling gruffness to tease them apart. But from the sounds coming through the slight crack of the open kitchen window, it seemed that his brothers had settled down in the family room to wait things out.

He explored the back of Rob's T-shirt and worked his hands under an oversized SFFD hoodie that Rob stole from the back seat of Mace's car a few weeks ago. The gray fleece was ratty, and the patches stitched on the sleeves were slightly faded by sun and saltwater exposure from fishing down at the pier, but Rob apparently didn't care. Mace got a curious delight from walking into the shop and finding Rob wearing it, its too-long sleeves rolled up past his sinewy forearms so he could work unhindered.

Now the hoodie was in his way, and Mace could only think of stripping it from Rob's body, along with everything else he was wearing.

"Tonight was supposed to go a lot differently than you coming up here to hold my hand because... of my father," Mace murmured into the crook of Rob's neck. Then he ran the tip of his tongue across the strong pulse beating beneath Rob's skin, blew on the wet spot, and bit it lightly when Rob shivered. "We were supposed to eat a good dinner here and then maybe go to a movie or, I don't know, a bookstore or maybe the Irish pub down by the pier. I wanted to take you home and make love to you tonight. I wanted to spend the night taking care of you, and instead you're here, and I'm not sure if I should be crying just so you have something to wipe away from my face.

"I don't *feel* anything," he admitted, his voice breaking. "I mean, I don't feel anything for him. I feel relieved for myself, for Grandma Yu, and happy that I don't ever have to worry about him coming after you, because I think I was burying the fear he eventually would."

"There's nothing wrong with feeling like that," Rob consoled him and cupped Mace's face in his strong, graceful hands. "You survived him in life. And you shouldn't feel guilty for surviving him in death. The only thing good about him was you. I think I can safely say that. And as much as he tried to break you—even if you think he did—he *didn't*. I mean, you can talk to Luke, because it seems like he's got a whole bunch of degrees and some pretty long words to justify how you're feeling, but I think it's okay for you to be relieved he's gone. Because he can't lock you back in that closet anymore, even if it's only in your mind."

"Now you sound like Luke." Mace couldn't hold back his laughter. It started from the depths of his belly and then worked through his chest to break through the pressure built up there. Wrapping Rob into a tight hug, he breathed in the warm, masculine scents on Rob's skin and hair. "Thank you for pulling me back together, or at least showing me how to get started on it."

"Not a problem," Rob whispered. He stamped his feet. "But I'm getting kind of cold here, and I don't know where this is coming from, but I have a deep need to ask you if you've eaten and if you've taken any of your medication. Because I think with all of this going on, you were more focused on taking care of your brothers than what you needed. Am I right?"

"You might be," he confessed with a wry grin. "Gus and Rey brought pizza with them. They've got Chris tonight, and it seemed like the safest bet. Apparently there's not much difference in eating habits between a three-year-old and a house full of tattoo artists. So, if you like pepperoni-pineapple-jalapeno pizza, I'm pretty sure we have that and maybe something with a lot of meat. I'm going to guess they're counting olives and onions as vegetables tonight."

"I count olives and onions as vegetables every night. Even the jalapenos count." Rob made a face at Mace's disgusted snort. "I only keep in shape to fit into my jeans. You keep in shape because you have to drag people up and down stairs. For you, vegetables are a lifestyle. For me, they're a garnish. So, let's get some pizza and maybe some pills into you, and then let's go back to your place. And if you need me to spend the night holding you so you can get some sleep, I will."

"Might need you for more than one night," Mace whispered.

"Yeah?" Rob tilted his head back and gave Mace a teasing sidelong glance. "How many nights do you need?"

"I don't know," he replied and then gave Rob a gentle kiss. "I'm thinking could be maybe a lifetime of them."

TWENTY

ON WEDNESDAYS Rob welcomed the jangle of the front door's bells as much as he did his first cup of coffee in the morning after a long, hard night. Business was slow enough for Gus, worn out from staying up with his sick kid, to take a nap in the back room. Wednesdays were always slow, but the inclement weather kept people off of the sidewalks, so their drop-in traffic had been nonexistent all day. He had a couple of hours to go until the second shift walked in, and he'd made tentative plans with Mace to grab food at the pub down the street, providing Mace wasn't stuck at the station if they had a call.

And the suckiest thing about a slow Wednesday morning shift was there was only so much art he could do, and Earl wouldn't show up until about six, when Bear came in.

"Couldn't you have at least brought the dog?" Rob grumbled, his complaint directed to Gus, who, being dead asleep and on the other side of the building, couldn't hear him. "My brain is going numb from playing this stupid game on my phone all day. Next time, I'm bringing my tablet so I can at least read."

He'd cleaned the shop in the first hour, to the point of having to open the front door to air out the bleach smell. Then he scrubbed the floor until he worried he was scraping some of the finish off the poured concrete. Organizing his stall took him another hour, mostly restocking and then fiddling with a tattoo machine he felt was sticking. When he glanced over at the other stations, he got an itch to rearrange things there, but he liked his fingers and knew he would be putting them in danger if he so much as breathed on Ivo's equipment. Gus probably wouldn't mind, but he wasn't going to chance it, especially after Gus stumbled in looking like he'd gone on a six-week bender instead of spending the night wiping the sick off of his kid's face.

Another bout of rain brought in a cold wind and the delightfully pungent scent of sea lion, fish, and bus exhaust, so Rob buckled down and closed the door, hoping he didn't asphyxiate himself with the cleaning supplies. After about the third hour, he could see falling exploding jewels when he closed his eyes, and every single one of his tattoo machines hummed like Earl during a belly rub.

So when the bells jingled, Rob was ready to throw himself at the feet of whoever came in and give them any tattoo they wanted for half price.

He spun around on his stool and stood up to greet the shop's first customer of the day, but his breath was stolen by the sight of Mace in a slightly damp white T-shirt, old jeans, and holding two steaming cups of Vietnamese coffee.

"Tell me one of those is for me," Rob whispered, hoping Gus wouldn't wake up so he could drink in both the coffee and Mace by himself. "Your brother's passed out in the art room, so I can't make coffee without going back there and making noise. He apparently had a rough dad night. Don't take this wrong, but I hope the kid got food poisoning, because the last thing I need is the stomach flu. I've got a six-hour session on Saturday, and why are you here so early? It's not even four yet. Aren't you supposed to—"

"They cut me loose. Now, as adorable as you are, these little cardboard sleeves don't do much to hold back the heat, so I'm going to need you to take one of these or I'm going to put it down," Mace interrupted with a chuckle. "And from what I heard, Chris woke up bouncing off the walls and demanding Pop Tarts, so I don't think it's the stomach flu. Take a coffee, give me a kiss, and tell me why you're looking so wild."

The coffee was warm, but Mace's hug was warmer. Rob liked that they were close enough in height so he didn't feel like an Oompa Loompa, a significant change considering the last few guys he dated had towered over him, and he never felt awkward about not having a perfectly cut body or classically beautiful features. Mace made him feel comfortable and appreciated Rob for who he was and what he did.

Standing in the middle of the tattoo shop, Rob realized Mace gave him something no other man had done before—respect. Dating another artist was an exercise in battling egos, a lot of one-upmanship about art and money. Since he'd come into the game older than most, Rob had to work extra hard to carve out a place for himself, and even now, he swallowed down a lot of attitude when Ivo or Gus told him how to do something. Still trying to find his place and his style, he needed a solid home life, but Rob hadn't wanted to tie himself down to a volatile dating situation until Mace shoved his way into his life.

Then Rob's brain seized the words Mace had so casually flung out between them, and his heart clenched. Adorable was an admission of fondness, an almost confession of Mace *liking* Rob in his life. Hearing the bemused humor in the poured heat of Mace's melodic voice pulled Rob up short. They'd come so far from the place they started, and stopped along the way to christen the shop's floor with a bout of hard, hot sex that Rob still jerked off to. It was as though they built their relationship backward, getting the physical out of the way and then scraping down through the layers to discover the men inside.

He *liked* Mace. Rob would have committed to an even stronger emotion, but he didn't know where he stood. There was so much between them—a convoluted tangle of blood, tears, and a violence so horrific Rob couldn't accept that Mace had been raised in it. But they'd come through the horror of it all to a tenderness and honesty Rob never imagined he could share with another man—

Much less Mace Crawford—someone he now felt very comfortable teasing.

"Did you just say you think I'm adorable?" He took the coffee cup and silently agreed that the zarf was purely for show. "Dude, you just don't drop that and then hand a guy his coffee. *Adore* is a word you use for kittens and puppies, and you just used it on me."

"Yeah, I think I did. It just came out." Mace grinned at him and then gave him another quick kiss—again with a nonchalance Rob didn't know how to take from someone who usually spent his life wound up a bit tight. "I know Gus had a rough night. Rey told me all about it today when he came to start his shift."

"Is it one of those things you just say? Like in the South when someone says 'bless her heart' when they really mean 'Jesus, when is she ever going to screw in that lightbulb in her brain?' I'm *adorable*? I'm not sure how I feel about that." Rob grabbed Mace's coffee and easily found an open spot on his station to set both cups down. "Never mind. Don't answer that. I don't think I'm ready to have a conversation just yet. Maybe in a couple of hours, because I need time to absorb and—"

"I don't know where it came from. Look, I have a hard time saying 'you're cute' to the dog. But it just sort of slipped out so… I don't know. I just realized when I came to the door that I really missed you and I was happy to see you. It's not like I said you were precious or anything." He looked around the empty shop. "Do you think you have time to do some work on me? I don't want to take you away from your busy schedule."

"Okay. Did you get hit on the head?" He stood and stared at Mace, not sure if he heard correctly. "Did you just ask me to ink you? On top of the 'you're adorable' shit?"

"You really *are* having a bad day. Yeah, I'm asking you to work on me." Mace stripped off his T-shirt and slowly revealed a long stretch of mouthwatering muscles and golden skin. His jeans hung low on his hips, and the cut of his abdomen disappeared beneath his waistband, along with the light line of hair that trailed down under his navel. "I asked the doctor if it was okay to repair the damage from that gouge I got way before, and he said it should be fine. It shouldn't affect the healing on the other side. So, do you have some time?"

The adorable thing was funny, but Mace asking him to work on his skin was something totally different—it was serious in a way Rob didn't know if he was prepared for. He never—*ever*—imagined putting ink on Mace. He had three experienced, amazing artists for brothers, and he wore some of their best work. Even though the Neo-Traditional knight on his shoulder appeared to be simple, Rob knew better. The balance of the elements and the saturated gradation of the piece were so clean, and they were done when Bear was just starting to ink. If anything, that piece alone marked the standard of ink on Mace's body.

Being asked to touch up anything on it or even to add to what Mace already had was mind-blowing. He'd been cocky when Mace came in the first time, working off steam about something he thought he would never be allowed to do, but there Mace was, shirt off and showing him what needed to be repaired.

"It's that tattoo you have over... *that* scar. You never got Bear to fix it?" Rob stammered, his tongue tripping over the words. "You don't let anyone but family touch you. And you're asking me?"

"Yeah," Mace replied softly and turned around so Rob could see the spot on his powerful back. "I think it's healed over smoothly enough that you could probably fix it. What do you think?"

Mace's damaged skin was a tattoo artist's worst nightmare. There were layers of scar tissue under an elaborate Japanese-style dragon wading through a pond. He hadn't taken the time to appreciate Mace's tattoos during the one time he'd seen him naked on the floor, but Rob had his mind on other things then.

He couldn't yet look at the other side of Mace's back, or at least not without feeling a hell of a lot of guilt. The scar there was fresh, an angry pink that time would eventually soften, but for right now it was a constant reminder of how close he'd come to losing Mace before ever truly having him. Still, Rob silently left a small kiss on the healing spot and chuckled when it made Mace shiver.

The piece itself wasn't large, or at least not as massive as some of the Japanese back work he'd seen come out of the shop. It was definitely Bear's work—an organically flowing piece that followed the line of Mace's shoulder. It was done in strong vivid colors, but on a more muted background with a lot of open skin to allow the art to breathe. It was a style Ivo and Gus had mastered as well. They packed in more colors and detail than Bear, but their older brother was the best at inking over scar tissue.

Rob could barely see the keloid hidden in the dragon's folds, but his fingers easily found the scattered mass. It was solid in one spot and spidered out into uneven jagged lines. If there had been any symmetry or sense to the original shape, Rob couldn't find it.

But he couldn't help but notice that Mace flinched when he first touched the spot.

"You did catch it really good over here," Rob commented lightly as he traced over the three-inch scar that cut through the dragon's frilled tail. The gouge wasn't deep, and it sliced over the space diagonally, which gave Rob a good idea of what it looked like before. The span itself was thin and long, rather than wide. It was an easy repair, but he would have to work hard to color match and in a few spots, blend in a black gradient.

"You think you can do it?" Mace twisted his head around to peer over his own shoulder. "I've been meaning for Bear to take a look at it, but I thought I'd see if you felt like you could do it."

There was a lot of power in Mace's back and stretches of untouched skin Rob would've loved to paint with ink. He had a nice undertone for color—a bit of olive and gold—a good base to make blues and purples pop. The reds and oranges they used were richer, earthier than Rob normally liked, but the hues were bold and strong enough to hold their own against the brighter colors. The stippling worried him a little bit, but as he inspected the outer edges of the tattoo, Rob noticed the other faint scars that crisscrossed Mace's back.

He didn't need to ask about them. He'd met the man who put them there, was nearly a victim of his cruelty and violence. Rob longed to trace up the length of Mace's spine with the tip of his tongue or spend a lazy afternoon counting the faint freckles on his shoulders.

"I can do it," he finally replied. When he glanced up into Mace's deep, sultry blue eyes, Rob couldn't help but smile when Mace winked. "The question is, are you sure? Because if I fuck it up, Bear isn't just going to fire my ass, he's going to kick it."

"It's my skin," Mace reminded him. "Besides, you look bored enough to chew off your own foot for amusement."

"Yeah, but at least if I do that, it's just my foot," he muttered and gave Mace a light shove toward the chair at his station. "Let me start mixing up some inks and we can get started. And if I jack up in the lines, I'll blame it on the Vietnamese coffee you brought with you."

ROB ONLY had a few more minutes of shading to do when the door's bells rang for the second time that day. There was little hope that Gus would be any help. He'd woken up five minutes after Rob laid his first pass of orange over the dragon's tail and made a loud scrambling dash toward the shop's bathroom. It sounded as though he hit every wall and door with his body along the way. Then came the distinct liquid gushing sounds of someone emptying their stomach.

"I'm not cleaning that up if he gets it on the floor," Rob said as he continued to layer in the color. "He's on his own."

"I'll do it," Mace promised. "It wouldn't be the first time I've cleaned up after Gus puking. I doubt it will be the last."

His back was to the door, his chair angled so he could get full light on Mace's back, so Rob couldn't see the customer who came in. He was about to ask them to hold on when he glanced up at the mirror hanging on the wall above the counter at his station and caught sight of the top of a very familiar head.

"Don't look now," Mace said as he met Rob's startled gaze in the mirror, "but I think there's a gelfling here to see you."

"That's my mom!" He fumbled to find a place to put his machine and pulled the cords to the side as he untangled himself from his chair. He had a slight ache in his back, mostly from clenching up with nerves while he worked on Mace, so he groaned when he stood up. "Shit, umm… stay here. Or… crap… hold on."

He'd been thirteen when she got short, but Rob had grown up believing his mother was the most beautiful woman in the world. Now in his midtwenties, he still hadn't found any woman who'd changed his mind. There were subtle hints that she came from a stocky people—a musculature he'd inherited—but her generous curves hid a powerful strength from years of workouts and limited carbs. It was her outrageous fashion sense that shaped much of Rob's own tastes, and although she refused to do anything crazy to her long black hair, she wasn't afraid of color in her wardrobe.

Today was no exception. Her magenta skinny jeans were paired with a frothy yellow blouse that was dotted with an explosion of purple circles. If Ivo were in the shop, he'd probably have something to say about her chopstick-thin metallic-gold stilettos. Her sunglasses sat on top of her head, a pair of enormous pink cat's-eyes dazzled with rhinestones. Her silky brown skin might have had more wrinkles than when he was a child, but her smile still lit up the room for him, and when she enveloped him in a tight hug, her light floral perfume soothed his rattled nerves.

"Don't stop working because I'm here. I just came by to say hello because I had a dental checkup down the street." His mother peered around his shoulder, smiled at Mace, and then said through gritted teeth in a low whisper, "He's nice. I wouldn't take my hands off of him. Very pretty. Look at all of those muscles."

Apparently he'd gotten his no-filter mouth from her as well.

"*Mom.*" He matched her whisper—a hot hiss of mortification and resignation. It wasn't the first time she'd boldly commented on a man's physique or his looks, and once she accepted his sexuality, she oftentimes nudged him in the ribs to point his attention toward her object of momentary lust. "That's Mace. Let me… just come over and meet him. And try not to drool on him."

Mace was still straddling one of the chairs when Rob brought his mother over. As they approached, he stood up, exposing his bare chest and abdomen, and Rob's mother sucked in her breath.

"Mace, this is Nina, my mom." Rob rolled his eyes at his mother's now even broader smile as she held her hand out. "Mom, this is Mace. The guy I was telling you about."

His mother literally cooed. She sounded like a flock of pigeons descending on a scatter of birdseed. Rob spent five minutes listening to his mother exclaim admiration over Mace's tattoos and then express her delight in discovering he was a firefighter, something Rob had mentioned to her nearly a month ago.

"Why don't I finish up, and the two of you can continue your lovefest," Rob grumbled at Mace as he rolled his chair back into place. "Sit down. Mom, let me get you a seat."

He braced for a long, drawn-out battle about how she didn't need a chair, but Mace walked over to Gus's stall to grab one, and that cut it short before it began. He watched his mother ogle Mace's ass and then shoot him a flirtatious smile when he returned. Judging by her gratitude, anyone eavesdropping would have imagined Mace parted the Red Sea to let her people go free. Getting Mace back into position was easy enough, but as he turned on his machine and the needles began to jump, Mace did the one thing Rob prayed he wouldn't do.

"So what was he like as a kid?" Mace shifted in his chair and leaned his chest against its back so Rob had better access to his tattoo. "I've got four brothers. Lots of embarrassing stories."

"You're so fucking lucky that I have pride in my work and I don't poke you deeply," he muttered into Mace's ear as he edged his chair closer. "And don't think I'm not going to ask your brothers about the shit you used to do when you were younger."

"My life is an open book, babe." Mace turned his dazzling smile toward Rob's mother. "I can tell you they really like him at the shop here. I'm one of the owners, although Bear is the one in charge. Technically Rob and I shouldn't be dating, because he's an employee, but you know him… just irresistible."

And with that, Rob's mother was off and running.

It was hard to tattoo a laughing man. It was harder not to die of embarrassment as his mother proceeded to drag out probably the most mortifying moments of Rob's life. He had to pull back the machine from Mace's skin when she recalled when he was eight and she caught him shaving his hair into a mohawk using her epilator. Her recollection included a reenactment of him screaming like a pterodactyl on fire, and he stopped so he could give her a death glare.

"Mom, I did not sound like that," Rob protested to apparently deaf ears as his mother and Mace burst out into hearty laughter at his admittedly petulant tone. "And unless you want to sit in this chair all night, stop giggling so I can finish."

The ten minutes left stretched into forty-five following an interruption by Gus, who was a color of green only seen in the Chicago River during St. Patrick's Day. His mother subsequently coddled Gus and oohed over the pictures of his toddler as she made him hot tea. Rob set Gus back down into the art room, finished up, wiped Mace down, and then leaned back to scrutinize his work.

"Okay. I think I'm done, but you've got a little bit of swelling going on, so let's see how that does, and if we need to go back over it, we can. I don't want to overwork the area, because you've already had trauma there, and the last thing I want to do is cut you. Let's see how the scar takes the ink." Rob rolled his seat back and gave Mace room to stand up. "Take a look in the mirror and tell me what you think."

All he needed to see was Mace's wide grin to know he'd done well.

"That looks great. I think it's going to heal really well. You did a fantastic job." Mace turned and gave Rob a deep kiss that left him breathless and tingling. "I think Bear will be very impressed with it. You nailed it."

There were moments of pride Rob lived for when tattooing, and each moment was different and special in its own way. But seeing Mace's face and hearing his words intensified his satisfaction over the work. He loved to ink. He loved everything about tattooing, from the feel of skin and how it moved to the constant struggle to replicate his art onto a living canvas. A cover-up was a challenge he always embraced, and the occasional touchup was probably even more nerve-racking because he had to make it look as seamless as possible and match another artist's skill level and design choices.

The fact that he brought that glorious smile to Mace's beautiful face just made nailing the tattoo even better.

"Oh, that looks so pretty." His mother beamed at him. "You can't even tell where the scratch was."

"Yeah, I hope he'll do a whole piece on me someday," Mace told her.

"Let me get this covered up before you start making me even more nervous about inking you." Rob gestured him over, holding up a piece of dermal film. "Do you need the aftercare instructions, or are you sick of hearing them?"

"I think I know how to get hold of my tattoo artist if something goes bad," he teased. Then he lifted his arm out of the way so Rob could stretch the film over the newly inked area. Mace bent his head and whispered, "I'm kind of hoping he'll make a house call tonight. We can order in some food and put in a movie that we're not going to watch because we're making out on my couch."

"Let me get my mom out of here and we can definitely talk about it." He fought back his smile and worked out all the air bubbles as he lay the film down. "Actually, who am I kidding? So long as I get to pick the movie we ignore. I'd say we can go now because it's so dead, but Gus is useless, and Bear isn't going to be here for a little while."

Saying goodbye to his mother took nearly as long as it did to finish Mace's tattoo. First she had to check up on Gus and then invite a now-dressed Mace over to dinner with the family. Rob tried to derail that, but despite his best efforts, they were locked into a Saturday meal with probably just his parents in a restaurant he would have to wear a tie for. By the time she left, Mace wore an imprint of her lipstick on one cheek, and Rob was fairly certain his face was covered in pink gloss from the butterfly kisses she gave him before she headed out.

"Sorry about my mom taking up so much time." Rob looked in a mirror and caught sight of the war paint she left on him, so he started to wipe his face with a paper towel. "She's not usually down this way so I like to stop and talk to her when she comes by."

"No, it was nice. I know you and your dad have issues, and she's probably stuck in the middle of it, right?" Mace gave him a sympathetic grimace when Rob nodded. "I liked her. You're a lot like her. And I can see how much she loves you. Kinda made me jealous because I don't have that. And don't get me wrong, I love the guys, but a mother is kind of special. It's different, and it's good to see."

"Yeah. My dad and I are okay. Or at least I think we're good now. Last time I went up to the house, he was telling one of his friends to drop by the shop and have me cover up some crappy flash he got overseas. 'Bout blew my mind listening to my dad talk me up," Rob said. He sidled up to Mace to wrap his arms around him. "Dinner's going to kind of suck because there'll be about seventeen forks and five hundred spoons and my father will go on about the state of the city and how I either need a haircut or a real job. We might even get a special appearance by one of my older brothers or sisters, but I doubt it. I can promise you the food will be good, because my dad really likes to eat well. There will probably be lots of meat. Just so you know."

"I like meat. And it doesn't matter what we eat so long as you're there with me." Mace pulled him closer and fit Rob into the dips and valleys of his body. "Do you want me to keep you company? Or should I head out and maybe pick up my dirty clothes off of the living room floor?"

Rob was about to answer when a massive gurgling sound erupted from the back of the shop. If he hadn't known better, listening to the gushing noise, he would have thought a pipe broke. He patted Mace's ass. "Tell you what. I'm going to take you up on your offer to clean up after your brother, because unless I'm wrong, he didn't make it to the bathroom this time. And as much as I love having you in my life, it doesn't extend to your immediate family and the stomach flu."

TWENTY-ONE

ROB GASPED and pulled his head back to get some air. "Shit, I was really looking forward to that movie."

Something was digging into Rob's spine, and he briefly wondered if it was the open zipper of his jeans. At any other time, he would've stopped what he was doing to yank the pants out from underneath him, but Mace half lying on top of him made it difficult to move, and he was busy trying to get Mace's T-shirt off without breaking the stream of kisses being left on his throat.

He could've sworn Mace only had two hands, but it seemed like they were everywhere. And they *were* everywhere. They were everywhere with a wicked skill and a seemingly instinctive knowledge of Rob's body, because no matter where Mace touched, he left a trail of fire banked under Rob's skin.

"We can always go back to the living room," Mace muttered, his words half lost in Rob's hair as he began to explore Rob's ear with his tongue. "If you really wanted to watch it. Funny thing is, I don't even remember what movie you picked."

It was beginning to be a pattern with them. Starting with the afternoon Rob repaired Mace's Japanese dragon, they often made plans for dinner in and to watch a couple of hours of television before Rob went home. Rob couldn't name one movie they'd ever watched, and as far as going home went, more and more of his clothes were taking up space in Mace's closet, and Rey's old apartment key now hung on Rob's keychain. He'd gotten used to helping Mrs. Hwang take out her trash and sort through her recyclables, and he'd picked up a few words in Cantonese. He marveled at Mace's near fluency in the language, because he struggled with it.

They'd even gotten a damned fish, a brilliantly frilled orange-and-red betta they called Namor, whose colors caught Rob's eye and were reminiscent of the dragon he'd worked on. Neither one of them knew anything about fish, so it was a crash course with a friend of a friend, and now the apartment's living space was filled with the gentle burble of a five-gallon aquarium set up in Mace's working area. There were other fish in the tank besides Namor, brilliantly colored but small-finned dart-like creatures the aquarium guy reassured them would get along well with their bruiser of a betta fish. Snails were okay. Shrimp were a buffet. And after a panicked phone call down to the fish store when Rob found Namor building a pile of bubbles in the corner of the tank, Mace suggested they buy some books and get at least a little bit smarter about what they brought home.

Their dinner with his parents went better than Rob expected. His mother flirted with everyone under the sun, typical of her when she was happy, and from the oddly indulgent looks his father gave her, there seemed to be a peace between them Rob had never seen before. Mace was a hit, and his presence unearthed a long-hidden childhood desire his father once had to become a firefighter. They left the restaurant with a promise to have a dinner at the house, and his father only once asked him if he'd found a real job. But he softened the criticism with an unexpected offer to give Rob money if he needed it.

He caught the gleam of something akin to admiration in his father's steely eyes when he reassured his parents he wasn't only just doing fine, but was building a successful clientele. Mace remained silent, smiling and giving a supportive murmur or two, but for the most part, he didn't step in. He let Rob stand on his own accomplishments. Rob liked that. He knew he could look to Mace for backup, but Mace wasn't there to save him or to validate what he did. Even though he'd spoken openly about Rob's work at the shop, he kept his comments to artistic skill and technique rather than reassuring Rob's father that his son was a functioning adult.

There were other dinners, some more formal with Rob's family and others with Mace's, mostly backyard stuff where they grilled large chunks of meat and the occasional zucchini to say they had their vegetables. They learned their boundaries. Mace didn't like anyone reading what he wrote until he was ready, and Rob adjusted to some constant noise in the background, although Namor's tank went a long way to soothing Mace's quirk.

He celebrated Mace going back onto the trucks and was thrilled when the physical therapist gave him clearance to go back into the fray. Mace had been impatient about it but reasonable, something Rob appreciated not fighting about, especially after dealing with a seemingly endless stream of crazy clients down at 415 Ink. And even though he'd been invited countless times before, there was no way in hell Rob was ever going to join Rey and Mace on their insane game of full-out sprint-and-tag through Chinatown in the early mornings.

There was also the small matter of trying not to dissolve into a puddle of ugly tears the first time Chris called him uncle, and as hard as he tried to save the world from impending doom, Ivo and Lilith became very close friends.

Although with as much trouble as Rob was having with Mace's shirt, he was seriously doubting his functioning-adult status and wondered if he shouldn't have brought a scissors in with him from the kitchen.

"Quit squirming," he scolded. "You're making this hard to get off of you."

The bed squeaked and moaned, its frame protesting their continuously moving weight, but Rob was past the point of caring. The thing could break underneath him and he would just keep going. Pushing Mace back onto the mattress, he tugged the shirt off of his lover's arm and tossed it aside. Naked, Mace lay spread-eagle on the bed, his erection pressed into the crease between Rob's cheeks.

Mace was simply beautiful. From his position straddling Mace's hips, Rob drank in his fill, still slightly awed he'd ended up with the man beneath him. Mace's form was a balance of grace and power, his muscles honed by backbreaking work and embellished with art that Rob nearly lost himself in. As beautiful as Mace was, Rob enjoyed the *man* even more. His disciplined exterior masked a playful boyishness tempered by a subtle compassion many would never see.

"What? You're staring at me like I've got something on my face." Mace wiped at his cheek and glanced at his hand. "Other side? *What*?"

"I'm going to tell you something, and I don't want you to feel like you owe me anything in return. Okay?" Rob raked his fingers through Mace's hair, grateful Mace finally grew it out enough for him to play with. The sun was lightening it, streaking the strands with caramel and gold, but the scruff on Mace's jaw was as dark as his roots and more than a little bit scratchy when Rob rubbed his cheek against Mace. He'd complained about the beard burn he got until Mace finally shaved. "I guess I've been thinking about us these past couple of days, and I just wanted to tell you that I love you."

The shadows hid the blues in Mace's eyes, folding dark grays over the luminous hues, but Rob still saw the confusion in them dissipate, replaced by a softness Rob saw more and more. Mace ran his roughened hands up Rob's naked thighs. Then he gripped his hips and squeezed lightly.

"You just had to go and have this conversation while we're both naked and I'm on my back." His hands were on the move again, stroking at the small of Rob's back, and then he passed a thumb over Rob's hip bone. "I've been trying to figure out the right time to tell *you* I loved you. Let me finish before you get started, because you're kind of like a chainsaw if I don't get a word in edgewise. Now it's going to be difficult for me to cut in, and I need you to hear me."

He pulled Rob down until they lay chest to chest, and Rob propped his chin up to see Mace's face. Once the words were spoken, everything seemed to fall into place. The universe clicked down as though Rob had found the final puzzle piece he'd been missing his entire life.

"I think I fell in love with you at the diner when you spent the night talking, and I could have listened for hours longer if only they hadn't needed the table. Or maybe it was even before that, because you would challenge me and growl at me when I came in. That made sure I couldn't put you into a box and set you on the shelf like I did other people who worked there. I found myself looking for you when I came in. And it used to piss me off because I felt like I had no choice, like I couldn't help myself. I would hear you laugh, and I would get angry because you never laughed with me. And then that day when we decided to say 'fuck it' and give in, I spent weeks afterward reliving every single moment.

"You've seen where I come from—hell, you were caught in it—and you didn't turn away. You stuck with me, telling me I was worth being loved and worth healing past all of the shit I carried for so long." Mace exhaled. With his fingers, he followed the rounded curve of Rob's butt and then traced back up his spine. "This isn't the *when* I thought I would do this, but I can't imagine waking up tomorrow morning and not having you here with me. I love you, Rob, and I really want to wake up next to you for the rest of my life. So if you'll have me, I'd like to marry you."

ROB SAID yes.

Or at least Mace thought the deep, soul-touching kiss he got was a yes. He would've stopped and asked, but they quickly moved on to other,

more interesting things, like Rob's mouth around Mace's cock and his
fingers cupped around Mace's balls.

"Babe, you've got to move your elbow," Mace gasped when the
offending joint dug deeper into his thigh. "Okay, not that direction. Up."

"I kind of lost the lube somewhere," Rob grumbled as his head
disappeared beneath the sheets. "I was going to try to be all sexy and get
you slicked up, but I can't find the damned bottle."

"That's because I've got it here." Mace plucked up the lubricant
from its place next to the pillow. "See? Now, who wanted to do this?"

"Exactly the way I started," Rob purred and climbed across Mace's
body with a slow slink. "Just lean back and let me do all the work. Okay,
maybe you could moan a few times."

"I don't know. I kind of like a fifty-fifty deal most of the time." He
stretched his arm out and kept the bottle out of Rob's reach. Rob knew all
of his weak spots, starting with the ticklish area along his ribs and how
turned on he got when Rob kissed his collarbone. This time, Rob went
for the ultimate prize of raking his fingernails along Mace's inner thigh,
an erotic blend of sharp on sensitive skin that immediately hardened
Mace's cock until it nearly ached with his arousal. "*Shit*. That is not fair."

He handed over the bottle.

The lube was warm and slippery, an odd sensation around his
naked cock. They'd come home from dinner out, satiated and slightly
buzzed from a round of new brews at their favorite pub. The cab driver,
for the most part, kept his eyes on the road, but his attention definitely
drifted toward the rearview mirror whenever Rob leaned over to nibble
on Mace's ear. They probably made too much noise coming in, and they
*shush*ed each other in that loud whisper most drunk people used. Coming
upstairs, feeding the fish, watching a movie and having a bowl of ice
cream had been the extent of their plans, but a single kiss turned into
many more, and the next thing Mace knew, they were tangled up around
each other in the bedroom.

"You make me feel safe, do you know that?" Mace murmured as
he cupped Rob's face. The press of Rob's hard cheekbone into his palm
was a comfort no amount of noise or candles could ever match. "I don't
think I even understand how much I love you and need you. But I want
to spend the rest of my life figuring that out."

"I'm totally on board with that." Rob returned his whisper. "Hold
on to me and let me take you for a ride."

Rob straddled him and then eased Mace into his velvet warmth. The fit was tight, and Rob's stomach clenched. He held in his breath until he seated himself down onto Mace's hips and enveloped him fully. Mace thought he was about to lose his mind from the sensations overwhelming him, but then Rob began to move, and he fell into the rhythm of his lover's body.

Their lovemaking changed constantly, with a fluid range of emotions and mood. It ran from playful to lazy and sometimes wild. They'd broken a shower curtain rod and once left a hole in the hallway wall that Mace had to patch up the next morning. There was a Sunday where they tested the dining room table's sturdiness when Rob innocently sucked on a very large strawberry and Mace decided to put himself exactly where that fruit had been.

This time was different.

The first time they made love, Mace discovered Rob pulling him in deep was like running his fingertips through the stars. They moved slowly, felt every thrust, and built up the heated tension between them. Rob arched his back and thrust down onto Mace's cock, and Mace angled his hips and pushed up into Rob's tight hole.

"Turn over. I can't... I want you to feel me in you, having you under me," Mace pleaded. Rob nodded, and they shifted. They nearly lost their joining, but a bit of laughter and careful movement drove Mace back into Rob's clench. "God, yeah. Right there. Hold on to me, okay?"

With his legs spread open and his heels digging into the small of Mace's back, Rob dug his fingers into Mace's arms. Their bodies were already damp with sweat, and their soft grunting bled into the sounds of the bars in the alleyway—a punch of music and rapid-fire Chinese spiced with a bit of raucous laughter.

"Shit... okay," Rob groaned as he tilted his head back into the pillows, his eyes hooded and glazed. "Fuck. Damn, Mace."

Rob shivered and tightened around Mace's cock on every downward stroke. Grunting, Mace thrust in deep, his back and hip muscles straining to slide his cock against the nerve center tucked into Rob's body. His lover's plump asscheeks were spread apart enough for Mace to glance down and see his cock sliding in and out of Rob's hole, the lubricant running slick and releasing its sweet citrus scent from the growing heat of their feverish thrusts.

When Mace tilted his hips and ground out a steady rhythm, Rob's moans nearly masked the sharp slap of their bodies coming together. He liked being able to make Rob lose his mind with a few long thrusts and a couple of filthy kisses. Working in deep, Mace broke their pace, quickening some of his strokes and agonizingly slowing others. He felt the tug of Rob's muscles around his breadth and the hot sear of his body down his shaft when Mace began pounding into him again. He also really loved the way Rob whimpered when he slid nearly all the way out and then inched his way back in and filled Rob to the brim.

Their friction and pace thickened the air with the musky scent of their exertion. A faint sheen glimmered on Rob's chest and belly. He bit his lower lip and worked at his already-kiss-swollen mouth, and a tiny bead of sweat gathered at his temple. It shook with every thrust Mace made and held on until Mace hooked his hands under Rob's lower back and lifted him from the bed so he could go in even deeper. The clear drop plunged down Rob's high cheekbones and coursed past his jaw, where Mace caught it in a kiss.

Rob twisted at Mace's nipples with his clever fingers and tugged them into sharp peaks. Then when Mace arched his shoulders back, Rob took advantage of the space between them and bit at the turgid point, creating a shock wave through Mace's body.

Overwhelmed, Mace fought to hold back, but the rise of his seed broke the trembling, fragile control he had left. Rob's nip on his nipple drove him insane, and he twisted. He knew the pleasurable pain would make him lose control, and he wanted this moment between them to last as long as it could.

The curve of Rob's ass on his hips and thighs centered Mace, but his thrusts became short and erratic. He hitched Rob up, bent forward, captured Rob's mouth again, and tasted the salt of their sweat on his tongue. He'd trapped Rob's cock between them, and its damp tip smeared a wetness on Mace's belly. The first pearling of Rob's release on his skin ignited a trail of sparks across Mace's body. Its lightning strike grabbed at Mace's balls and demanded he release himself into Rob's heat.

Rob's golden skin flushed, and the color worked its way up over his chest. He grabbed at Mace's sides, and a stream of indecipherable words poured from his panting mouth. Gasping, Mace ached with the effort to keep himself from climaxing, but at the same time, he longed to see Rob go over the edge. He leaned forward and captured Rob's mouth with his, their kisses broken from gasping pants and soft, murmuring encouragements.

"So fucking close," Rob gasped. "Jesus, you drive me crazy."

"Just let go, babe." Mace took another quick sip from Rob's mouth and coaxed him to the edge. "Let me see you go."

His own climax struck him without warning. Focused on Rob, Mace let his tentative grip on himself slip away, and the universe came rushing up to engulf him. It felt like the stars were no longer out of his reach. He could see them burn brightly on Rob's skin in an inked constellation along his ribs, and their brightness pushed away everything but the man he held in his arms. Another stroke of his hips and Mace gave in to the showering light.

Rob's release struck as Mace's first shuddering explosion of hot come reached deep inside of Rob. The shaking in his limbs grew, and Rob cried out. A splash of his climax coated Mace's stomach. Half-blind from his pleasure, he reached up to touch Rob's sweat-moistened face and worked the pad of his thumb across Rob's teeth-dimpled lips.

"Love you," Rob panted, and he arched again as another orgasmic wave hit him.

"I love you too," Mace murmured, and resting his weight on his elbows and continuing to rock his hips, he took Rob the rest of the way.

They thrust again, slower as their bodies gave in to the lessening tide of their release. Exhausted, they lay against each other and struggled to take in every breath. With Mace quivering from the effort of merely drawing air into his lungs, Rob complained about being empty when Mace slid out of him. But he didn't have enough energy to do anything but whimper his complaints, and they soon turned to soft contented sighs when Mace curled up against his side.

Lying in the aftermath of their lovemaking, Mace realized the tension he'd been holding in for years had slowly been chipped away, a lot of it by the love he had for Rob. He felt good about where he was and who he was, secure in the faith and love of his brothers and the awesome sensation of spending his life with the man who not only got under his skin but refused to leave him.

"So," Mace finally whispered into the alleyway-chatter-filled shadows around them. "I'm going to guess that's a yes, then."

"I don't know. That could have just been a maybe. Give me five minutes and I'll be up for another round of convincing." Rob heaved an exaggerated, dramatic sigh and rolled over, his sleepy expression at odds with the soft flirtatious look in his amber eyes. "Or better yet, how about if I ask you to marry me and I be the one to do the convincing?"

EPILOGUE

"I AM really glad we're staying the night," Rob said, resting his chin on Mace's hunched shoulder as he hugged him from behind. "I don't think I'll be able to walk after eating all the food that's laid out. This is insane, but not as insane as my dad and Chris's grandpa talking about social justice in the family room. The old man's done practically a one-eighty in there. Almost didn't recognize who was talking."

"I love you, but you've got to let me go because I need some onions." Mace gestured toward the basket of onions on the counter. "We vastly underestimated how much salsa we would go through."

"I think you vastly underestimated who would show up for this," Rob teased as he walked by the onion bowl. He tossed one over to Mace, who caught it easily. "Okay. So far we know you can cook beef stew, mac and cheese, that weird taco lasagna thing you do—which I love, but it's fucking weird—and now salsa."

"You do *not* cook salsa." Mace began to mince the onion. He wouldn't win any awards for knife skills, but he figured they didn't invite any Iron Chefs to the cookout, so he was safe from condemnation. "If you see Luke, ask him to get me some cilantro from the garden, unless you can sneak past everybody and clip it without him seeing. Apparently none of us know how to cut it right."

"So you just don't yank it up from the ground?" His boisterous laughter mocked Mace as Rob opened the back door. "I'll find Luke."

"He's playing ball with Chris and Ivo. The herb scissors are hanging on the wall next to the grill." Bear padded into the kitchen, his bare feet silent on the wood floors. He tucked empty beer bottles he brought with him into the recycle bin and glanced over at Mace. "Do you need help?"

"Nah, I just wanted to make sure I had enough cilantro, but looking at what I already cut, I think it'll be good, but you never know." Mace edged in closer to the counter to give Bear room to go behind him. "Gus and Rey have any luck with the kiddie pool? How hard is it to inflate that?"

"Pretty hard if you don't attach the pump to it properly. Kind of funny watching them trying to figure out what's wrong when the pump hose is dangling when they lift it up. I think Chris called them out on it." Bear chuckled. His expression shifted and grew serious, but a smile still brightened his eyes. "It's good to see you happy. I like you and Rob together. Complicates things a bit down at the shop, because you know now I can't fire him, but you being happy is worth it."

"You could always fire him. You just won't because you're a marshmallow. It's why Ivo knew he had to fire that intern. If he'd left it for the morning when you came in, the guy would've given you a sob story and you'd have been stuck with him until the next time he pissed Ivo off."

"Well, we've got a new one starting soon. He's just wrapping up some work he's doing and then he'll be joining the crew in about six months. Older, but I'm looking forward to seeing what he can do. I like his art." Bear nudged Mace's side with his knuckles. "I'm proud of you, you know. Back on the trucks, going to get married, setting up house with Rob, and your book's going to be published. You've come a long way since that angry kid I met years ago."

"It wasn't hard," Mace scoffed and put down his knife. "And don't get too excited about the book. Romantic urban fantasy is a hard sell, but I liked writing it. They want a sequel already. Took me almost two years to write the first one. I'm hoping to knock out the next one in six months. It's easier now. Rob kind of settles me, so I'm not all over the place when I get home. What about you? When are you going to find your happily ever after?"

"I don't know if I'll ever have one, but I imagine after all of you guys have found yours. I don't think I could let myself fall in love with anyone unless I knew you guys were… the four of you are my life, and I just want you to be happy."

Mace wrapped Bear into a tight hug and squeezed as hard as he could. He'd grown up embracing Bear. Their bodies thickened with muscles and their shoulders burdened with more and more responsibility, but their connection and their hugs remained strong.

"Just don't let life pass you by," Mace whispered into Bear's ear and caught his mouth on Bear's beard. The he let go and slapped Bear's back one last time. "You, of all of us, deserve to be happy. Although I could use less face fuzz when giving you a hug. You're getting woolly. Now grab the chips, and I'll bring the salsa. We've got a family to feed, and if I'm not mistaken, I think it's my turn to man the grill."

"Hey, how much cilantro do you need? Luke says you can have two handfuls, but only if you need them," Rob called out from the open back door. "Apparently that shit's like gold."

Bear chuckled and picked up the salsa and chips. "I'll take the stuff out and grill. Why don't you spend some time with your future husband? See if he can lay tile or something. We've really got to update that upstairs bathroom."

THE FOOD was spicy and messy. His family was loud and even more messy. Filling up the kiddie pool became a water fight with a couple of hoses and no prisoners taken. In the end mostly everyone was soaked to the bone, including Rob's father, who Chris felt needed a thorough explanation of every single plant in the garden and any bug he could find.

Cuddling on one of the backyard couches was Mace's idea of a perfect evening. With Rob curled up across his lap, they watched the sky fold in a blazing array of oranges and yellows before dipping down into a sea of soft blues spangled with yellow bursts from far-off streetlamps. The deck was fairly empty, just them on the couch with an exhausted Earl lounging on a dog bed a few feet away. Ivo and Gus were leaning on the deck railing, sarcastically commenting on the volleyball game Lilith and Luke had set up and drafted more than a few family members into playing.

"I somehow don't think that's the volleyball rules I remember," Gus muttered around a mouthful of beer. "The whole point of the game is to not let the ball hit the ground. What is this one-bounce shit?"

"They're playing on a driveway that's half cobblestones and half concrete. It's kind of like a golf hazard." Mace shrugged off the criticism. "It's also why we switch sides after every five points, because the garage is counted as a hazard, so if it bounces off of the wall, that's considered a play. Trust me, it'll all make sense to you in a couple years."

"I've worked down at the shop for two years now. None of you make sense." He toed the dog, found Earl's sweet spot on his back, and scratched it with his bare toe. "You all are crazy, but I'm glad you asked me to be part of the family."

Rob's kiss was even sweeter than ever, and Mace savored every moment of it. Tomorrow would mean work for both of them, with a few short scraped-together moments and meals during breaks in Mace's day-long shift. They'd talked about doing something with the other bedroom in their place, turning it into a workspace for Mace or perhaps even sharing the room, fitting a lighted drafting table against one wall for Rob.

It was good their lives had gotten to the point where figuring out what to do with a spare bedroom was the most complicated thing on their to-do list.

"Where do you want to get married?" Rob tilted his head back so he could look at Mace. "When do you want to get married? Or is that too… I don't know how this works. Who's in charge of what and who gets to ask when?"

"I'm pretty open. I never even imagined getting married." Mace remembered the days of struggling with his attraction for men, wondering if the beatings he'd gotten from his father had been justified because he was broken and less of a true man than he should've been. Bear helped him see things in a new perspective, and when the others began to join the household, Mace realized his masculinity was defined not by who he loved but rather by how he cared for those around him. "I guess I never thought about it. Maybe something romantic, where I'm not wearing a 415 Ink bowling shirt and we have somebody else provide the food so nobody has to cook."

"Do I have to dye my hair one color?" He stopped scratching the dog, and Earl cast a forlorn look over his shoulder until Rob started up again. "How formal is this thing?"

"How about if we get married at the gardens, rent out the diner for the night, and invite everybody we know to come eat trash food and just dance with us?" The gleam in Rob's eye was enough for Mace. "Honestly, I don't care if we get married in jeans and T-shirts, just so long as we're together and our families are there. I'm going to probably be saying this for the rest of my life, but just so you understand—here and now—loving you saved me. And I know you're going to say you were just there, but honey, that's what I need most. So, wear a rainbow in your hair if you want to, because I'm going to love you no matter what. For the rest of our lives."

MONDAY MORNINGS were hard enough without nursing a slight hangover and nearly killing himself walking out of the parking garage in high heels during a heavy rain, but Ivo pulled the short straw and was tagged to open the shop. He liked getting in early. It meant a full pot of hot coffee brewed as strong as he liked and having the music blasting through the place as he readied the shop to be opened.

415 Ink was his second home. He'd done school work in its office, learned the tricks of the trade in its art room from men and women who'd spent their entire lives inking skin. If anything, the shop was as much his baby as it was Bear's, and he was fiercely protective of who worked there and anyone who'd come in to get a piece of their souls put on their body.

"Still," he said to himself as he reveled in the emptiness of the space, "it's damned fucking nice to be in here by myself."

He took care of Gus's stall first, knowing Gus would be in to do a job at noon, and considering Chris spent the night, he didn't know how much sleep Gus got. He hadn't known how thirsty three-year-old boys got in the middle of the night and how quickly it took them to require a sheet change after a few sips of water.

Halfway through stocking the paper towels, he caught his heel on a bubble in the concrete floor. It was stupid. He knew it was there. He'd tripped on it at least five times in a single week, but normally he caught his sneaker on the bump. Snagging a thin stiletto was a different story, and Ivo flailed to catch his balance. Years of walking in stilettos probably saved him, but Ivo was inclined to believe the rock-steady stall walls Bear installed years before had more to do with him not falling on his ass or face than any skill on his part.

"*Fuck*. I better change my shoes before I kill myself," Ivo grumbled. "Or with my luck, Bear will show up and catch me in them."

He dragged out his old pair of red Converses he'd stashed in his station and carefully limped over to the couch in the waiting area. His ankle was a bit tender, but it didn't feel too out of line, nothing a couple of hours of babying it wouldn't cure. He'd just tossed the Converses onto the couch so he could sit and put them on when a loud knock rattled the front door of the shop.

It was the cop.

The shock of seeing Nicholls framed in the doorway wiped away any thought of the ache in Ivo's ankle. Instead, other parts of his body clenched, uncomfortable and unsure. But at the same time, an electrifying excitement crackled through him.

He had a few days of beard growth on his strong jaw, and the rain had dampened his dark brown hair and turned it almost black. He had on an ebony peacoat over a deep gray button-down shirt, his coat collar turned up to protect his neck from the cold, biting wind, and his jeans were dark in spots from where the fabric soaked up a bit of water. Ivo couldn't see his feet, but he guessed the cop was wearing the same pair of cowboy boots he'd seen him in before. His green eyes were stormy, flinty hard, and his mouth was set into a firm straight line. His jaw tightened as he met Ivo's gaze, and he knocked on the door again.

"Open up!" the detective growled, pointing through the glass toward the doorknob.

"The shop doesn't open until noon. You want to make an appointment, call and leave a message on the answering machine and somebody will get back to you as soon as we can," Ivo replied as he took slow, deliberate strides toward the front door, his treacherous heels tapping on the floor. "I don't know what everyone's schedule looks like, but mine's full up, so you're going to have to go to somebody else."

"I don't want anybody else. Just *you*," Ruan snarled at him through the glass pane and then glanced down at Ivo's feet. "And what the *hell* is it with you and those shoes?"

Rhys Ford is an award-winning author with several long-running LGBT+ mystery, thriller, paranormal, and urban fantasy series and is a two-time LAMBDA finalist with her Murder and Mayhem novels. She is also a 2017 Gold and Silver Medal winner in the Florida Authors and Publishers President's Book Awards for her novels Ink and Shadows and Hanging the Stars. She is published by Dreamspinner Press and DSP Publications.

She's also quite skeptical about bios without a dash of something personal and really, who doesn't mention their cats, dog and cars in a bio? She shares the house with Harley, an insane grey tuxedo as well as a ginger cairn terrorist named Gus. Rhys is also enslaved to the upkeep a 1979 Pontiac Firebird and enjoys murdering make-believe people.

Rhys can be found at the following locations:
Blog: www.rhysford.com
Facebook: www.facebook.com/rhys.ford.author
Twitter: @Rhys_Ford

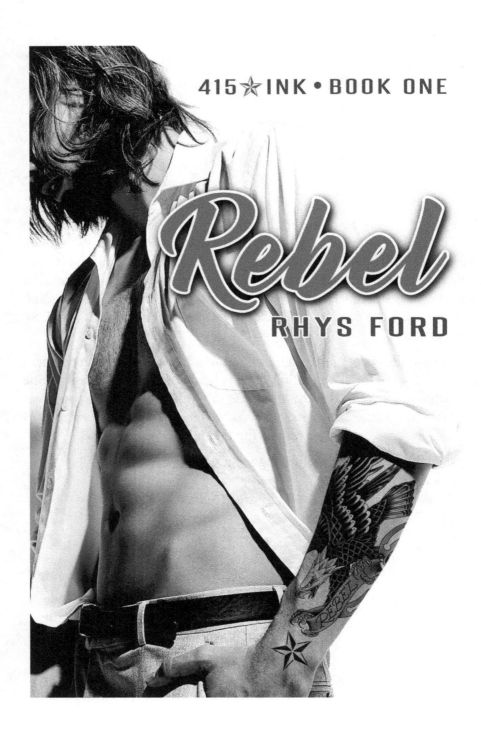

415 ☆ INK • BOOK ONE

Rebel

RHYS FORD

415 Ink: Book One

The hardest thing a rebel can do isn't standing up for something—it's standing up for himself.

Life takes delight in stabbing Gus Scott in the back when he least expects it. After Gus spends years running from his past, present, and the dismal future every social worker predicted for him, karma delivers the one thing Gus could never—would never—turn his back on: a son from a one-night stand he'd had after a devastating breakup a few years ago.

Returning to San Francisco and to 415 Ink, his family's tattoo shop, gave him the perfect shelter to battle his personal demons and get himself together… until the firefighter who'd broken him walked back into Gus's life.

For Rey Montenegro, tattoo artist Gus Scott was an elusive brass ring, a glittering prize he hadn't the strength or flexibility to hold on to. Severing his relationship with the mercurial tattoo artist hurt, but Gus hadn't wanted the kind of domestic life Rey craved, leaving Rey with an aching chasm in his soul.

When Gus's life and world starts to unravel, Rey helps him pick up the pieces, and Gus wonders if that forever Rey wants is more than just a dream.

www.dreamspinnerpress.com

MURDER AND MAYHEM

Murder and Mayhem: Book One

Dead women tell no tales.

Former cat burglar Rook Stevens stole many a priceless thing in the past, but he's never been accused of taking a life—until now. It was one thing to find a former associate inside Potter's Field, his pop culture memorabilia shop, but quite another to stumble across her dead body.

Detective Dante Montoya thought he'd never see Rook Stevens again—not after his former partner falsified evidence to entrap the jewelry thief and Stevens walked off scot-free. So when he tackled a fleeing murder suspect, Dante was shocked to discover the blood-covered man was none other than the thief he'd fought to put in prison and who still makes his blood sing.

Rook is determined to shake loose the murder charge against him, even if it means putting distance between him and the rugged Cuban-Mexican detective who brought him down. If one dead con artist wasn't bad enough, others soon follow, and as the bodies pile up around Rook's feet, he's forced to reach out to the last man he'd expect to believe in his innocence—and the only man who's ever gotten under Rook's skin.

www.dreamspinnerpress.com

CPSIA information can be obtained
at www.ICGtesting.com
Printed in the USA
LVHW04s1508120918
589921LV00011B/810/P